A Novel

NIGHT ANGEL 9

Peter Telep

BERKLEY BOOKS, NEW YORK

This is a work of fiction. Names, characters, places, and incidents are either the product of the author's imagination or are used fictitiously, and any resemblance to actual persons, living or dead, business establishments, events, or locales is entirely coincidental.

NIGHT ANGEL NINE

A Berkley Book / published by arrangement with
the author

PRINTING HISTORY
Berkley edition / January 2001

The Penguin Putnam Inc. World Wide Web site address is
http://www.penguinputnam.com

ISBN: 0-425-17813-7

BERKLEY®
Berkley Books are published by The Berkley Publishing Group,
a division of Penguin Putnam Inc.,
375 Hudson Street, New York, New York 10014.
BERKLEY and the "B" design
are trademarks belonging to Penguin Putnam Inc.

PRINTED IN THE UNITED STATES OF AMERICA

10 9 8 7 6 5 4 3 2 1

For
Mike, Jim, Larry, Sue, Kim and John.

And for two Orlando, Florida, medics
whose names I never learned. They treated my
daughter when she had a febrile seizure. Those medics
have long since forgotten the call,
but I never will.

Acknowledgments

I began this project with the "simple" goal of writing an entertaining and technically accurate novel. I wanted to surround my lies with as many truths as possible. The catch? I'm a writer and university English instructor, not a firefighter–paramedic. I needed a crash course in EMS, and I needed one fast.

The dedicated professionals of Fire Station 35, Seminole County, Florida, willingly and graciously opened their doors to me. Fire Service Technician/ Paramedic Michael A. Scott showed and explained to me every piece of equipment on the station's engine, squad, and rescue. He also read excerpts from this manuscript and served as the inspiration for many of its scenes. Lieutenant Mike Hammonds, a nationally recognized extrication expert, provided me with many of the details on how to get people out of wrecked vehicles. Lieutenant Michael Johansmeyer gave me a much appreciated copy of the EMS protocol manual, and Lieutenant Steve Jones answered my questions and shared several interesting stories. Kevin Welday, Dennis Miller, Eric Borns, Christopher Cahill, Heath Gifford, Ed Michalowski, Wayne Bernowska, and David Scott loaned me their ears and offered many insights.

EMT–Specialist Sue Hunter helped me break

ground. Her Web site (http://www.firefighting.com/emtsue/) and expertise really aided me when I found myself overwhelmed by practice parameters, protocols, algorithms, and terminology. Thanks, Sue!

Larry Levy, M.D., FAAEP, read these pages from a seasoned ER doctor's perspective and offered me the kind of insight and experience you often won't find in textbooks. His time and generosity have vastly improved my research and my writing.

Jim Newberger, a full-time nationally registered EMT–paramedic working out of North Memorial Medical Center in Minneapolis, brought his twelve-plus years of working the streets to this manuscript. Jim was always quick to point out how "medics really do it in the street" and how my passion for technical accuracy sometimes clouded the drama. Should you still find errors in this book, E-mail me. I will supply you with Jim's home phone number. I know he would love to hear your quibbles and would particularly enjoy a 3 A.M. chat with a stranger.

My editor, Kim Waltemeyer, helped me shape the opening chapters of the novel and advised me on the finer points of characterization. I'm extremely grateful for her assistance.

John Talbot, my agent, is one of those people I call when I need an adrenaline fix. You get him on the phone, and five minutes later you're so fired up that rejection seems more laughable than tragic.

Without my family's support, I could not take on projects as challenging as this. Love doesn't conquer all, but it sure does help.

Author's Note

The Valley Police and Fire departments and San Fernando Medical Center are products of my imagination. They are in no way meant to represent the actual police, fire, and medical services presently available and operating in the San Fernando Valley. The EMS system in this book is based on a number of different organizations, some located in Los Angeles, one in Florida, one in Minnesota, and one in New Mexico. Logistics and creative freedom informed this decision. I received my hands-on training in Florida, gathered notes from my consultants in Minnesota and New Mexico, and relied on materials from several West Coast organizations. Those who work in EMS will tell you that all systems have basic similarities; much of what you'll read here could very well occur, but in deference to the wonderful folks working in Los Angeles, their procedures and protocols are, in some cases, different from those described in this novel.

1

"Engine Nine, Rescue Nine. Engine Nine, Rescue Nine. Sick child. Thirty-nine-twelve Laurel Canyon Boulevard. Apartment two-zero-two. Cross street Ventura. Both units respond code three. Time out: one-oh-five."

Firefighter-paramedic Stephanie Savage glanced at her mobile data terminal as a text version of the radio call spilled across the screen. "Valley, Rescue Nine responding," she acknowledged the Tactical Area Radio Operator, a veteran dispatcher named Rueben Mordova, known by everyone in the Sixth Battalion as TRO Six.

At least Savage and her new partner, Abe Kashmiri, a firefighter and rookie paramedic beginning his three-month probationary period, were already on the road, having just dropped off a diabetic patient at San Fernando Medical Center, the closest hospital and the valley's level 1 trauma center. They should make good time, although Murphy's Law dictated that the shortest distance between your location and the scene was usually under construction.

Abe, a gangly kid of twenty-two, squinted through his safety glasses and guided the one-ton ambulance known as a "rescue" in a right turn so sharp that it nearly took them up on two wheels. As Savage flicked on the siren, she slammed into her door. She wished she were at the wheel, but the medic in charge of the rescue always rode shotgun in "the seat." She swore and rubbed her arm. "Training for NASCAR or what?"

"Sorry, ma'am."

"*Ma'am*? That makes me feel like I'm already in my box."

"My parents taught me to respect my teachers."

"One reason why I like foreigners."

"I'm not a foreigner. My parents are Pakistani, but I was born here."

"Wasn't talking about you."

"Yeah, but—" Abe lifted his slender index finger and pointed at the red light rushing toward them.

"So what? Opticom should take care of that," Savage said.

The Opticom device mounted on the rescue's roof transmitted an infrared beam to the traffic light, which would remain green until they passed, yet the signal's synchronization would not be compromised. Abe gunned the diesel engine.

"Slow down so I can check the right!" cried Savage.

They streaked through the intersection.

"Damn! Sorry," he said. "Going too fast."

"Thank God we were clear," Savage said. "Look, Abe, for some reason they picked me to be your Field

Training Officer, so here's a first lesson from your FTO. We got three rules for code 3 driving that'll keep us alive: No one can see our lights. No one can hear us. Everyone else on the road is an idiot. Got 'em?"

"Yeah."

"You're panting again."

"I know. I'm just nervous." Abe adjusted his headset's microphone as another unit reported over the dispatch frequency:

"Rescue Twelve on the air."

"Rescue Twelve," TRO Six responded.

More units from that station exchanged information with the dispatcher regarding a Dumpster fire behind an Albertson's supermarket, and Savage listened as the grainy night yielded to the Santa Monica Mountains ahead. She gazed longingly at the million-dollar homes dotting the ridgelines, then remembered that those same homes afforded their owners splendid views of the homeless "concrete inspectors" pushing stolen shopping carts along the boulevard and the row of cuffed gang members now sitting on the curb, awaiting transport by their "racist and corrupt" chauffeurs who were probably being videotaped from an apartment balcony.

At Riverside Drive, Abe slowed so Savage could check the right, then pushed sixty miles per hour toward a Thrifty drugstore on the southwest corner of Laurel Canyon and Ventura. The store's neon sign cast an otherworldly glow over an all-night newsstand that wrapped around the building's east side. Across the street, a pair of five-story apartment buildings reared up against the mountains.

"First one's 3930," Savage said, reading a map off

her palmtop computer, then gazing at the mauve-colored structures whose stucco showed few signs of aging or earthquake damage. Higher-rent district to be sure. For once Savage might be spared the wretchedness of flash-lighting her way through a condemned building and stepping over crack addicts to rescue a child from his HIV-positive mother.

"See it," cried Abe, then pulled a hard U-turn and slowed in front of the complex.

"Valley, Rescue Nine is on scene," Savage told TRO Six.

"Rescue Nine, Valley."

Savage grabbed the metal clipboard holding their run forms, tucked it under her arm, then jumped down from the rig. She moved swiftly but calmly to a bay just past her door, where she nearly ran into Abe. He jingled like a janitor with shears, forceps, Mag-Lite, two pagers, ra-dio, and multipurpose pocket knife bound to his belt, along with holsters loaded with bandage scissors, a seat belt cutter, window punch, and penlight. His navy blue pockets bulged with 4x4 pieces of gauze and a pocket mask for CPR. And, of course, his stethoscope dangled in front his white golf shirt with paramedic patches on the sleeves.

"Still think you need all that?" she asked, tugging open the compartment.

"Makes me feel better, m—Ms. Savage."

She withdrew the pediatric bag, tossed it to Abe, then went to the back of the rescue and grabbed the orange drug kit, a converted fishing tackle box sealed by a small lock. "Let's go with Steph, huh?"

"I'll try, ma'am."

Savage sighed and bounded up a flight of stairs leading to a pair of glass doors trimmed in brass. The intercom system was on the wall to their right, and she dialed the apartment.

"Hello?" came a woman's quavering voice.

"Fire department. Did you call 911?"

"Yeah, I did. Come on up!"

The buzzer sounded, and Abe all but dived for the door handle.

Inside, black marble tile shimmered across the entrance foyer to floor-to-ceiling mirrors. Neat rows of mailboxes stood to their left among potted ferns. A short hall to the right terminated at twin elevator doors.

Abe jogged over and punched the elevator button.

Savage crossed to the stairwell door beside the elevator. "It's only two flights."

He followed her up the stairs. On the second floor landing, they charged onto a terrace overlooking a meticulously landscaped courtyard replete with palm trees, benches, and a fish pond fed by four miniature waterfalls.

"Damn. What you think the rent goes for here?" asked Abe.

"Place like this in Studio City? You don't want to know." Savage's gaze flicked over door numbers.

They reached apartment 202. Savage lifted an ornate knocker, banged twice, then she and Abe moved to the side of the door. You never knew who or what would greet you. She had walked into countless homes where one person had called 911 while the others there saw her as an authority figure and hated her for that. One pusher had even decided to clean his gun while Savage worked on his girlfriend. "Fire department."

The door yawned inward, revealing a petite Hispanic woman of about thirty. She wore a black silk robe, and even without makeup, her olive skin appeared remarkably clear. Savage could only dream of having a body and skin like that, but for a husky blonde with blemishes, she had done all right with men since her divorce ten years earlier, never letting a single boyfriend abuse her the way Tim had.

The woman motioned them in, then led them over an ivory shag rug, past a small kitchen with adjoining bar, and into the living room, where a boy of about four, a cute munchkin with dark bangs and amazingly blue eyes, sat on a leather sofa. Savage recognized the boy's wheezing as stridor, a sound typically produced by constriction of the upper airway.

"I'm a script supervisor, and we got out late tonight," the woman explained. "He didn't look so good when I picked him up. I thought it was just a cold. But he woke up crying about an hour ago. I took his temperature. It was 103. I'm scared. I think maybe it's croup. Oh, I'm sorry. I'm Roberta Villanueva."

Savage introduced herself and Abe, then added, "Don't worry. We'll take care of your son. What's his name?"

"Carlos."

After handing Abe the clipboard and instructing him to get a patient history from the mother, Savage slowly approached the boy, who, as he coughed and drooled, turned slightly blue—evidence of cyanosis, decreased oxygen in the blood due to poor ventilation.

The boy shrank deeper into the couch. Seeing this, Savage hunkered down, unzipped the pediatric bag, and removed a small, blue teddy bear. "Hey, Carlos? Don't try to talk. I just need your help. Can you hold this bear for me?"

His gaze riveted on the toy. He managed a nod.

"Okay," she said, as soothingly as possible and proffering the bear. "Your mommy called us because you don't feel good. We're here to make you feel better. We won't hurt you, I promise. And you can help by taking care of that bear, okay?"

Carlos winced through another nod.

"Now what I want to do is see how many times you breathe, and I want to find out how much air is in your blood. I can do that last part by putting this little plastic thing on your finger. It doesn't hurt at all, see?" Savage placed the pulse oximeter's thimblelike sensor on her finger and held it up. The sensor would measure the transmission of red and infrared light through an arterial bed like the ones in Carlos's finger. "Wanna try?"

He scrutinized the sensor and attached leads for a moment, glanced at the bear, then half-shrugged. Savage placed the sensor near Carlos's leg, and he took it into his hands.

"Put it on your pointer," Savage said, miming it for him.

Once Carlos had the sensor on his finger, Savage turned on the pulse ox, a newer model no larger than a cell phone. She waited for the SpO_2 and the pulse rate to come up on the monitor: 92, with a pulse of 160, told her enough. "Carlos, I'm going to put my hand on your chest. It won't hurt. I just want to see how many times you breathe. I'll put on this glove, see? It's kind of like a balloon." Savage clawed into the latex glove, then slid her hand beneath Carlos's Barney print pajama top. She applied firm pressure to his chest and gently stroked his hair with her free hand. Normal respiration for a boy his age fell between twenty and thirty respirations per minute. Carlos's came in high at thirty-eight.

"Got a history," Abe said, drumming a knuckle on the clipboard and run sheet. "No allergies. Not taking any meds. No major medical problems in the past. Last meal at 7:30 P.M. Looks like his airway's compromised. You wanna tube him?"

"Is he all right?" the mother pleaded.

"He'll be okay," answered Savage. "But we need to transport him right now. It could be epiglottitis."

"What is it?"

"There's a flap of cartilage behind his tongue that protects the airway during swallowing. That flap is swelling up because he might have a bacterial infection, probably *Haemophilus* influenza."

"Influenza? My God, that's serious, right?"

"It can be. Epiglottitis is considered life-threatening. Get me a robe, a blanket, something to wrap him in. And get what you need. What hospital do you want to go to?"

"Uh, SFMC, I guess."

Savage rose. "Can I pick him up?"

"Yeah, sure."

As Carlos's mother dashed into the bedroom, Savage removed the pulse ox's sensor from the boy's finger, then hoisted him into her arms. "As his airway becomes more obstructed," she told Abe, "he'll exhibit nasal flaring and pulmonary hyperexpansion."

"He almost looks septic," Abe observed. "But why do you think it's epiglottitis when you didn't visualize the airway?"

"You *never* visualize the airway in these patients. It's contraindicated in every text you've read, and could result in laryngospasm or complete obstruction."

"So what do you do?"

"When they're crying, sometimes the tip of the epiglottis can be seen posterior to the base of the tongue."

"So you saw it?"

"No. Last week we had three kids come down with it in this neighborhood. Carlos is number four."

"Books don't help for that call," Abe said with a shrug.

"Right. You gotta know the 'hood. Go down to the rescue and set us up for humidified O_2. We'll get a BP down there. I peg Carlos for seventeen kilograms. Use your tape and get us ready for a needle cric, just in case. Check the dosage for albuterol."

Abe packed up the pediatric bag, then started for the door. Down in the rescue, he would unfold the color-coded Broselow resuscitation tape and figure out which color belonged to a seventeen-kilogram child. Then he would unroll a tool bag with plastic, color-coded pouches Velcroed inside. Each pouch contained an IV starter kit, endotracheal tube, and oropharyngeal airway sized for a particular weight group. All you had to do was match the colors. Thus, you'd have the right equipment and a cheat sheet to make sure you never overdosed a child or used the wrong size catheter or ET tube.

Savage called the system "rookie-proof." The bag and tape were often employed for trauma cases, the tape stretched out next to the child to determine his or her weight class.

"Okay, I'm ready," said Carlos's mother.

Cupping the boy's head into her shoulder, Savage nodded and moved gingerly out of the apartment.

"What can they do for him?" the mother asked as they hit the stairwell.

"They'll take a soft-tissue X ray of his neck. They'll give him some drugs intravenously, and we'll probably use what we call inhaled bronchodilators. Thing we worry about most is keeping his airway open."

They reached the front doors. Beyond them, Abe waited at the back of the rescue, giving a heads-up to the three firefighters of Engine Nine, who had just arrived. Savage carried Carlos inside the ambulance and set him down on the stretcher. Abe buckled the boy in an upright position, the most comfortable for epiglottitis patients, then pulled off the small miracle of sliding on the BP cuff and pumping it up before the kid knew what was happening. "This will just squeeze your arm a little bit," he told Carlos.

Lifting her voice over the two rumbling engines, Savage directed the mother to a red bench opposite the stretcher and asked her to buckle in, then hold her son's hand.

"Okay, Carlos. See this mask? Just like Halloween, only air comes through this one. Your mom's going to hold it near your face. It won't hurt at all, and it'll help you to breathe." Savage handed the mask to Carlos's mother, and she held it near the boy's nose and mouth in a technique for ventilating pediatric patients known as the "blow-by" method. The transparent air tube snaked away from the mask and attached to a water bottle and the oxygen supply up front.

Abe reported the boy's BP at ninety, then hopped down from the rescue. He locked the folding bumper into its upright position, then shut the rear doors.

"It's gonna be okay, honey," said Carlos's mother, just shy of tears.

Savage unclipped the mike from the wall-mounted radio and adjusted the frequency. "SFMC, this is Paramedic Stephanie Savage, Rescue Nine."

"Nine, SFMC," answered Medic Controller Charti Darunyothin, a dispatcher who handled all incoming paramedic calls for the district.

"Request MCEP for report."

"Stand by."

After fifteen seconds a familiar voice came over the radio, an attending physician Savage knew very well. "Nine? This is Doctor Joanna Boccaccio. Copy?"

"Copy, Doctor. En route to your facility with a four-year-old Hispanic male, ALS unstable. Patient found exhibiting signs and symptoms of epiglottitis with temperature of approximately 103. Vitals are BP 90, pulse 160 and thready, respirations 38 and labored with stridor, pulse ox 92. Administered humidified O_2 at fifteen liters via simple face mask. Prepping to administer 2.5 milligrams albuterol via nebulizer. ETA code three of five to six minutes."

"Copy, Nine. Peds team will stand by. If total airway obstruction occurs, avoid intubation. Perform needle cric."

"Confirm needle cric if total airway obstruction occurs. Nine out."

Savage knew that words and phrases like "thready," "labored with stridor," and "albuterol via nebulizer" might scare Carlos's mom, so she explained that the first simply meant that Carlos's pulse was rapid and a little weak, and that the second meant that he was wheezing a bit. She added that they would attach a device known as a nebulizer to the mask and that Carlos would breathe in albuterol, one of the bronchodilators she had mentioned earlier. The drug would help open up his throat. Savage avoided the subject of a needle cricothyrotomy. The possibility of her having to stick a catheter into the front of the boy's neck to help him breathe would only further unravel the woman.

The rescue lurched forward, and the siren blared, sending a jolt through the little boy.

"Easy, Carlos," said Savage as she slid on her wireless headset. "Abe? Let's cheat a little and spare this young man some of that racket. Just lights."

"You got it, Steph."

Savage grinned weakly, then eyed Carlos's mother, whose face was etched with anguish. "I have a son. He's twenty. Yesterday, he was four years old."

"Any others?" the mother asked.

"No, he's my only."

"Me, too."

They shared a look of understanding, one mother to another, as the rescue thundered on.

James Robertson stifled a yawn and squinted through the windshield of his Taurus station wagon. Amazingly, his was the only car on that section of the 405 Freeway. But in just four hours or so, the ungodly rush hour would begin. Robertson had just exited from the Golden State Freeway, but he had no recollection of how he had wound up on the 405. He had driven the route so many times that he figured he had slept through the turns. In less than an hour, he would climb into his own bed after a weeklong vacation of boating and fishing at Lake Arrowhead. He stole a glance at his wife, Casey, who rested her chin on her palm and slept quietly. His eight-year-old son, Trent, and his twelve-year-old daughter, Trisha, had fallen asleep two hours earlier, after a heated battle over something too trivial to remember.

Robertson dreaded the return home during the wee hours, though he had argued for staying the extra two days and driving all night to be home by early Wednesday morning. Back at the campsite, the drive had sounded easy and had conjured up memories of the all-night driving sprees of his college days. Now he felt his forty-one years all too painfully.

Repressing a second yawn, Robertson turned on the radio and listened to a banal talk show, lulled by the cadence of the speakers' voices. He lowered the window a little more, stuck his face in the breeze for a few seconds, then swallowed and tightened his grip on the wheel.

Still clear road ahead, with no traffic on either side of the freeway, yet something seemed missing. No, it wasn't the lack of other cars. Something else. He couldn't put his finger on it. He set the cruise control to sixty-five and gave his tired foot a break. His head dropped forward a little, eyes closing . . . closing. . . .

"Shit," he whispered. *Don't fall asleep, you idiot.*

From the corner of his eye he spotted a speck of light. Two specks now, well ahead of him, maybe a pair of UFOs strafing the canyons but more likely some teenager begging for a ticket with busted taillights. Those damned lights came up swiftly on Robertson, and he checked the dash to see why the cruise control had increased his speed. He frowned at the gauge: sixty-five.

When he glanced up, he realized that the reflectors set into the pavement were not shining as brightly as they should be, and for some odd reason a road sign was facing the wrong—

"Oh, shit!" he cried.

The two lights congealed into one harsh beam that all but swallowed him. A shrill horn and the screech of brakes split the air as the broad windshield of an eighteen-wheeler peeked through the veil of light. Robertson yanked the wheel toward the shoulder, but the truck's massive chrome grill materialized on the passenger's side, just a heartbeat away.

He thought of his wife. Of his children. Of his failure to protect them.

As the truck hit.

2

Isabel Vivas of Rescue Squad Ten sucked in her gut and scowled at the can of French vanilla Ultra Slim-Fast. "Lose weight, feel great," she muttered, reading the label.

"Wanna lose weight?" John "Doe" Smith asked from his seat opposite her in the hospital's cafeteria. "Don't eat." Her partner took a ravenous bite out of his turkey sandwich, then added with his mouth full, "But either way, you ain't got a prayer. You're a Latina mama with big bones. Listen to the Doeman. It's genetics. You can't screw with genetics. But don't off yourself. Some guys like 'em big. Like your ex, right? So what're you worried about?"

"I'm worried about what I'll do to you if you don't shut up and eat." Vivas tensed as she popped open the can, took a long swig, then shook her head. "For your information, I used to be a model when I was in high school." She leaned forward and grabbed her chin. "You see this face? Guys killed each other over this face." She unclipped her long, ebony hair and let it tumble over her shoulders.

"I'll give you that," he answered, chewing with his mouth open. "But then you had your kid. Hey, if it makes you feel better, I'd do you."

She jerked the can of Ultra Slim-Fast, tossing some at him.

"Aw shit," he cried, sliding back from the table. "You're wasting it."

"I know. Give me the other half of that sandwich."

"You got no willpower."

"Look who's talking."

"Hey, Izzy. It's medicine—"

"You get naked," she finished, having heard him say that tired line for the nth time.

Still, he smiled, and when he did, Vivas could see why his digital answering machine repeatedly ran out of memory. If his dimples got any deeper or his eyes any bluer, even *she* would jump on him—and that was saying a lot, because she had suffered through his Peter Pan antics for nearly two years and had consoled at least four of his romantic casualties.

"Let me tell you about my trip to Orlando," he said. "By the way, Mom says hi."

"She like it in the new place?"

"That expensive raisin farm? Hell, yeah. They're all waiting to die. But they're doing it in style. Dad hates it. He drives over to the beach a couple times a week to check out the babes. I hope I'm still horny when I'm his age."

"I think you'll have worn it out by then," Vivas said

through a sigh. But she wouldn't chide him too much about it now; his sandwich tasted too damned good.

"So I hooked up with a buddy from NASA while I was down there. Couple engineers around the office came up with this new condom made out of some space-age material. I got samples."

"Samples?"

"Seriously. I'm gonna try one out. I'll let you know." He winked.

She made a face.

"Almost experimented on one of my sister's friends," he continued.

"What happened? She got to know you?"

"Guess so."

"So your sister's still living there? How're the kids?"

He pursed his lips in disgust. "All I get is, 'John, you're thirty-two years old. You need to figure out what you're gonna do with your life. You can't just work your job and play with your toys. There's more to life than motocross and snowboarding and parasailing. When you gonna settle down?' "

"That's a pretty good impression," Vivas said with a knowing smile. "So, what're you going to do? Start a family or die a lonely old man?"

After a prolonged yawn, Doe stood, abandoning the question. "I'm done. Let's go bust Charti's balls before we leave."

"Not again."

"C'mon, he's had a week's vacation from me."

Vivas stole a last bite of the sandwich, then followed Doe out of the cafeteria.

They headed across the emergency department to

where critical patients arrived "off the ramp" and were immediately taken to a special procedures and trauma stabilization area known as "C-booth." The booth, which could accommodate up to five cases at one time, was empty at the moment. All too often Vivas had watched emergency room physicians and surgeons working together in C-booth to stabilize and quickly resuscitate trauma patients. Decisions to intervene, transport to the OR, or triage to surgical admitting were made there, and Vivas had learned a hell of a lot about emergency medicine just by observing the trauma teams going about their business.

Gunga, the triage officer on duty, gave them a passing nod as they moved past C-booth to the nurses' station. Fenced off by gray counters and harshly lit by fluorescent lights, the station served as home to the nurses of 7700, an eclectic group who could handle any "emergent" situation from navel lint to cardiac arrest.

Doe paraded to the end of the counter, where Medic Controller Charti Darunyothin sat, brooding over his computer screen.

"Surfing the Internet on company time again?" asked Doe.

After a dramatic pause, the slightly built Filipino looked up, dark eyes burning, jet-black spike cut screaming to be rubbed. "You're violating the no Doe zone. Get lost."

"I missed you, too." Doe leaned over the counter. "What? You don't feel the same?"

"Charti, I'm sorry," said Vivas, assuming her most sympathetic look. "He's a jerk."

"What's the matter, Charti?" Doe asked with an exaggerated frown. "Do you really hate me that much?"

Poker face unchanged, Charti answered, "You're in violation of the no Doe zone. If you don't withdraw in ten seconds, I will call security."

Sauntering behind the counter, Doe came upon a stack of forms piled up next to Charti. He *tsk*ed as he tossed them all over Charti's impeccably neat station.

Charti bolted to his feet, mouth agape, cheeks flushed. "Out!"

"Did you say *ouch*? Or *out*?" Doe asked. "Or is that a Filipino curse?"

"Listen, you trauma monkey—"

"Got him!" Doe cried. "Got him! Mr. Charti Darunyothin, always so neat and never, *ever* gets upset. Look at him now: workspace a shambles and shouting with the worst of 'em." Doe's voice grew mock serious. "You're a disgrace to this hospital, Mr. Darunyothin. I'm you, I resign immediately and spend a few years thinking about my unprofessional behavior."

"Leave him alone," Stephanie Savage hollered as she trudged down the hall toward the station. Her new partner, Abe, hustled to catch up with her. Vivas had to laugh at the rookie's overzealous utility belt.

"And a good evening to you, too, Beast," Doe answered, coming around the counter. "How'd you make out with that epiglottitis patient?"

"They almost had to cric him, but he'll be all right. 'Bout time we came across a parent who actually cares about her son. I mean, look at my kid. If it weren't for me—"

Vivas and Doe groaned in unison. If they had to listen to another word about how well her son was doing in college or how good-looking he was or how many girl-friends he had or how many employers wanted to scoop him up after he graduated from that big Florida school he attended, they would remove her tongue with their seat belt cutters.

"Hey, I got a right to be proud," Savage hollered. "Dysfunctional families all over the place. Lunatics walking into community centers and high schools and gunning down people. It's a mean world. You're luckier than the Irish if you can keep a kid on the straight and narrow."

The sound of hands clapping drew everyone's attention to Dr. Joanna Boccaccio. Even Doe straightened as she came forward, her mane of curly hair pulled into a tight, dark bun, her gaze sizing up the quartet as though she were a drill instructor wearing olive drab instead of hospital green. Though she could not be much older than thirty, the experience of four years of residency showed in her eyes. She neared Savage, who stood nearly a full head taller. "That's a pretty good sermon. But it's two-thirtysomething in the morning. I'm used to these hours, but it's still too early for sermons. So what're you doing, Doe? Other than showing off your tan and standing around."

"I am *not* standing around," he answered. "I'm refamiliarizing myself with the emergency department of this fine hospital after a much-needed vacation." He broke off and surveyed the area, nodding comically at this corner and that.

"He's bothering me again," Charti called from his station.

"All right, ladies and gentlemen, let's take this love

fest outside," Boccaccio said, tipping her head toward the exit and drawing Doe's groan.

"I'll catch up with you," Vivas told Doe as he headed out. She turned back to Boccaccio. "Hey, Doctor, got a sec?"

Boccaccio drew in a long breath. "What's up, Izzy?"

"I'm trying to lose weight, and it ain't working. I'm doing the Slim-Fast thing, but I gotta eat more than 'a sensible meal.' Got any suggestions?"

"Come and see me at eight. We'll have breakfast together. I mean we'll just talk. I know a few people who can help."

"Yeah, good. And see what you just said? Our society is all about food. I go home, and the whole day is planned around when and what we're gonna eat. Sometimes I blame my mother, but that's how she was raised, and it's why we're all fat horses. It's like you can't socialize unless it's about food."

"Or sex," Boccaccio added.

"Hear that. I'll see you later." Vivas moved off, then TRO Six's baritone voice came over her portable:

"Engine Nine, Rescue Nine. Engine Nine, Rescue Nine. Code three to an MVA on northbound Four-Oh-Five Freeway at Roscoe Boulevard. CHP en route. Multiple victims reported."

3

"Okay, Abe. All calls are BS until proven otherwise, but I got a feeling about this one. Looks like we'll beat our engine on the scene, so remember your mechanism of injury. You size up the situation and anticipate injuries or injury groups even before you make contact with the patients. You've got your motion, your momentum, your acceleration, your deceleration, and your energy. Use 'em to predict injuries. The old saying 'Speed kills' is a scientific fact."

If Abe's pulse did not slow down, he would demonstrate that scientific fact in about five seconds. Never mind the fact that he should have peed back at the hospital and that Savage's reminding him of what he already knew made him feel even more inadequate. He sat in the rescue, hands locked on the wheel as he barreled down the 405 Freeway toward the motor vehicle accident. Vivas and Doe, having responded to the second alarm, raced about a thousand yards behind, xenon strobe lights flashing, siren preaching the good word from the book of Get the Hell out of My Way. When faced with a racing emergency vehicle on their tails, some drivers would, for some stupendously idiotic reason, develop acute blindness and deafness. Twice Doe had to swerve around cars whose drivers refused to yield.

Abe shuddered as he contemplated the wreck ahead. TRO Six had given them an update as reported by the CHP units on the scene. Station wagon versus eighteen-wheel car carrier, with four patients in the wagon. Your typical "grinder." He ordered himself to remain calm and remember his training. In most typical MVAs, there are actually three collisions. The first occurs when the vehicles collide. The second collision involves the human body, which is moving independently of the vehicle and comes to a sudden stop against whatever is around—seatbelt, air bag, steering wheel, dashboard, another passenger, what have you. The third and least obvious collision happens when an organ, often the brain, slams against the inside of the body. The impact can result in contusions and/or bleeding that can create enough pressure to cause brain death.

"Show time," muttered Savage.

They had just reached the crest of a hill and now looked down on an eerie crimson glow produced by a semicircle of flares lit by officers from two California Highway Patrol units. The car carrier sat fifty yards up, on the right shoulder, which meant that the driver had recovered some control after the collision and might not have been seriously injured. A Honda Accord and an old Ford Mustang lined up behind the eighteen-wheeler;

they probably belonged to the middle-aged black man in the security guard uniform and the teenaged boy with pink hair and nose ring who stood at the perimeter of the flares.

"Damn," Abe gasped as they pulled beyond the wreck and slowed to park. He studied the wagon, which had been smashed out of the carrier's way and lay on the shoulder amid a glittering carpet of safety glass. The forward two-thirds of the passenger's side had been smashed in twenty or even thirty inches. The front tire had been blown out and bent at an improbable angle. Thankfully, the car had not burst into flames, though thin columns of smoke still rose from beneath its tented hood, and fuel pooled near the rear bumper. A miasma of gas and burned rubber lingered in the air and wafted in through the rescue's AC unit.

"Speed of the wagon?" Savage asked, her voice unmoved by the shattered vehicle.

"I'd say about sixty. Truck was probably braking."

"Yes, it was. Check your tire tracks." She cocked a thumb over her shoulder. "You'll see that the wagon was dragged for about twenty feet before it broke away. Somehow this rocket scientist was traveling in the wrong direction. Also, think about that eighteen-wheeler. Is it carrying any hazardous material? No, just new cars, with not much gas in their tanks. Now, talk to me about the wagon's occupants."

"Driver could be drunk. No doubt we'll find head injuries. Patients will be in varying states of consciousness. Compression against the lateral chest and abdominal wall may have injured the spleen, liver, and/or kidneys. Shoulder compression may have produced midshaft fractures of the clavicle and/or lateral flail chest. Might even find a pulmonary contusion or injury to the solid organs. Occupants on the driver's side are vulnerable to splenic injuries, since the spleen is a left-sided organ, while those on the passenger's side are vulnerable to liver injuries."

"Very good. Let's see how you apply what you've learned." Savage grabbed the mike and muttered, "Hope we got enough people out here." Then, "Valley, Rescue Nine. On scene of T-bone MVA. Request two air squads and additional CHP units to close northbound side of freeway and set up LZ for our choppers. Contact Cal Trans for cleanup. Will update as needed. Rescue Nine is command." She slammed out of the rescue and marched toward one of the officers as Abe switched on the rescue's powerful side lights, focused twin beams on the wagon, then hustled out. He opened a compartment and snatched the c-spine bag, then grabbed the airway bag off the stretcher as Rescue Ten rolled up.

"Somebody took a wrong turn," Doe said as he knifed out of his rescue, then jogged toward Savage and the CHP officer, who had been joined by a second cop and a heavy-set guy with a Santa Claus beard and black leather beret, probably the truck driver.

Indeed, Abe and the others had responded to a whole lot more than their routine fender bender, and once the engine arrived, Lieutenant Juan Martinez would take command. Accidents of this magnitude were invariably multiresponse and organized using the Incident Command System. In a few minutes the freeway would swarm with well-trained rescuers walled in by gleaming apparatus.

"You okay, Abe?" Vivas asked, gripping her own airway and c-spine bags.

"Yeah."

"Don't sound like it. C'mon. I bet you've seen shit worse than this. Let's go."

For a moment, Abe leaned shakily on the back of the rescue, wondering why he was kidding himself. *I don't belong here. I belong back in Pakistan with my folks. I can't do this anymore. I have nobody here. Nobody.*

"Abe," cried Savage.

He took a deep breath and jogged over to the wreck. He *had* seen worse shit, but the sight of a family of four crushed in their car and converted into bloody hunks of meat tied knots in his stomach. He swallowed and, as he had been taught, circled the vehicle, assessing the damage, asking himself how and why the accident had occurred. Perfect little family of four clinging to life. *Thanks a lot, God.*

Doe gingerly opened the driver's side door to assess a white male in his forties while Vivas headed for the unconscious ten- or twelve-year-old girl on the rear passenger's side. Savage lay across the hood, trying to squeeze past the shattered windshield to evaluate the mother, also in her forties, who lay inert and pinned beneath the dash and roof. One rule of thumb in extrication Abe knew all too well: what you cannot see is trapping your patients. He jogged behind Doe toward a whimpering eight- or nine-year-old blond boy still seated and belted, leaning on the window. Doe asked the driver, "Are you okay? Are you okay?"

"What are you doing?" the driver rasped, then emitted a strangled cry.

"Just hang in there, sir. My name's John Smith. I'm a paramedic, and I'm gonna help you out." Doe directed his penlight into the man's eyes. "Hey, Beast? Got evidence of flail chest with obvious paradoxical movement. Open fracture to right arm. Possible broken jaw from the airbag. Pupils reactive. Evidence of concussion. He could also have a ruptured spleen. I'll get a collar on and board him. No apparent evidence of ETOH," Doe added, referring to alcohol by its medical name. He turned to one of the CHP officers standing nearby and holding a blood draw kit. "You guys'll have to get your draw at the hospital. How 'bout a little help with a c-spine?"

Abe eased open the driver's side rear door, leaned into the compartment, and clicked on his penlight. "Hey there, my name's Abe," he told the boy. "I'm a paramedic. You okay?"

"I'm bleeding. And my head hurts. Mom? Dad?"

"Don't worry, we'll help 'em. What's your name?"

"Trent."

"Okay, Trent. Can you do two things for me? Don't move, and think of your favorite thing in the whole world."

"Okay."

The kid had suffered minor lacerations to the head and face, and his speech told Abe enough about his airway, at least for the moment. Blood seeped from one of his ears, and Abe immediately pulled out a 4x4 from his pocket and allowed some blood to drip on the gauze. A dark red circle appeared, surrounded by a lighter one— an indication that cerebrospinal fluid had mixed with the boy's blood and that he had suffered a skull fracture. In the coming hours, the boy might exhibit Battle's sign, a black-and-blue discoloration behind the ears, and/or bilateral periorbital ecchymosis, commonly known as "raccoon eyes," as blood traveled into the periorbital subcutaneous tissue to give him two black eyes and confirm a basilar skull fracture.

"Hey, Steph," Vivas called. "This girl's unconscious, unresponsive. Trach is midline. Lungs clear bilaterally. Definite blunt trauma to the head. Possible closed head injury. Pupils unequal. Crepitus in the hips. Possible pelvic fracture. She's also got fractures of the right femur and right arm. There's barely enough room, but I ain't waiting for extrication. I'm gonna try tubing her."

"Do it. And I've got decreased breath sounds and evidence of blood in the pleural space over here," Savage said. "Possible closed tension pneumothorax. We have to get in here, tube her, then decompress while we're waiting for extrication. Abe, how's that boy doing?"

"He's alert," Abe answered, picking the highest of four levels of consciousness: Alert, responsive to Verbal stimuli, responsive to Painful stimuli, and Unresponsive. "Evidence of CSF in the ears. Possible basilar fracture." The scary part about treating kids was the fact that they could maintain a normal appearance for a long time, then, suddenly, wham! They went critical and died on you.

"Need another c-spine?" one of the CHP guys asked.

Abe glanced back at the young, pale-faced man with shaven head. "You know what to do?"

"Been here, done this, unfortunately," the officer said. He slid past Abe and positioned himself at the boy's midtorso, angled so he could face the boy with one knee almost touching him. Then he began head immobilization, gripping the boy's face and neck like an expert while Abe attached the collar.

Breathing an inaudible sigh of relief, Abe scooped up the airway and c-spine bags, then circled around to Savage's side as Vivas announced that her tube was in the girl.

The enormity of the moment struck again. Four people still lay in the car, two of them trapped, while four paramedics and two Highway Patrol officers hovered over them. A third officer joined the rescue to provide a c-spine for the mother, who had been shoved toward the driver's side and now lay on her husband's shoulder. Rescuers literally swarmed over the car. In a few moments, three more would arrive in the engine, to begin foaming down the fuel spill and extrication.

"SFMC, Rescue Nine," Savage said into her portable.

"Nine, SFMC," replied Charti back in the emergency department.

"Request MCEP for category 1 report."

After a brief pause: "Nine, SFMC, Doctor Boccaccio on line. What do you got?"

"Four criticals. Multisystem traumas from an MVA. Two adults, two kids. Father and son coming in via ground. Mother and daughter via chopper."

"Copy, Nine. We can take them all. We'll have the booth ready for you."

"Roger that. We'll update ETA en route. Nine, out." Savage dialed a different frequency. "Air Squad Nine, Roscoe command."

"Roscoe, Air Squad Nine. Go Savage," responded the medevac chopper pilot.

"What's your ETA?"

"About four minutes. Eight's just behind me."

"Copy. Roscoe out." Savage turned to her partner. "Okay, Abe. You're smaller than me. You're gonna squeeze in there and tube her."

Repressing a shiver, Abe zipped open the airway bag, retrieved the Ambu bag, also known as the bag valve mask, and handed it to Savage. The first step in a visualized orotracheal intubation was to hyperventilate the patient, using a simple airway adjunct like the mask. Correction. The first step was to calm down.

Meanwhile, Doe had been fitting the father and daughter with cervical collars from the c-spine bag Vivas had brought over, thus relieving the CHP officers. Doe finished with the father's collar, then, with the help of the officers, he rotated the driver ninety degrees and lowered him carefully onto a long backboard. Doe had already taped a splint and bulky dressings to the patient's flail chest in an attempt to reduce motion of the flail segment, which would lessen pain. Concurrently, another officer maintained positive-pressure ventilation by squeezing the bag valve mask he held fast over the man's nose and mouth.

With the driver out of the way and ready for packaging Abe wriggled in, gently pushed the seat's release and reclined the woman a few precious inches, then maneuvered behind her head. Once in position and with Savage ventilating the patient, he yanked the laryngoscope handle from the airway bag. The handle was a stainless steel cylinder about eight inches long, and it housed batteries, much like a flashlight. Abe quickly attached a flat, curved blade known as a MacIntosh to the

handle. He'd use it to lift the patient's tongue and epiglottis out of the way. Laryngoscope blades came in
sizes from 0 for an infant to 4 for a large adult. Abe had
pulled a 3 from his cache. A tiny light glowed on the
blade's tip and would illuminate the patient's throat.

Next he pulled out the proper size endotracheal tube,
whose bottom had been cut at a forty-five degree angle
and came with an inflatable cuff to seal the trachea. A
second, thinner tube called the inflation tube was attached to the main one near the top, and a 10cc syringe,
inflation valve, and pilot balloon helped to inflate the
main tube's cuff.

Finally, Abe slipped out the stylet, basically a long
wire covered with plastic. The wire had a loop on one
end and was slipped into the endotracheal tube to pull
the tube into a J or hockey-stick shape, often making it
easier to insert.

"She's hyperventilated," Savage said.

Abe pulled back the plunger on the endotracheal
tube's syringe until he had drawn in about ten milliliters
of air, then attached it to the one-way valve on the inflation tube. He held the whole setup in his right hand,
with the laryngoscope in his left.

*Okay. You got no more than thirty seconds. Should
take you no more than ten. Think you can do it while
you're squashed into this car? Is this what you wanted
your life to be? Stop thinking! Concentrate. . . .*

He widened his eyes, forced the tremors out of his
hands, and began earning his paycheck.

4

Abe inserted the laryngoscope blade, and once it was properly placed in the woman's mouth, he applied gentle traction. As he had been taught, he carefully avoided touching the upper incisors or using them as a fulcrum. Still leaning over the woman, he glanced up, and a cool breeze raked over his face. The *thump-thump* of approaching choppers, accompanied by more sirens, grew louder.

Two more CHP units had arrived, and four officers had lit flares and had placed them at the four corners of their makeshift chopper landing zone, an area of freeway about three hundred feet square. Then they had positioned two patrol cars on the north side of the freeway and facing the center of the zone. Both had set their headlights to low. A firefighter wearing a reflective orange vest spoke with the chopper pilots.

All while Abe was trying to get his tube in.

It was one thing to perform an intubation in an apartment, a shopping mall, an auto repair shop, or the cool confines of a classroom—he had done so in all of those environments—but at a crash scene, so many distractions vied for his attention that he made a conscious effort to reduce the world to just him and the woman. No stench rose from behind the car. No shouts of CHP officers or beeping radios assaulted his ears. No vibration from the rocking vehicle jarred his legs.

"You see the cords?" Savage asked.

"Got 'em," he responded, then slightly advanced the endotracheal tube between the woman's vocal cords until the cuff just passed through. "Going in about another inch. Cuff's good. Stylet's coming out," he said, withdrawing the plastic-covered wire. Then he inflated the cuff and removed the syringe from the one-way valve. Savage handed him the disposable bag valve mask, which he quickly attached to the adapter on the endotracheal tube. The woman would now receive pure oxygen supplied by an attached tank inside the airway bag.

"Okay, I'm on the bag," said Savage. "Now, this might be the field, but it's your classroom, Abe. And maybe you're not used to talking like this out here, but we're gonna do it. What do we do before we secure the tube?"

"Visually check for adequate chest rise and auscultate for good breath sounds at the midlung field," Abe answered, then slipped on his stethoscope. He strained to hear breath sounds on the left. Good sounds. Then he checked the right. "Sounds strong on the left, weak on the right."

"Exactly. She's got a partial pneumo. You secure the tube, then I'll decompress."

"Old Fitzy's here, Steph," came a gravelly voice from behind. "Looks like y'all need a hand."

"Take over bagging," Savage said, then waited until the freckle-faced man in his fifties with a thick red mustache and fiery blue eyes had reached into the car and seized the bag.

At the same time, Abe attached the tube to the woman's face with a Veni-gard, a very sticky, looped piece of tape. Then he reached into the airway bag and fished out a fourteen-gauge large-bore catheter over a needle. He opened the package, then pulled a latex glove from his hip holder. He cut off a glove finger and threaded the catheter through the end of it from the inside. He handed this setup to Savage, who had already cut away the woman's shirt, had prepared the site with an antiseptic swab, and now firmly introduced the needle into the affected pleural space on the upper right side of the patient's chest.

"You watching me, Abe?" Savage asked. "The landmark for insertion is the second intercostal space in the midclavicular line. Feels like pushing a knitting needle through shoe leather, right? You watching?"

"Maybe he's watching you, but I ain't," said a nearby CHP officer. "That's a big ass needle."

"You hear it?" Savage yelled, then pulled Abe's head down toward the woman's chest.

Air rushed through the catheter, relieving the pressure in the woman's chest and demonstrating a successful pleural decompression. Abe nodded as Savage secured the catheter with a Veni-gard. "Gotta make sure the catheter doesn't kink." She checked the glove flapping over the end of the catheter and forming a flutter valve. Pressure now flowed from within the woman's pleural cavity to the outside. Abe hurriedly covered the area with occlusive dressing and a sterile gauze pad. The flutter valve would remain unobstructed outside the dressing.

Savage crawled across the hood, jumped down, then jogged back to the rescue to fetch fluids and the "stick box," a thin, transparent container that served as an IV starter kit.

"You the new guy?" asked Fitzy.

"Yeah."

The older man smiled. "They just call me Fitzy, and you're lucky you got a real good one here. You missed a real nasty T-bone about two weeks ago. We pulled four out of this little Honda. I couldn't believe anybody survived, but old Jack Daniels saved the driver. I don't think he even knew he was in an accident. Kept telling us he had to get home to vacuum."

After a cursory nod, Abe accepted the equipment from Savage and rushed to start an IV line on the woman's right arm while Savage did likewise for the left. Normally they would start lines en route, but sometimes prolonged extrication didn't allow for that. He set down the bag of 1,000ccs of normal saline with its attached plastic tubing, then applied a tourniquet to the woman's arm, making sure to leave one end of the band's slip knot exposed to assure rapid release when the procedure was done. The rest came quickly, almost without thinking:

Find vein. Antecubital (AC) vein. Big one in the woman's arm, where her elbow bent.

Prep site with an antibacterial solution.

Keep bevel up. Insert needle and catheter.

Feel pop. See flashback of blood. Reduce angle.

Ease catheter all the way in.

Hold hub firmly in place. Withdraw needle.

Attach IV tubing to hub. Open flow regulator.

Run bag wide open. Secure with Veni-gard. Pull off tourniquet.

And you're out of there.

As Abe hustled off to get the cardiac monitor and pulse ox, he noticed that the real spectacle had begun. Lieutenant Juan Martinez had arrived and had sectored out personnel. Two paramedics from Rescue Eight arrived on scene to transport the little boy, who was already being packaged by firefighters from Engine Ten. Vivas and Doe had already left with the driver.

Abe assumed that the decision to take the mother and daughter by air and the father and son by ground was due largely to the severity of injuries and the extrication time. Although the choppers would take only about four minutes to get to SFMC, while the rescues would take seven, maybe eight minutes via ground, extricating the mother and daughter would take no more than three to four minutes—if Martinez had anything to say about it. The rescues would probably still beat the choppers—an unusual but not unprecedented occurrence, and Martinez would want the air squads ready to fly the second his team freed the most critically injured patients.

Beyond all of the commotion, the choppers had finally landed, one behind the other after the CHP officers had set up their blockade. In the meantime, a transportation sector officer was already waving a colossal tow truck toward the eighteen-wheeler, whose driver was now complaining of cervical spine pain and being treated by two firefighters from Engine Eight. The security guard and teenaged boy who had pulled over had given their statements to the CHP and were leaving.

Three firefighters from Engine Eight began foaming down the fuel that had puddled near the wagon's rear bumper. One firefighter guided the hose while another directed the nozzle, laying down a thick spray of alcohol-resistant foam that separated the fuel from the air and suppressed the release of flammable vapors. The third fireman monitored the system's bladder tank.

While the foaming continued, Squad Nine rolled up in their colossal apparatus, its engine growling. The "squad" vehicle represented the rolling hardware store of Station Nine's Special Hazards and Operations Team. It packed an astounding assortment of special equipment ranging from HAZMAT suits to multiple types of stretchers to an onboard computer and weather station. A boom atop the squad began rising and, once it was erect, a powerful spotlight would further illuminate the scene. Three firefighters leaped out, pulled open drawers along the squad's bottom, and removed long pieces of wood screwed together to form miniature staircases and fitted with nylon straps for handles. This "cribbing" was used to brace vehicles because excessive rocking during the extrication could result in further injury to the patients. The firefighters shouted and jammed the cribbing into place. Then, electric pumps aboard the squad rumbled to life as the team broke out two of their Hurst tools: a large C-shaped cutter with attached hose snaking back to a reel and a fifty-pound spreader, a needle-nosed instrument also linked to a hose.

The extrication team would need to work fast—and

not just to clear the freeway for the already incensed early-morning motorists. Research by the Maryland Institute for Emergency Medical Services revealed that severely injured patients who undergo surgery within one hour after their accident have a much higher rate of survival than those who do not. This "golden hour" begins at the moment of the crash. It might take another two or three minutes for the incident to be reported, then another minute for the call to go in to the 911 center. The call itself might last another two minutes, then the units nearest to the scene would be dispatched. The crews of those units might take a minute or so to double-check the address; then, finally, the units would drive to the scene, which could take anywhere from one to twenty minutes, depending upon distance and traffic. All of that time was set, so efficient extrication was the best answer to the problem of on-scene time. But those firefighters were working with the Grim Reaper on their backs, and Old Death had eternal patience and never got flustered or depressed.

"All right, let's get the roof off," cried Lieutenant Martinez. A lively, dark-haired, mustached man nationally recognized for his work in extrication, he directed one firefighter who brandished a reciprocating saw while, behind him, the two others began working on the driver's side front and rear doors, their cutter and spreader wailing in competition with the engine that powered them.

Savage now sat in the back seat with the unconscious girl whom Vivas had assessed and tubed. The fracture of the girl's right arm was not life-threatening, but the pelvic and femur fractures could easily kill her because they often resulted in severe internal hemorrhage, some-times in excess of two liters. Savage had already started IVs, eighteen gauges, in the left arm; another firefighter lay on his belly and bagged the girl through the shattered rear window.

"How's she doing over there, Abe?"

"Still unconscious, unresponsive," Abe shouted over the racket. "Pupils constricted but reactive. BP was ini-tially 100/60, but now it's 140/100. Pulse was 90, now it's 80."

"Indicating what?"

"A late sign of increasing intracranial pressure. The systolic blood pressure rises as the pulse falls during compensation. Then, during decompensation, the pulse rises dramatically while the pressure drops. If we weren't bagging her, I might find Cheyne-Stokes respi-ration, central neurogenic hyperventilation, or even medullary-type breathing." Those terms described breathing pattern changes in patients with head injuries, and Abe knew them well, though he had never worked on a patient who exhibited them.

"You sound like a textbook. Knock it off."

"But I thought—"

"Any signs of decorticate posturing?" she asked.

Abe examined the woman for signs of flexion or bending of the upper extremities, with the lower extrem-ities rigid and extended. Medics who enjoyed black hu-mor called it "positive Honda sign," referring to the signs of many motorcycle crash patients. "Got nothing yet."

"Expect it any time now."

"Starting to see some evidence of CSF," Abe said,

referring to the cerebrospinal fluid leaking from the woman's ears, the same fluid he had found on the boy. He daubed it with a 4×4 and spotted the halo.

Without warning, heavy blankets dropped over Abe, Fitzy, and the woman as well as Savage and her patient, so that all would be protected from broken glass, saw sparks, and metal shrapnel.

The two firefighters wielding the Hurst tools began peeling off the wagon's roof. Metal and plastic creaked in protest. Another rule of extrication: You disentangle the metal from the patient, not the patient from the metal. It was all about keeping the trapped patient as immobile as possible. Abe figured they would have to use rams to push up the dashboard, although Martinez was saying something about getting the woman out by removing both front seats. Abe was elbowed by a firefighter gripping a ratchet.

"Pretty wild shit, huh?" yelled Fitzy, as the wagon vibrated under the extrication team's efforts. Despite striking up a conversation, Fitzy did not miss a beat with his ventilations.

"How many times have you done this?" Abe asked as he took a quick blood pressure reading and winced over the noise.

"Bagging someone? Or coming to a wreck?"

"Both."

"Don't know. Been a firefighter for twenty-six years. Maybe I've seen a thousand wrecks like this and a thousand poor women just like this one."

"It ever get to you?"

Fitzy chuckled. "Nope."

"So what's your defense mechanism? Budweiser or Heineken?"

"Sex."

"You kidding?"

"Me and the old lady go at it just fine. And when I'm with her, feeling just how good it is to be alive, I can look at all this stuff and think—I don't know, think I'm invincible. Like it won't touch me. I know I'm living in denial, but I never once woke up in a cold sweat. And let me tell you, son, I've seen some pretty god-awful things, burns you wouldn't believe."

"All right, fellas, we were thinking about playing with the seats, but let's just get a ram in there and lift that dash," said Martinez. "Let's get a board under her back. We got sixty seconds."

Abe helped guide the long backboard under the woman's back and down to her waist. Another firefighter came in through the passenger's side window and helped hold the board while yet another set the yardlong, pole-like ram in place.

"Get ready," Martinez warned.

The ram hissed and rumbled. The dashboard slowly lifted off the woman's trapped legs. Her blood-stained jeans indicated that she might very well have open fractures to her right leg, though Abe spotted no signs of gross hemorrhage. In a flurry of activity that caught Abe wholly off guard, the firefighter who had set the ram guided the woman farther up the backboard, while the one who had come in through the window made sure her legs did not bang against the board's side. Suddenly, she was fully on the board and being pulled from the wagon, Fitzy having abandoned his ventilations for a few seconds to join the others outside the car. Abe leaped down from the hood and followed the group over to the treatment sector, which Martinez had established on the shoulder about ten yards ahead of the wagon.

While Fitzy resumed bagging the woman, the fire-fighters began packaging her, and a third held up the IV bags, Abe cut long slits in the woman's jeans, then applied a sterile pressure dressing to her fractured tibia as foam cushions called "Head-ons" were placed on either side of the woman's head. Straps helped brace her forehead and chin. Still more straps bound her tightly to the backboard.

Meanwhile, the girl had been extricated from the back seat and was also being packaged. Savage looked grim, though miracles did happen. Abe bet she had seen them firsthand, and that when one happened before your eyes, it was really weird. He rose as the firefighters lifted the backboard. Without warning, and as it had before, the moment struck him inert. Engines hummed. Choppers thumped. Rescuers hollered. Lights flashed. Broken glass twinkled. The sky seemed to pale and descend upon him. And damn it, he still hadn't peed.

"If you don't learn how to manage stress, you won't make it," one of Abe's instructors had said. "You need to recognize the early warning signs of anxiety. And remember, some stress is valuable because it can protect you and improve your performance. You have to discover your own optimal stress level and figure out a way to maintain it."

He knew what he had to do—but being able to do it, well, that was the challenge, wasn't it? He had to come to terms with the fact that the job required him to assume many roles and responsibilities; that things would often go unfinished; that he would rarely see people at their best; that he would forever be racing against the clock; that routine runs would always get old fast; that his energy, patience, and emotions would always be taxed; that restrictions on his ability to administer care would drive him nearly insane; that his workplace would always be an unstable one; that he would continually lack recognition and forever be referred to as "an ambulance driver"; that there wasn't much mobility in his profession; that abusive patients and dangerous situations would always cross his path; that no matter how well he adapted, caring for critically ill or dying patients would never, ever be easy.

All that for a meager paycheck.

What had possessed him to get into the profession? Was it that rush of adrenaline at the sound of a siren? Was he just living out a boyhood fantasy? Did he really need this? Did these people make him feel any less alone in a country that his parents said was not his?

"Hey, son," Fitzy cried. "Come on!"

They carried the woman to the chopper, mindful of the tail rotor. An air medic in a khaki jumpsuit listened attentively as Abe updated him on the woman's condition via the tactical frequency, and an air nurse secured the backboard to a stretcher. Then, their work complete, they jogged away as the chopper kicked up a maelstrom of dust and debris. On the LZ's perimeter, Abe looked back to watch the chopper vanish into the early morning haze.

5

While Isabel Vivas barreled down the freeway, the rescue's siren shattering the otherwise tranquil air, John "Doe" Smith sat on the bench seat and Firefighter–EMT-I Timothy Avalty took the "captain's seat" at the head of the stretcher and facing the patient's head. Avalty, a muscular twenty-five-year-old with thick, Buddy Holly–style glasses, worked the Ambu bag, ventilating the father, while Doe monitored vitals and recorded his findings on the back of his latex glove. Later he would transfer his scribbling to the official run form. As he stared at the cardiac monitor between the patient's legs, the call to alert the hospital rang in his ears:

SFMC, Rescue Ten en route to your facility with a major trauma patient. ETA, six minutes. Patient is an approximately forty-year-old male, restrained driver in an MVA. Required minimal extrication. There was major deformity to the vehicle with significant intrusion into the passenger compartment. Patient initially alert but

confused, with closed head injury, and is now unrespon-
sive and unconscious, currently intubated. Patient also
has obvious flail chest, possible intraabdominal hemor-
rhage, fractured right forearm, and fractured jaw. Vital
signs as follows: BP 128/80. Pulse 82 and regular. Res-
pirations 30 to 32, shallow and irregular, assisted with
bag on one hundred percent O_2, sats one hundred per-
cent. Pupils are unequal. Left responds to light briskly.
Right dilated and sluggish response. GCS is 5. TSS is
10. Patient has two IVs in left arm with NS running in
each. Right arm bandaged and splinted. Chest is also
bandaged and splinted. Patient is fully immobilized on
LSB with c-spine. Patient remains unconscious and un-
responsive. No change in vitals since initial assessment.
Updated ETA is four minutes.

The GCS, or Glasgow Coma Scale, was a scoring
system to evaluate patients with head injuries. Patients
received one to four points for eye opening, one to six
points for best motor response, and one to five points
for verbal response. Doe had given the father a 1 for
eye opening because he did not open his eyes when
pinched. The man's best motor response came in at a 3;
he flexed his body inappropriately in response to pain.
The man scored a 1 on verbal response because he made
no sounds. Patients with scores of 12 or less were immediately transported to level 1 trauma centers. A score
of 7 or less usually indicated coma. Doe would assess
the patient's score in each category at least twice more
before they reached the hospital.

Another system for rating patients, the Trauma Severity Score, had been revised a few times over the years
and often included the GCS as one of its categories. The

simplified system Doe used gave patients zero to four points for respiratory rate, zero to four points for systolic blood pressure, and zero to four for GCS. The man scored high in the first two categories but only half on his GCS. Patients in Doe's district with scores of 10 or less were immediately taken to SFMC.

"How's he doing?" Vivas asked over the intercom.

Doe slid over his headset's mike. "Looks like his pressure and pulse have stabilized. Maybe that spleen isn't ruptured after all. But we won't know jack until they do a belly tap."

"You're right. God, is this a bad one or what? Did you see those kids? They were just a few years older than my baby. That could've been my baby in there."

"Here we go," Doe groaned. "Every time we get a kid. . . . Yeah, it could've been your daughter—but it wasn't."

"I hear you, Izzy," Avalty said.

After smirking at his colleague, Doe added the present time and vitals to his gloves. The man's pulse had increased a little. Doe took another GCS; still a 5. He grabbed the clipboard and filled out a few items because the man's condition didn't look like it would be changing anytime soon and Avalty had the ventilation covered. The run form included columns for respiration/SAO_2, pulse, blood pressure, consciousness, pupils, skin, medications, and blood sugar, as well as boxes for time of alarm, time on scene, time to hospital, time at hospital, time in service, mileage start, and mileage ending. Although Doe still found the forms tedious, a by-product of a lumbering bureaucracy, he understood their importance. The one on his clipboard would become a permanent part of the patient's medical record, detailing the care the patient received from the field to his ultimate discharge from the hospital, should he survive. Moreover, the form might also come to Doe's defense, should his patient's care be questioned in a court of law or by medical control. "We live in a litigious society," a lieutenant had once told him. "You fail to properly fill out that report, and you're leaving yourself wide open for a lawsuit. You know what they say: If you didn't write it, you didn't do it." Doe knew of paramedics who had been sued for negligence and had ultimately lost their jobs. Whether they had actually been negligent or not, he never knew; but he had seen how the accusations all but ruined their careers, despite support from their buddies.

As Doe finished the notes, his thoughts took him back to the last phone conversation he had had with Geneva, a hairstylist whose dark, secret-filled mane had become a familiar sight on his pillow during off days. Six months earlier, twenty-seven-year-old Geneva Bowers had entered his life matter-of-factly during a simple haircut. Doe found it unnerving how much he thought about her and how he had kept her existence a carefully guarded secret from his comrades, in an attempt to preserve his womanizing image. He had lied to Vivas about trying to hook up with his sister's friend down in Florida. His sister had been the one who had tried to fix him up; he had declined because he could not stop thinking about Geneva. When he had returned to Los Angeles, he had immediately called her.

"Hey, you. I'm back," he had said playfully.

"I'm glad."

"What's wrong? You sound a little off."

She had hesitated. "Nothing. Just tired, I guess. Long day."

Doe had leaned back on his sofa and had kicked bare feet up onto the coffee table. "You cut a lot of hair today or what? Think I could use a trim myself. How 'bout I stop over?"

"Now's not a good time."

"How 'bout later? I'm on tomorrow, so this is all the time we'll have for a couple of days."

"Maybe when you get off, we'll go get something, and I'll cut your hair. I just don't feel so good right now."

"What's wrong? Can you describe the pain?"

"It's nothing you can fix."

Doe had frowned. "You sure 'bout that? Some people say I'm a pretty good medic."

"I'm sure. Just come by in the morning. We'll talk then."

After turning off his cell phone, Doe had thrown his head back and had sworn under his breath.

Now, with his pen balanced over his run form, he traced back through his memories of everything he had said and done during their last date, attempting to identify his fault. He had never heard her so distant. *Maybe I'm just going nuts*, he thought. *Maybe she's just not feeling good. Maybe it has nothing to do with me*. Doe shrugged off his insecurity and continued his entries.

San Fernando Medical Center had been classified as a level 1 American College of Surgeons–approved trauma center and had, in its twenty-three years of existence, become one of the largest in the United States, with approximately six thousand trauma admissions per year. Sixty percent of those admissions were for blunt trauma, forty percent for penetrating trauma. A dedicated division of trauma and critical care included nine full-time faculty members, one critical care fellow, and six research fellows. According to one brochure, the hospital's mission was to provide "convenient, affordable, and culturally aware health care, one patient at a time."

Convenient? Well, Doe agreed with that claim. The facility was located smack in the middle of North Hollywood, making it accessible from just about anywhere in the San Fernando Valley.

Affordable? That seemed a bit of a stretch, given the obvious nationwide rise of health-care costs, the costs and limitations of medical insurance, and the expenses incurred in operating a facility as large as SFMC.

Culturally aware? Was that this month's buzzword for avoiding racial slurs? Maybe so, but Doe deeply respected SFMC's division of trauma surgery and critical care. He had more than once witnessed doctors in precarious situations with foreign patients. Language and cultural barriers were continually broken down in an attempt to deliver the best care possible.

Because Doe's patient had already met the criteria for trauma team activation, Dr. Yokito Masaki, one of the attending trauma surgeons, had summoned a trauma team to meet them in the emergency department. Doe knew that attending physician Dr. Joanna Boccaccio would also be there to pitch in. He had to hand it to her—for four long years she had tolerated his antics and advances. Any woman capable of that deserved his respect; ignore the fact that she was on call for twelve hours every third day, that she spent many precall days in the clinic, and, on top of all that, she was supposed to do research and publish papers. Doe had twice invited her to go out on his boat and water-ski, but both times she had declined.

"What do you do with your free time?" he had asked her, wearing his wounded boy face.

"I've never had any free time," she had answered. "Four years of college. Four years of med school, two in the classroom, two doing student rotations and clerkships in teaching hospitals. I got my degree and my restricted medical license, then went right into my residency program. After that, I did a fellowship and eventually became an emergency department attending here because I enjoy teaching. What I don't enjoy is you trying to pick me up. I just don't have the time."

"You mean you don't have the time for me. You're a doctor, and I'm just a medic. Old story. I know how it is."

She had glared. "Do you really? Do you know the kinds of sacrifices I've made?"

"I think I do. And I think because of them you believe you deserve somebody better. That's okay. I crossed the line. I shouldn't have. I'm sorry."

That had widened her eyes. "Really?"

"Really. It won't happen again."

Since then Doe had tried his best to avoid any personal conversation with Boccaccio, but now and again he slipped in a word or two because he sensed a kind of electric tether between them that hummed with current every time their gazes met.

Vivas switched off the siren, and Doe stole a look through the rescue's side door. They had reached SFMC's ambulance entrance, and Vivas navigated around two private buses to get them close to the sliding glass security doors. The rescue rumbled to a halt. In a pair of heartbeats she stood at the rear doors, pulled them open, then unlocked the stretcher from the floorboard. Doe unhooked the two bags of saline, rested them momentarily between the patient's legs, then helped her guide the stretcher out of the rescue as Avalty continued his rhythmic squeezing of the Ambu bag. Vivas steered the stretcher toward the doors, then keyed in a security code. The glass doors slid easily apart, no dramatic banging. They calmly rolled the stretcher inside, where Triage Officer Gunga waved them on toward C-booth.

Boccaccio was coming down the hall as they approached the booth. She had already been notified of the patient's injuries, so Doe simply issued a rapid-fire update of the vital signs and level of consciousness.

"What's his name?" she asked.

"James Robertson," Vivas answered, having been the one to search for the man's ID.

"Mr. Robertson, I'm Doctor Joanna Boccaccio. You've been in a very bad car accident and now you're at the hospital. We're going to treat you."

Whether Robertson had actually heard the doctor, Doe could not be sure, but Boccaccio always spoke to any patients who might be aware. She had admonished Doe more than once to watch his mouth around supposedly unconscious or incoherent patients.

They reached the booth and, in a flurry of coordinated activity, Robertson was transferred to a gurney. Avalty

handed over the job of ventilating the patient to a respiratory technician while an RN detached the cardiac
monitor and a third hooked up the patient to the trauma
team's BP, cardiac, and respiratory equipment. That
third nurse inserted a Foley catheter for urinary drainage,
then checked the patency of the IVs, a simple procedure
to make sure the lines were not blocked.

Next came the hardest part for Vivas, Avalty, and
Doe.

Standing back.

Their job of helping to save James Robertson was all
but finished. They would complete their run form, turn
over the white copy to Charti, keep the yellow for themselves, then begin the long and arduous task of cleaning
up and inventorying their equipment. After that, barring
another call, they would return to Station Ten to update
their database and allow Avalty to return to riding on
the engine.

While they came down from the extraordinary world
of saving lives, Boccaccio, Masaki, and the trauma team
would catapult themselves into it by getting arterial
blood gases via an "arterial stick." They would supply
lab personnel with blood samples for type and cross
match for transfusion and give type O negative un-
crossed blood (called the universal donor) in the interim
before type-specific or cross-matched blood was available. Boccaccio would also ask for a trauma blood panel,
or rainbow draw (as in every color of the rainbow, referring to the different color of the top of each of the
blood tubes that would be filled). The blood panel was
the first test most emergency room doctors ordered for

the vast majority of their patients, and was composed of twenty-one complete blood count chemistries, including electrolytes, liver and pancreas functions, and cardiac and clotting studies.

Meanwhile, X-ray technicians would set up for "trauma shots," which included a lateral cervical spine and flat chest and abdominal to include the pelvis. Doe suspected that the patient was developing a tension pneumothorax and would need pleural decompression. They would probably perform that procedure, then place a triple-lumen central venous catheter in his right sub-clavian vein for fluid access. Doe would never attempt to access central veins in the field because of the time it took and the higher complication rate.

If the patient's vitals remained stable, he would be sent for helical/spiral computed tomography scans of his head, neck, chest, abdomen, and pelvis. For the scans, which would take about fifteen to twenty minutes, he would be transported to a room adjacent to the booth. After that, Dr. Masaki and his residents would reevaluate him, look at his films, and consider his lab work. More than likely the surgeon would decide to rush him up to the operating room as an RB, a term specific to San Fernando Medical Center and applied to all superemergent operative cases. In the old days, a red blanket was thrown over the patient as the gurney was whisked to the OR, hence the term. There, he would be treated by the surgical resident, who was assisted by Masaki, and once-tired medical students would excitedly observe the action. All injuries were the domain of the trauma resident, and it was up to that person to request consultation from other surgical specialties, which in this case might include a neurosurgeon who could perform a craniotomy, a hole or incision in the skull to allow access to the brain. It was all part of a resident's training.

"My good friend, Charti," Doe said, tearing off the white copy of the run form and handing it to one of the nurses. "Mother and daughter come through yet?"

Charti shook his head curtly, his gaze never meeting Doe's. "Landing now."

"You really do hate me, don't you?"

The controller ignored Doe in favor of the data glowing on his computer screen.

"Hey, man, you there?"

"I am. And you, sir, are in the no Doe zone."

"You tell him," Avalty said.

"What's with that?" Doe asked Charti.

"Come on," Vivas said, seizing Doe's bicep.

Doe leaned over the counter. "Charti, you're a weird little man."

"Come on," Vivas repeated, then dragged him toward the exit.

Just then the doors parted to reveal two medics from Rescue Eight, who rolled in the boy. Doe knew one of the guys, Michael Troft, a know-it-all in his late twenties pretty enough to model underwear. Troft had once worked a little overtime at Station Ten, filling in for Vivas when she was on vacation, and that had been one of the longest weeks of Doe's life. Not only had the curly-haired wiseass questioned every move Doe had made, but he had made even more questionable decisions himself. Add to that his terrible driving, and you had yourself a migraine by the end of each shift. Vivas had said that Doe and Troft did not get along because they were two of a kind.

"Hey, Pooh," Troft said, straight-faced and concentrating on his patient.

Doe coughed through a curse, then regarded Vivas, who stood there transfixed, eyes misting. She had been a firefighter–paramedic for nearly four years herself; hadn't she learned to remove herself from the job?

"Hey, Izzy, you all right?" asked Avalty.

"Yeah," she answered hollowly.

As the boy rolled by Charti's desk, the lean Filipino shot up and locked his gaze on the kid, assuming the same stricken expression as Vivas.

"What's going on around here?" Doe asked. "It's a trauma case. We've been on 'em before, we'll be on 'em again. There's nothing special about this one. Family of four in an MVA. Happens all the time. Could have been us or someone we know, but it wasn't. Nothing profound about it." Doe rolled their bright yellow stretcher outside, lowered it to the ground, then removed the cardiac monitor before lifting and sliding the heavy stretcher into the back of the rescue. The engine purred steadily and seemed to ease his frustration.

"Hey, don't you wanna go up and see how the mom and daughter are doing?" Vivas asked. "We got time."

"Nope." Doe zipped the cardiac monitor's nylon covering closed. "Let's get cleaned up and get back."

"Let's at least talk."

"Izzy, I know you're into this whole situational support thing, and you always attend those debriefings, but haven't you learned by now that I'm the wrong guy to make you feel better?"

"I'll talk," said Avalty.

"Shuddup," snapped Vivas, then faced Doe. "What I've learned is that you need to come with me later. It's a Critical Incident Stress debriefing—not some New Age crystal worship to find inner peace. They're helpful."

"When I first started, I went to one after these two little kids got run over by a garbage truck. And you know what? I've been doing everything right. I get enough sleep, I leave the job at work, I balance my work and fun time, I exercise, I have friends in and out of the profession. I can see what we just saw and deal with it. Just part of the blur."

Vivas gritted her teeth. "Yeah, you deal with it, all right. You just pretend our patients are not real, just hunks of meat that you have to fix. That whole family might die up there. Means absolutely nothing to you, because whatever was in you that cared already died."

Doe leaned back on the rescue's bench seat and folded his arms over his chest. "So we work together for two years, and this is what you really think of me? Where's this coming from? What the hell is the matter with you? It's just a goddamned trauma case! It's the kinda shit we live for. All the drunks and overdoses and diabetics are just fillers. Why do I even have to tell you this?"

"Because you know I'm right, and you just won't admit it. You don't get into this job because you *don't* care. You get into it because *you do*. You're just too afraid to admit that."

"Okay," Doe said in a placating tone. "I'm a cold

bastard. After two years, you've finally figured me out. Now, you mind giving me hand?"

Vivas cursed under her breath and marched toward the driver's side door.

"I'll help," said Avalty with a shrug.

6

S avage sat in the captain's seat, taking inventory, while Abe diligently locked down the stretcher and placed the drug box, cardiac monitor, and airway bag on the stretcher's blanket. He checked the valve on the oxygen bottle mounted at the stretcher's foot to make sure it was closed, then the valve on the main oxygen line mounted on the driver's side ceiling. He picked up the stick box and used a seat belt to secure it to the back end of the bench seat.

They had handed off their patients to the air crews, and that had turned Abe's expression from wide-eyed and intense to soft and dour. Savage sympathized with the young man. Though you might work with a patient for only a short time, you developed an instant bond— even if he or she was unconscious. You saw that individual as depending upon you, as a representation of your work, and if you could make a difference in that person's life, there were few things more rewarding. But you often felt bad about breaking that bond, and more than a few paramedics who viewed themselves as "paragods" wished they could stabilize a patient in the field, drive to the hospital, wheel the patient into an OR, and perform the surgery themselves. Afterward, they would speak with the relatives and enjoy the accolades. These people were a royal pain to work with and rarely admitted mistakes. Savage had learned over the years that you had to recognize when your contributions to the team effort ended and when others' began.

A cabinet with sliding glass doors hung above the stretcher, and Abe made sure the doors were sealed over the first compartment, where they stored stuffed animals like the one Savage had given Carlos earlier in the morning. A locking compartment below held some of their drugs—atropine, epinephrine ("epi"), Benadryl, lidocaine, bretylium tosylate, Narcan (naloxone), adenosine, morphine, Versed (midazolam), and Valium (diazepam) in plastic boxes—spare nitrous oxide bottles, and drug manuals. The adjoining four compartments made up an advanced life support (ALS) department, with extra IV fluids and tubing, syringes, tourniquets, needles, masks, cannulas for breathing oxygen through the nose, and a multiport airway valve that would allow them to put up to seven people on oxygen at one time. Beneath the ALS equipment and just to Savage's right lay an open compartment with steel countertop on which they stored the standard-size pulse oximeter. To its left was the coiled hose of the onboard suction unit used to clear mucus, blood, or vomit from a patient's mouth, nose, or throat. The puke bucket sat just behind the stretcher; the rule was that the medic closest to the bucket had to reach for it when a patient was about to vomit. If that medic didn't get to the bucket in time, then he or she had the fun job of cleaning up.

Savage slid open the upper right door of the ALS supply cabinet and took note of the fluids and administration sets they had used. Beyond the open doors of the rescue, the sound of voices moved near.

"Excuse me," called an approaching CHP officer, trailed by a news reporter and cameraman. The brawny, crewcut officer cocked his thumb over his shoulder. "Sorry, but she's been bugging me to talk to you. Found out you were the first medics on scene."

"Why should that matter?" Savage asked. "I'm sure one of my buddies will talk to her."

The reporter, a petite brunette with the bloodshot eyes of a woman who had rushed out of bed, elbowed her way past the officer. "Hi. Lara Linnmeyer, News 5. Would either of you mind answering a few questions?" Her smile did nothing for Savage.

Abe glanced at Savage for approval. "I wouldn't mind."

"Just the facts," Savage cautioned. "Remember patient confidentiality, and that whatever you say could come back to bite you later."

With a quick nod, Abe climbed down from the rescue and began talking with the reporter.

"Mind if I have a seat?" asked the CHP officer.

Savage nodded.

"Been standing out there a long time," he said, then sighed as he took off a load. "I'm trying to figure out how this bozo gets on the freeway going the wrong way. I mean, we've all dozed while driving, but he had to drive up the ramp, pass the Do Not Enter, Wrong Way signs, then keep going. I'm thinking that takes some serious exhaustion or some serious drinking."

"Or some serious stupidity," Savage added. "No shortage of that on the freeways."

Outside, a bright light appeared on top of the camera, and the reporter thrust her microphone in Abe's face. He spoke evenly, his expression sober, squinting a little at the light. He was going to hate how he looked on TV, but speaking to that reporter would help ease the stress and serve as a first reward for a job well done.

After a few moments of silence, the cop hauled himself up. "Well, thanks for the break. Nice work out there."

"You, too."

Savage glanced down at her inventory report and realized her hands were trembling.

Abe bounded into the rescue. "She said I'll be on the six o'clock report but that it'll probably run a few times during the day and be on tonight at six,"

"We'll set the VCR when we get back, though I have to tell you, you'll never live down the teasing."

"Yeah," replied Abe. "But I don't care. I've never been on TV before."

With the inventory complete and their equipment stored, they climbed into the cab and watched in silence as the shattered station wagon was dragged onto a tow truck's flatbed. Valley Police's photographer had finished his work, and a Cal Trans crew had begun clearing the freeway of debris.

Savage grabbed the mike. "TRO Six, Rescue Nine."

"Rescue Nine, TRO Six."

"Nine on the air and returning to quarters. Copy?" As the dispatcher replied, Savage glanced suddenly at Abe. "Oh, yeah. Don't let this go to your head, but you did okay."

"I was too nervous."

"Doesn't matter."

Abe shrank a little. "I've done 320 hours of didactic and skills, 160 hours of hospital and clinical training, 480 hours of field internship with forty ALS patient contacts, and now I'm doing three months of probation."

"What are you saying?"

"I'm saying that passing the national registry doesn't mean jack unless I calm down."

"For what it's worth, this job already has enough pressure attached to it. You don't need any more from yourself."

Abe threw the rescue in gear. "If I'm going to do this, I have to do it well. Otherwise, my parents were right."

"About what?"

"About me wasting my life."

Fire Station Nine, located in the heart of Studio City, just behind the Mary Tyler Moore Studios, had been constructed on a dead-end street to minimize local traffic disruptions. Like most fire stations, the focal point was the large, three-door garage accessible from the front and rear and capable of berthing the massive squad vehicle, the standard engine, the rescue, and even the dive team's step van and zodiac rescue boat. Known as the apparatus floor, the garage had a high ceiling, shelves holding spare hoses, and rows of metal lockers in which firefighters stowed their "turnout" or "bunker" gear: soft yellow coats, pants, hats, and boots made of heavy water- and fireproof materials.

As Abe backed up the station's driveway and activated the automatic garage door, Savage turned her back to him and held up a hand. In her fifteen years as a firefighter–EMT, the last five as a firefighter–paramedic, she had never gotten such bad shakes after a call.

"Want to get out and check it?" Abe asked, referring to his positioning of the rescue on the apparatus floor. The lieutenant was particular about where each of the vehicles was parked and how far inside the building he wanted them. He had even gone so far as to make marks on the floor—but that was only to tease Abe.

"Don't worry about it," Savage said. "Looks good."

The engine and squad were still en route back to the station. Rescue Five, which had been moved up to Station Nine to take over while Savage and Abe were busy at the Roscoe incident, had left just before their arrival, so theirs was the only fire rescue vehicle inside, save for the dive van.

They hopped out, and the garage seemed uncharacteristically quiet, save for TRO Six's occasional reports through overhead speakers. Savage moved past the traditional fire pole that ran up through a catwalk. She crossed to a door and entered the office area, where a wide desk unit wrapped around the walls to her left. Firefighter–EMT Joe Tenpenney and Firefighter–paramedic Paul Cannis, men in their late twenties with shaven heads and even builds that made them look like twins, sat at computers and reviewed database entries. The lieutenant's office was opposite them. Martinez had several bookcases atop which he displayed his score of trophies. A notebook computer lay on a secondary desk, and dozens of framed photographs of the man in action adorned the paneled walls. The lieutenant often wore a huge fire truck belt buckle, had so many firefighter decals on his pickup's rear window that he could barely see out of it, and had seen the movie *Backdraft* over thirty times (he owned it on VHS cassette *and* DVD) and had hung the movie's poster in his office. He also owned four dalmatians and an antique fire truck, and had married a firefighter. Despite his excessive zeal, Martinez represented the best of the best, and Savage and the other twenty-five people of Station Nine could not help but admire his commitment and unending enthusiasm for the job. He had found a career that he loved, embraced it with everything he had, and did it better than most people.

Beyond the lieutenant's office lay the dayroom, an open area divided into three sections: kitchen, an area with a conference table, and a den replete with leather sofa, love seat, and nine well-padded recliners facing a wall unit with large-screen TV and stereo equipment. In one corner, a stairwell led up to "the hood," a basic cots and lockers affair retrofitted to accommodate the needs of both sexes.

Savage reached the conference table, and before taking a seat, she scanned the marker board for any phone messages. Because he kept college student hours, her son Donny liked to call in the middle of the night. No, he hadn't called. The board reflected only the ever-present and ever-changing fire equipment, EMS supply, and grocery lists. She gave the general information, communications, fire suppression/rescue operations, tracking, and EMS clipboards below a cursory glance for new reports, then took a seat beside Abe, who leaned back, pillowing his head in his hands. "Hungry?" he asked.

"Nah." She looked to the kitchen. "Make something if you want."

"It's okay." He closed his eyes. "Isn't this when you give me the speech?"

"What?"

"Well, this is only our second shift together, and we just came off a major trauma call, so I'm figuring you'll give the veteran's debriefing. You know, you ask me if I'm all right, if I know how to deal with the stress, if I've learned not to take every case personally. I got that a lot at my old station."

"I take it you've read the CIS sheets?"

He nodded. "Alternate exercise with relaxation within the first twenty-four to forty-eight hours. Stay busy. Keep your life as normal as possible. Talk to people. Do things that feel good. Eat right. Get enough sleep. Keep a journal."

"You rattle that off pretty well, and I've noticed that you have a really good memory for practice parameters. That'll come in handy."

"Yeah, I know what to do. Not sure I can do it."

Savage considered that. "So, what do you think about that call? You talked to that little boy. How do you feel about that?"

Abe squirmed a bit before answering. "I made a big mistake out there. I guess somewhere in the back of my mind I imagined I was him, sitting there, looking at my sister all bloody and crushed, looking at my mother and father hurt real bad, and just being really, really scared and wondering if my whole family is going to die. How do I feel? The answer is way too much, which makes me too nervous. I mean, at first, I had a hard time going near the wreck. I've talked to people who would have paid me to take my place on that call. And I just kind of stood there for a moment, trying to figure out if this is what I should be doing with my life. Which begs the question: Why do *you* do this?"

Savage tucked her still jittery hands under her thighs and leaned toward him. "I took this job because I thought it would save my family. My husband always had a problem with the routine of a nine-to-five job, so we never had any steady money. A friend of mine led me by the hand and got me into this. My husband already worked crazy hours delivering pizzas and newspapers, so I figured working twenty-four hours on every third day wouldn't be too bad, and might actually give me more time to spend with my son."

"So at first you had no desire to fight fires or help people? You just wanted steady money and time with your son?"

"That's right. I wanted to save my family." The old feelings simmered in Savage's gut. She saw Tim's smirk beneath his large, bald head and heard the threats underscored by his grating voice.

Abe looked slightly dumbfounded. "This job takes such a commitment. Don't get me wrong, but wouldn't it have been easier to work at Wal-Mart?"

Savage grinned. "I told myself a million times I should quit, especially in the beginning. Most people think I'm this tough chick or militant feminist who wants to prove she can fight fires and rescue people. The gender thing has nothing to do with it. Sure, I got harassed a lot in the beginning—there are a lot of misogynist assholes who wear our uniform—but I'm just here to do the job, and the only thing I've ever wanted to prove was that I'm a good medic. I think I'm here now because I want to be remembered."

"I hear a story coming on."

"You've been around firefighters long enough to realize how many stories we have to tell," Savage said. "So we got this one call, turned out to be a little girl who was being abused by her father. Guy burned her with hot barbecue tongs. Tried to make it look like an accident, but I took one look at his wife, and I knew. Anyway, Boccaccio helped us get the father arrested, I hooked up the mother with Family Services. Like two, maybe three, years go by, and I'm on line at a supermarket checkout, and I get a tap on my shoulder. It's this woman and her daughter. I barely recognize them, but she goes on and on about how much I changed their lives. She's even telling the checkout guy all about it."

Just as Savage finished, a high-pitched and rapid beeping resounded, followed by two lower-pitched and slower tones, then the familiar rising siren. "Engine Five, Rescue Nine. Engine Five, Rescue Nine. Possible medical emergency. Sixteen-eight-oh-one Vineland Avenue. Sun Tower Apartments. Apartment one-nineteen. Cross street Magnolia. Units respond code three. Time out: Five-twenty-one."

M edic Controller Charti Darunyothin entered SFMC's surgical intensive care unit, a state-of-the-art facility with sixteen isolated, computerized beds overhung by monitors, IV bags, oxygen lines, and sundry other hoses and equipment that flashed and hummed. Charti moved furtively along the hallway, checking rooms until he came upon Trent Robertson, the eight-year-old blond boy who had been brought in. He lingered near the open door.

"Hey, Charti. We don't get to see you up here too often," said Nancy Rodriguez, a jovial thirty-year-old in blue scrubs who had just received her CCRN certification. Rodriguez narrowed her emerald eyes and pulled off a pair of latex gloves.

"Saw him come in," Charti answered, tipping his head toward the boy, who appeared to be either sleeping or sedated. "Thought I'd check on him."

"You know him?"

Charti shook his head.

Rodriguez stared at him a moment. "What's wrong?"

"Nothing. How's he doing?"

She pursed her lips. "He definitely tore his dura. Hemorrhage migrated to the mastoid. You can see the Battle's sign and bilateral periorbital ecchymosis. His intracranial pressure was increasing, but his fracture actually helped relieve the pressure. We sutured his lacerations. He's stable now, and we have him sedated."

"How 'bout the rest of the family?"

"I haven't had time to follow up, but I think the dad's going to make it. The mother's real bad. So's the daughter. You want to see them? I think Doctor Masaki is presenting the father's case now, but you can slip in to see the mother and daughter."

"That's all right."

"Just the boy, then?"

He nodded.

"Well, I have to go. See you," she said, gazing quizzically at him before trotting off.

Charti had seen literally thousands of kids come through the emergency department's door, but never had one struck such a harsh and familiar chord. Tentatively, he moved into the room and stared gravely at the boy's blackened eyes, then glanced up through the window behind the bed. Ground lights still shimmered, but wisps of dawn crowned the distant mountains. When the boy awoke, his life might be changed forever.

Dr. Boccaccio abruptly came into the room and nearly choked on the coffee she was drinking from a foam cup. "Charti? What're you doing here? I thought you were helping Jaci contact the relatives?"

"I'm on break," he said. "We reached the mother's sister. She's coming down from Valencia. Found out the father's got a brother who lives in Chicago. We're trying to track him down. Mom's parents live in Orlando. No answer there. Father's parents are in Tucson. Left a message on their machine."

"Jaci told me some of that. The mom's an English professor over at Valley Community, and the dad's an entertainment attorney. They were headed back to their house in Toluca Lake." She stepped farther into the room. "What brings you up here?"

He averted his gaze. "Same thing as you, I guess."

"Does it have anything to do with what's been going on between you and Doe? I know he worked on this call."

"There's nothing wrong. Thought I'd just come up and see how this kid was doing."

"Okay," she said, her tone indicating that she hardly believed him. "I hate it when stuff like this happens to kids. They're so damned innocent. God . . . I hate it."

"Me, too." After a last look at the boy, Charti hurried out under Boccaccio's curious stare.

By the time he reached the elevator, tears trickled from the corners of his eyes.

"Possible medical emergency?" Abe groaned as he double-parked in front of the Sun Tower Apartments, three high-rent, ill-repaired, thirty-year-old buildings. "Looks quiet to me."

"Little kid probably had a bad dream. Mom called 911," Savage rasped. "I am *so* exhausted. Get me out of here."

Not a single light burned in the windows of the front units, and all TRO Six could tell them was that someone had called and that he had heard a crying child in the background.

With the airway bag in one hand, the drug box in the other, Abe rushed to catch up with Savage, who had already forced herself up a flight of steps and had entered a gated pool area bordered on three sides by apartments. Abe's boots thudded on pink concrete that rolled out to those first floor units facing the pool. Savage moved toward a unit near the south corner. She rapped loudly on the pea-green door as Abe arrived. "Fire department," she announced in her little singsong as they moved to either side for safety. "Fire department. Anyone home? Anyone call 911?"

A baby cried behind the door.

"Hear that?" asked Abe.

Savage paused. Another cry. "Fire department!"

More wailing from the child.

"Hey, in there," Abe cried. "You all right?"

Only whimpering answered.

Abe sighed. "What do you think?"

"I think we wait for law enforcement and make a joint decision to force entry."

"Time they get here, it might be too late. And you know how leery they are about forcing entry. I say we got a medical emergency and implied consent."

Abe knew that before treating any patient, he had to get informed, expressed, implied, or involuntary consent; however, lessons in potential medical liability were the last thing on his mind. That baby inside might need

help. He tried the window next to the door and found it
open.

"Valley? Rescue Nine," Savage said into her radio.

"Nine, Valley," responded TRO Six.

"What's the ETA on our police unit?"

"Unit two-four-one responding. ETA approximately
two minutes."

"I think we can get in this way," Abe said, showing
Savage how he could lift the inside screen off its tracks,
though he resisted the temptation to remove it fully.

"Wait a minute," urged Savage. "I don't think—"

A gunshot blared so loudly and shocked Abe so thoroughly that he flew back from the window and fell,
dropping the airway bag and sending the drug box skit-
tering across the concrete.

Two more shots cleaved the air, followed by a distant
clinking of glass.

Savage ducked. "Stop!"

Another round cracked in reply.

"Fire department," Savage screamed. "Don't shoot!
Fire department!"

As the gunfire echoed in Abe's ears, he frantically
checked his golf shirt for blood. Though he had not felt
the sting of a bullet, he knew that the adrenaline surge
often numbed the pain. His old lieutenant, who served
in Kosovo, had been shot in the abdomen and in the
calf. He had seen the blood. His internal voice told him
he had been shot. Finally, the panic had set in.

"Get back!" came a man's gruff voice.

The baby bawled louder.

Savage crawled toward Abe, her face knotted in
shock. "You hit?"

"I don't know," Abe rasped, still patting himself for wounds. "Shit. I don't know."

"That window belongs to the apartment next door," Savage said, alternating her gaze between it and Abe. "I'm a little late with that report."

"Get away from my place," the man warned from somewhere inside.

With a slight creak, the door to apartment 119 opened to a slit. "Who's out there?" called a woman with a quavering voice.

"Leave. Now," hollered the man.

"Fire department," Savage said, dragging Abe away from the door.

"Don't believe 'em, Lisa," the man yelled. "These are those bastards who broke into Mac's apartment last week. Well, you ain't getting into mine. And I've already called the police."

As though on cue, a Valley Police Department officer skulked along the building, shifting in and out of the shadows. The faint voice of his dispatcher echoed from his radio. Abe figured that the guy had responded to the original call. More units were probably en route. "Valley Police! You, inside, place your weapon on the floor and come out with your hands fully extended above your head. Now!"

Footfalls sounded to Abe's left, where a second cop now hunkered down near the corner of the building.

"This is bullshit," cried the man. "Lock your door, Lisa. They're trying to set us up." Just then, the man's phone rang, and he answered it.

Savage pulled Abe behind the first officer.

"Sir, this *is* the Valley Police Department," barked the

cop. "Put down the weapon and come out with your hands fully extended above your head. Now!" The cop craned his head toward Abe and Savage. "Either of you hit?"

"We don't think so," replied Savage. "Shots went over the pool and into the other building. Could be injured over there."

Apartment windows randomly glowed with yellow light, and five or six residents had already come outside.

Abe crouched down, close to Savage. After half a dozen labored breaths, a metallic chink came from the man's door.

"All right," the guy said. "I'm coming out."

The door eased open. The man behind the irate voice emerged, all graying, sagging, 250 pounds of him. Silver eyebrows arced high over glassy eyes, and his considerable paunch ballooned up plaid pajamas. Wire-rim glasses barely clung to the tip of his pink nose. "Aw, Jesus Christ," he moaned. "I'm sorry. Aw, Jesus Christ. Aw, Jesus Christ."

Wasting no time, the first officer charged the man. "Place your hands on top of your head." After patting the guy down, the officer handcuffed him, and the second cop ducked inside the apartment to retrieve the weapon.

Meanwhile, the woman in 119 eased past her door, carrying her small daughter. Lean, with shoulder-length red hair and bluish-green eyes, the woman clung to the collar of her bath robe and locked gazes with Abe. "Oh, God. Is everyone all right?"

"Ma'am, I need you to stay in your apartment," instructed the first cop.

"You'll want to talk to her," Savage told the officer as she rose then helped Abe to his feet. "Somebody in there called 911." Savage withdrew her radio. "Valley? Rescue Nine."

"Nine, Valley."

"Request second rescue unit and supervisor to the scene. Shots fired."

"Copy. Engine Five should be at your location now. Engine Nine en route."

A trio of firefighters from Engine Five kept close to the walls and shifted into the pool area. One of them, a tall brunette whom Abe had never met but whose gait and badge pegged her as the lieutenant, broke off from the other two and headed toward the first cop. In the meantime, the second officer had come outside, holding a pistol that he had placed in a clear evidence bag. He began taking a statement from the woman, whose daughter fought to free herself from her mother's arms.

The other two firefighters, both blondes with crew cuts and surfer's tans, came toward Abe. They offered curt nods, then questioned Savage, whom they obviously knew. As they spoke, Lieutenant Martinez bounded up the stairs, along with two other firefighters from Engine Nine. They had been on the road, and as usual, Martinez liked to check out as many calls as he could. In their wake charged four more Valley Police officers backlit by dozens of strobe lights from the street below.

Martinez caught Abe's attention and waved him over. "Everybody all right?"

"Yes, sir," Abe said. "We arrived on the scene, heard a baby crying inside. While we were waiting for VPD, I checked the window—just to see if it was open. Guess

I had the wrong apartment. Guy inside started shooting." Abe's voice grew thin. "I'm sorry, sir."

The lieutenant stroked his mustache in thought, then moved away from Abe without a word. He spoke rapidly with Savage, then stormed toward the first two officers.

"Ma'am?" Abe beckoned Savage. "Steph?"

She shouldered away from the other firefighters as more bleary-eyed residents padded outside for a look.

"Am I in trouble?" Abe asked, looking at Martinez.

"You? I'd say that old man's trouble. We're talking automatic felony offense. Then you and I will get him in civil court for pain and suffering. Shit. I was in v-fib back there."

"Yeah, but we forced entry into the wrong apartment."

"We didn't force anything," Savage snapped. "You *checked* the window. When you give your statement to these cops, that's exactly what you say."

"Okay. I know this might sound weird, but I don't blame the guy. You heard what he said. There was a home invasion here. We could've been bad guys in paramedic uniforms. I don't think that gives him the right to fire at us, but I don't know. . . . I doubt I'll pursue this."

"You nuts? You'll pursue this. Medic in San Diego got shot in the face by a mentally unstable patient. He sued and won. So'll we."

"Nobody got hurt here. I just want to forget it. I'll pack up." Abe trudged off.

"Excuse me," cried the woman with the baby. "You, sir? Can I talk to you?"

Abe frowned a little as he approached her. "Yeah?"

She wiped a stray tear from her cheek and took another second to finish composing herself. "I just wanted to say I'm really sorry about what happened. There was an accident yesterday at my little girl's day care. A kid fell or something. My daughter must've heard them calling 911, and when she woke up this morning, she tried calling it herself. I didn't even know that she recognized the numbers."

"Don't worry about it," Abe said with a half-shrug. "It's all right. I'm just wondering . . . why didn't you open the door or at least let us know you were in there?"

"That was stupid, I know. I guess I was just scared. I saw what they did to my neighbor. I should've answered. I'm sorry." Her gaze dropped for a moment to Abe's hands. "Can I buy you and your partner a lunch, a dinner, something?"

"It's okay."

"No, really. For God's sake, you almost got shot. Let me buy you dinner."

Now Abe was the one checking her finger for a ring. He had not been on a date in over a year. "All right," he said, disappointed that he could not see her hand very well. Time to test the waters. "I don't think my partner will come."

"That's okay. And you know what? I'll go one better. I'll cook for you. How 'bout tomorrow night? You working?"

"No."

"Then come over at seven."

"Seven."

"Guess you don't need directions," she said, widening her eyes.

Abe frowned. "I know why you're doing this, and maybe it's not the best reason."

"This'll make me feel better, and you get a free meal. Those aren't good reasons?"

"Guess so."

"Just wish I knew your name."

With cheeks warming, Abe satisfied that wish and learned that her name was Lisa Margrove. "My arm's twisted. I'll be here at seven." He started off, realizing that neither of them had asked if the other was involved. Could he assume she was available, only to have dinner seated next her boyfriend—or girlfriend? Maybe he just wouldn't show. The whole idea was just too awkward. Then again, the notion of a date thrilled him, no matter how bizarre the circumstances were. He suddenly felt alive, like he somehow belonged. He finally sensed an end to the loneliness he had felt for the past two years since his parents' return to Pakistan.

Then, out of nowhere, he shuddered. *Jesus Christ, you almost got shot. . . .*

8

After the shooting, Savage and Abe had carefully filled out their run report, which would be reviewed by the battalion chief, VPD, a judge, and the state's attorney. Lieutenant Martinez had thoroughly questioned them, as had VPD, then the lieutenant had taken them out of service and had turned over the rescue to Joe Tenpenney and Paul Cannis. Savage did not complain at being relieved. Exhaustion had set in, and she welcomed the opportunity to lounge in the den until eight A.M. and watch Abe pop up on the news every fifteen minutes or so. Meanwhile, the celebrity himself drew the laborious task of updating the station's database and making sure that their drug log had been signed. He had already seen himself on TV and had, as expected, winced over the dark rings under his eyes and half a dozen other physical flaws that he pointed out with grim fascination.

"The boy's nose does look awfully big," remarked

Fitzy, the only other firefighter in the day room. Everyone else was out on a fairly routine call to a nursing home. Fitzy had remained behind, staring jadedly at the TV. "Would you look at that nose?"

"I don't know, Fitzy. Remember that supermarket fire on Ventura? Remember when that reporter interviewed you? I think *your* nose looked even bigger."

Savage pushed up the volume to drown out his answer. The reporter, whatever her name was, now sat in the studio, and her practiced voice reverberated through the speakers: "Surprisingly enough, Jim, that same firefighter was involved in a shooting later in the morning. Apparently, a resident mistook him and his partner for home invaders." The reporter went on to give the details and concluded with the good news that no injuries were reported.

The angle widened to reveal Jim Newberry, the quintessential middle-aged anchor sporting pouffy gray hair and chiseled jaw. Savage had grown so used to him over the years that the news didn't sound right unless it poured from his lips. "Quite a night for those paramedics."

Savage closed her eyes. "If you only knew, Jimmy baby. If you only knew."

The phone rang. Savage looked to Fitzy.

"You don't think I'm gonna get it, do you?" he asked. "Where's the TV star?"

"I'll get it," Savage said with a huff, then hastened toward the phone on a wall near the kitchen. "Fire Station Nine. Stephanie Savage. Can I help you?"

"Hey, Ma."

"Donny? I thought you'd call earlier. How'd you make out on that Cornerstone exam?"

"Ninety-two. There were like only five people out of sixty who got As. Pretty good, huh?"

Savage shook a fist and grinned. "That's great. I'm so proud of you."

"So Ma, I'm not gonna be in the apartment for a few days. Eric, Tina, and the other guys are driving down to Miami and taking this art deco tour thing. It's only like three, four hours from Orlando. I'm going with them. My professors have already excused me from class. We're just starting some new chapters. It's no biggie."

Savage's grin began to evaporate. "Who's driving?".

"Eric. You know, he's got his mother's Expedition."

Drawing in a deep breath and holding it, Savage considered her response. Donny had not called to ask if he could go; he had called to say he was going. At least he had been considerate enough to let her know, so that she wouldn't worry. Trouble was, now she would worry even more. "So you're going to Miami? I don't think it's a good idea."

"Ma, I didn't call for your opinion."

"So you're going to take 520 over to 95, is that right?"

"Probably."

"You driving during the day or night?"

"We're leaving tonight," he said, his voice sharpening with tension.

"Damn it, that 520 is the worst road in Florida. Two lanes, unlit, going through miles of nothing. All it takes is one drunk driver. . . ."

"So maybe we'll go a different way."

"Why are you going in the first place? You're not into that art deco are you?"

"No, I'm into babes. And there's a lot of them there. So I'm going, Ma. I'll try to keep the cell on."

"Listen to me. You'll have a lot of time in your life to do a lot of traveling. I don't feel comfortable about you packing yourself into a truck full of college kids and driving all the way to Miami at night."

"And I don't feel comfortable about you sticking needles into AIDs patients and working on the side of the road where you can get run over. But I don't ask you to stop, do I?"

"That's my job. You're talking about a joy ride."

"Ms. Savage?"

"Who is this?"

"It's Eric, ma'am. Donny just wanted me to tell you that I'm a good driver. I never got a ticket. Never drove drunk. Don't worry. It's cool."

"You can be as cool as you want, Eric. But what're you gonna do when some drunk asshole jumps lanes and plows into you? How're you gonna feel when you're standing there and firefighters are cutting your bloody friends out of the truck? It doesn't matter that it wasn't your fault. It doesn't matter at all."

"Your mother's a loon," Eric whispered in the background.

"Ma, you there?" called Donny.

"I'm here," Savage said behind gritted teeth.

"Don't worry about me."

"All right, Donny. You do what you want." Savage bit her lip. "Just be careful."

"I will, Ma. I will. 'Bye."

The line that had once kept Donny close to her had grown so long and tenuous that Savage feared it would soon break. Her Donny was, quite obviously, a man capable of making his own choices. And he had chosen. And maybe she had overreacted. An only child herself, with both parents already gone, she knew she couldn't stop him and she knew she was being selfish. But he was the only family she had left. And now he wanted to risk that for some ridiculous ride to Miami? How could he be so stupid? Hadn't she taught him better?

"You look like you just got a call from the IRS," said Fitzy as he loped into the kitchen and yanked open the refrigerator door. "Damn, did that kid eat all my bacon again? And are you all right?"

"Steph?" Abe stood in the doorway. "I'm done."

"So what do you want? Applause?"

He rolled his eyes and snickered. "I'm going to read the protocol manual." He started for one of the recliners. "That okay?"

Savage lifted a hand and softened her expression. "I'm just tired."

"Yeah, whatever." He flipped open the manual and buried his not-so-big nose in it.

Every morning at seven, the on-call trauma team at SFMC met with the new on-call team in the surgical admitting area, Ward 1909, for pass-on rounds. All of the trauma consultations and admissions from the prior twenty-four hours were reviewed and critiqued by both teams. Patients in need of further observation or workup were handed over to the new team. Patients were directly examined and workup studies were reviewed, in an effort to generate a specific care plan. Attendance at pass-on rounds was mandatory, and the exceedingly busy residents often arrived in a flurry, rumpled, squinting, and late. On more than one occasion, Dr. Joanna Boccaccio had had to go down to their call room in order to drag one out of bed. At the moment, all were present and accounted for, and had already reviewed radiological studies and patient presentation in greater detail.

Once the rounds finished, Boccaccio headed downstairs to the emergency department and found Isabel Vivas, still in uniform, waiting for her near the nurses' station. "Damn, Izzy. I forgot about us getting together."

"I didn't. I got this gut to remind me." She pinched an inch. "Do you have time?"

"Sure. I know you don't wanna eat, but I need caffeine, fourteen gauges bilateral, or I'm gonna fall over." She led Vivas toward the cafeteria.

"How's that family doing?"

"Thought you wanted to talk weight loss program and not shop," said Boccaccio, hoisting a brow.

"Don't know what it is. Can't get 'em off my mind. Whole family like that."

"The father and son have a pretty good chance. The mother and daughter are stable, but the prognosis isn't good. Still, we have some pretty sharp operators up there. I wouldn't be surprised if mom and daughter pulled through."

Vivas shuddered. "Be nice. Two less ghosts."

"Know what? You're right. That call *did* get to you. Same thing happens to me. I can see fifty trauma cases in a row, but for some strange reason number fifty-one will do it. Maybe there isn't anything different about her case. She's just another patient needing my care. I should treat her with dignity and respect and keep a professional distance so I can maintain a professional demeanor."

"But something sets off a feeling," said Vivas. "Maybe it's just an expression or something they say. Maybe it's just an image. Used to make me question God's mercy. You know, the whole thing about God letting bad things happen to good people. All I see are bad things, and I don't question God anymore. I question myself for doing this."

"It's not the job that's the problem. It's life. Just gets in the way of too many people. Makes them do crazy things. A resident was telling me about one of those "real video" programs where kids were lighting themselves on fire and diving into swimming pools. He saw another one where kids were smashing metal chairs over each other's heads because they were mimicking TV wrestlers. Sounds great while they're doing it, but when they come in and see me and have to explain how they got injured, I have to tell you, I've seen so many kids realize right then and there how stupid they were. Yeah, there's always a few who won't ever listen. They're choking on their own blood as they're telling you that the next time they still won't wear a helmet. If we're going to change the world—"

"We'll do it one patient at a time. But I'm not worried about the world."

As they entered the cafeteria, Boccaccio headed off to buy a coffee while Vivas grabbed a table. With the heavenly brew in hand, Boccaccio sat and moaned over her stiff back and sore legs. "So, you're having a hard time with your diet. . . ."

"Yeah, but you know what? I don't even want to talk about that." Vivas's eyes grew out of focus. "You ever think about quitting?"

"Thinking about it right now," Boccaccio quipped.

"Seriously. You went through all that school, residency, fellowship, so you could become a workaholic with no life. I'll bet the money's good. But do you have any time to spend it?"

Boccaccio took a long breath and reflected on the sacrifices, so many sacrifices, and the many missed opportunities. The faces, the places, once blurred by time, now tightened into focus. A trip to Cozumel turned down. An engagement ring returned to the handsome young attorney who had offered it.

"I'm sorry," said Vivas. "That's not what I . . . I mean, you ever just look around and think, My God, what a terrible mistake I've made? Have you ever done that?"

Boccaccio smiled knowingly. "I think you need to be a little insane to work in an ED. I've heard some of the blackest humor of my life back there. People calling body bags 'to go' bags. Residents coming up with their own Academy Awards for worst acting performance by a patient. And just like you, shift after shift, I'm seeing people at their worst, people who look me straight in the eye and tell me they have no idea how they get foreign bodies stuck in their rectums or people who are real quiet because they're dying. I got a girlfriend who started her own Internet company. She makes twice what I make and works out of her house while she's raising her two kids. I haven't dated in almost a year. Maybe

I'll have time when I retire. And kids? I wouldn't want to curse them with my schedule."

"So is it worth it?"

Boccaccio gave a slight shrug. "Most of the time I think it is. Either way, though, I'm locked in. My father . . . he's like the most focused guy you'll ever meet, and he did so much for me. He was a corpsman in the Marines and served two tours in Vietnam. He always wanted to be a doctor, but he had dropped out of high school. Guess he lived through me. I know it would kill him if I quit. He's made a career of bragging about me."

"You can't be here just for him. What about your mother? She the same way?"

"My mother," Boccaccio said, breathing the words like a curse. "They're nothing alike." She took a long sip of her coffee, then a spontaneous analysis of the moment struck her with irony. "Izzy, you've been working out of here for something like two years now, right?"

The paramedic nodded.

"And in all that time, we've never really sat down and talked. We should've done this so much sooner. And I get the feeling that this is a kind of CIS debriefing. Don't you have counselors who come down to the station?"

"I'm tired of being the only one at the meeting. Most of the people at Ten think they're so thick-skinned, especially Doe. But all of it's just building up. That's why so many of them drink. They say you have to work hard, play hard. I don't know. I'm tired of it."

"You have a little girl, don't you?"

Vivas opened her purse, withdrew her wallet, and produced two photos of a darling little girl of about six with brown pigtails and a smile that beamed as brightly as the diamond chips adorning her ears. "I keep telling my-self that *she's* why I'm here."

"You can stop telling yourself that," Boccaccio said. "She's not why you're here."

"She's not?"

"She can't be. That's your problem. If you're doing it for her, later on you'll resent her for it. Know what? When I think about it, I love my father for pushing me. But I hate him for it just as much." Boccaccio's pager went off. "Excuse me." She checked the display, ex-pecting a typical message like 19YR OLD LVL1 TRAUMA MVA ROLLOVER ALS UNSTABLE. ETA: 3 MINUTES. Instead, an unidentified person had asked her to call her home phone number. Unless her parakeet had escaped and paged her for more birdseed, there should not be anyone home.

"Doctor, I know you're busy. Thanks for your time." Vivas stood.

"You don't have to go."

"It's okay."

"Same time, same place, on Saturday?"

The medic's gaze lit up. "Serious?"

"This felt good. And maybe I can refer you to a di-etician, if you're still interested."

"Yeah," Vivas said. "See you then."

Boccaccio anxiously unclipped her cell phone from her scrubs and dialed her home phone.

"Hello?" came a familiar woman's voice.

"Mom?"

"Joanna, sweetheart, I just can't believe the disaster I'm finding here. Have you ever cleaned this place? The dust on this furniture is an inch thick. And the refrigerator? I found yogurt that expired three months ago and a box of baking soda, and that's it. Don't you ever eat? And what about guests? What're we supposed to do? Eat this bird food? You're lucky that smell coming from your hamper made me lose my appetite. C'mon, sweetheart, you're not one of those residents anymore. You're that attending person, right? You're supposed to be driving around in a big Mercedes and spending most of your time playing golf and tennis while your domestics clean and cook meals. You obviously got no help, and it looks like you never use this place. I'm really disappointed. You knew I was coming. You didn't think to clean up for your mother? You haven't seen me in six months, and this is the reception I get?"

"Mom, how did you get in?"

"Oh, you wanna go there? I went to the front office last night and made a big stink about it because you didn't leave the key under the mat like you said. I had to show this snippy little bitch like twenty photos of you and tell her three, maybe four stories before she believed who I was. She wanted to call you, but I told her not to. I knew you'd be busy. I know you don't get off until eight."

"Mom, you never told me you were coming."

"See, Joanna? You don't listen to me anymore. I tell you things, and you just forget them. I fly in from Vegas, and you just forget about your poor mother. Oh, but your father, you don't forget about him, do you?"

A hot pain crushed Boccaccio's chest and radiated into her arms. That was the most common presenting sign of patients experiencing myocardial infarctions—or those speaking to a mother like hers. If she didn't get off the phone soon, dysrhythmia, congestive heart failure, or cardiogenic shock would result in her sudden death. "Mom, I didn't forget you were coming," Boccaccio said emphatically. "You *never* called. You *never* told me you were coming."

"You're calling me a liar?"

"I'm just saying—"

"You are! I get on an airplane, I take a taxi, all so my daughter can call me a liar." Her mother sobbed like a child.

"Mom, stop it."

"Are you . . . are you coming home?"

Boccaccio shut her eyes and massaged the bridge of her nose. "I don't know."

9

4848 Santola Avenue
Toluca Lake
Wednesday, 8:45 A.M. Pacific Time

Charti Darunyothin stubbed out the cigarette in his
ashtray, then brought his old Nissan pickup truck to
a halt in front of a four-bedroom home built over half a
century ago. The house had been renovated several times
and had been kept in immaculate condition. Its white
aluminum siding shone brightly, as did the tiles of its
roof. Still more sunlight glinted off a spectacular bay
window and puddled across a flower garden that looked
too perfect to be real. A wide, circular driveway provided access to a two-car garage, to the massive front
door with its quartet of octagonal stained-glass windows,
and to two automatic gates attached to the home's most
striking and ironic feature: a four-foot-high white picket
fence encompassing the property.

Something—Charti wasn't sure what it was—drove
him out of the pickup. He walked up to the fence,
gripped two pickets, and stood there, an American dream
fully alive before his eyes. He half expected a young

boy wearing a Dodgers cap to come pedaling by and toss a newspaper over the fence. He pricked up his ears, waiting for the automatic sprinklers to hiss on. He strained for the scent of scrambled eggs and bacon wafting out from the kitchen window. He waited for James Robertson to come out in bathrobe and slippers to fetch the morning paper. Better yet, he waited for the family's sheepdog to do that.

Next door, a bearded black man wearing a dark suit and driving a green Range Rover backed out of his driveway. Charti's gaze met his for a second, then the man pulled out and braked. "Need help?" he asked suspiciously.

Charti shook his head.

"Mind if I ask what you're doing here? There's a sign on the corner that says no soliciting. You see it?"

"Yeah, I did. But I'm not selling anything."

He eyed Charti's sweatshirt and torn jeans. "What're you, a landscaper?"

"No. I was just admiring the house."

"Uh-huh," the man said, then eased the Rover forward and withdrew a pad and pen from the center console. He craned his head and riveted his eyes on Charti's license plate.

"Hey, it's okay," Charti called back. "I don't want to rob the place. I'm going."

"I got your plate. And I got a friend who works in the Sheriff's Department," the guy said. "Anything happens in this neighborhood, I'm sure they'll come looking for you."

"You're kidding me. I just stopped to take a look at the house."

"Well, you don't look like a real estate agent."

"I'm not."

"Then you don't belong here." With that, the man consulted his watch, then offered Charti a final glower before roaring off.

Grimacing over the stench of exhaust, Charti climbed into his truck and took one more look at the house. He suddenly felt foolish for coming, yet his suspicions had panned out. The Robertsons were every bit the perfect family he had imagined, and Charti needed more than ever to believe that they would not be torn apart.

He drove away as a young girl whispered in his ear: *You'll stay with me, Charti, won't you? You won't leave, right? You'll stay? Keep me warm? I'm freezing, Charti. I'm freezing.*

Pauly's New York Bagel Shop stood at the end of an old strip mall two blocks from John "Doe" Smith's Van Nuys apartment complex. Sitting down in the quaint little place for a cinnamon raisin with cream cheese and a black coffee had become a postshift ritual that helped Doe relax. The owner, Paul Bruno, a retired New York City cop, repeatedly offered free bagels because he knew Doe was a firefighter. Once in a while, Doe accepted a refill of coffee, but nothing more.

Geneva had volunteered to meet him at Pauly's, and there was nothing like a fresh bagel, a hot cup of coffee, and a beautiful woman to help him forget the night's trauma case and Vivas's accusations about him treating patients like hunks of meat. That couldn't be true. Just couldn't.

He drew in a long breath. "Smell that?"

"It's good," Geneva answered somberly. She hadn't touched her plain bagel and had taken only one sip of her orange juice.

"Pauly's got the ovens in the back. I've been all over the valley, looking for a good bagel. Can't beat this place. But don't tell anyone about it." He winked.

Her blue eyes grew reflective before she averted her gaze to fiddle with her napkin.

"You gonna eat?"

"Sorry. I'm still not feeling so good."

"Come here." Always the medic, he reached toward her neck to palpate her carotid pulse for general rate and character.

"I don't need a medic," she insisted, then hunted in her purse and produced a large clip with big teeth. She rolled her long hair into a bun, then clipped it in place.

"You're not just sick," he said, staring blankly at his coffee.

"No."

"Then this is the 'Doe, I know you and I have been seeing each other for a while, but I just can't deal with your immaturity anymore, and I can't be worrying about you every time you go to work' speech," he said, mimicking the voices of the many women who had, over the years, delivered nearly identical renditions of that uninspired blowoff.

Geneva's cheeks sank a little. She took another sip of juice, then bolted up. "Be right back." She headed for the restrooms.

Doe fell in behind her. "You okay?"

"I just have to go," she managed. "Sit down."

He threw up his hands, whirled, then marched back

to the table. What had he done? Become involved with a woman who now showed clear signs of manic depression? Should he urge her to see a shrink who could write her a scrip for Prozac? He stuffed the bagel in his mouth, tore off a huge hunk, then chewed fiercely, barely enjoying it.

After five irritating minutes, Doe rapped on the ladies' room door, and Geneva angrily assured him that she was all right. Another five minutes passed, then she finally reappeared, looking even more pale.

"Maybe you got food poisoning," he said as she resumed her seat. "What did you eat last night?"

"It's not food poisoning," she moaned.

"Geneva, if you don't think this is working out, you don't have to pull this whole 'I'm sick' thing. You just tell me, and we do what we have to do. I know I'm irresponsible. I know I like to have too much fun. I'm Peter Pan. But at least I know exactly who I am and what I'm about. And you know what? I don't really wanna change, because I kind of like me. I know a lot of people just can't deal with that. It's not like I haven't been called a flake or a cocky asshole before. It's okay. But I think if I was a much more boring guy, we wouldn't be here."

"You're so goddamned consumed with yourself," she fired back. "Would you look at me? Would you listen?"

"I would if you'd say something."

"Isn't it obvious?"

"What?"

"That I'm pregnant."

Doe leaned back in his chair, chuckled, then shook

his finger at her. "All right, you got me. Just for a second. But you got me."

"I didn't want to tell you in a bagel shop," she said. "But I can't hide it anymore. I went to the clinic, took the test, and it came back positive. I'm six weeks into my first trimester."

"Bullshit," he said, folding his arms over his chest. "What are you doing? Feeling me out? Wondering what I might do if you really are? C'mon. There's no way you could be pregnant—unless it isn't mine."

"Oh, it's yours. And I knew you wouldn't be thrilled—but for you to think that I'd joke or lie about something like this. . . . God, give me a little more credit."

"You're serious?" he asked, envisioning a potbellied, emasculated version of himself wearing a lost look as he stood in a children's clothing store, waiting for his wife and kid to come out of the dressing room.

"I just puked in that toilet back there."

"You said you're still only in your first trimester?"

Her lip twitched. "Uh-uh. Don't even say the word."

"It's not so bad. It takes like five to ten minutes. I've talked to patients who've had it done. They dilate your cervix and insert a cannula attached to a vacuum pump. Outpatient procedure. Or I can get you involved in one of those RU-486 clinical trials. They give you a pill that blocks a hormone and ends the viability of the fetus. Couple days later they give you an injection to induce contractions and expel the fetus."

"I'm twenty-seven years old," she said. "And I've thought about this. I'm ready for a baby."

"So I have no say?"

"You can *say* whatever you want. I'm telling you that there's a little boy or a little girl growing inside me, and you're the father. You can cover up how you feel with all your medical crap, your 'viability of fetus,' but if I were you, I'd be really scared and confused. I understand that."

"I'm not scared or confused. I'm pissed off because you're being so selfish. The kid deserves a mother and father who—"

"Who what? Give a shit? At least one of us does."

"I care."

"Wow, I'm convinced."

"I don't think you get this. Your freedom will be gone. I've seen what my sister's going through. I mean, she can't even go to a movie without paying big bucks to a sitter and worrying the whole time. Yeah, they rent movies, but the kids scream through them. That kind of burden—"

"That's all this baby is to you—a burden. I'm not asking you for anything here. I know commitment's a problem, and once this baby is born, you don't even have to be a part of its life. I'll support us just fine. I just wanted to let you know." Her face tightened as she got to her feet. "I had a dream a couple nights ago that I told you, and you were really happy and supportive, and realized that there are things in life so much more important than playing with your toys or running around with your buddies. I'm glad I reminded myself that it was only a dream." She bowed her head and aimed for the door.

Doe did not stop her. He lifted his coffee shakily to his lips, then found it hard to breathe. He reflected on

what he had said to her, on his tone, on what his expression must have conveyed. He had just finished telling her how much he liked himself. The only thing he
liked now was his ability to realize what a cold bastard
he had been.

On her way home from the station, Stephanie Savage
had stopped off at her local Ralph's market and picked
up two six-packs of beer. She carried them into the one-
bedroom with a loft that she had occupied for the past
five years. Half a dozen times during the day, she opened
the refrigerator door, stared at the glowing cans, then
tore herself away. The old Stephanie would have finished them before noon. The clock above her TV stand
now read 4:09 P.M. She had not touched a single beer,
and her soap opera was already in full swing when the
phone rang. "Hello?"

"Your goddamned son calls me to say he won't be
home for a while 'cause he's traipsing down to Miami."

The voice struck Savage rigid. "Tim, what do you
want?"

"I want you to act like a mother instead of some butch
fireman. Don't tell the kid you got a problem with him
going down to Miami. Tell him to go ahead and have a
good time and to remember everything you've taught
him and stay out of trouble—'cause then the guilt will
work on him, and he won't get in trouble. But no. What
does the woman wearing the pants do? She pisses the
kid off, so that now he's going down there with a vengeance, and the chances of him getting hurt have just
doubled. He's got a father right here, you know. Let me
discipline him."

"Discipline him? Where were you when he was in high school—besides moving around with that slut you were dating? He's twenty years old. You missed your chance."

"Maybe we both did."

"Maybe one of us could've grown up and held a steady job."

"Look, I don't want to argue."

Savage snorted. "Then why'd you call?"

"I'm just worried about Donny."

"If you're so goddamned worried about him, why don't you drag your ass on a plane and go down to Florida to see him? You don't even know what his dorm room looks like, do you?"

"I call him every week."

"When's the last time you saw him? Don't tell me it was at his graduation."

"I got a lot of things going on right now."

"Tim, you talk out of both sides of your mouth. And my show's on. Why don't you just lose my phone number for a couple of years?" Savage hung up, swore as the soap returned from a commercial. Apparently someone had been shot.

"The ambulance drivers are here," announced Mitch Bartholomew, the heroine Tina's younger brother, an obligatory family rebel with a mop of frizzy hair dyed blond.

"Ambulance drivers?" Savage cried. "You're kidding me!"

Mitch opened the mansion's front door and turned to join the group gathered in the parlor: two maids and a chauffeur, all in black uniforms and looking aghast at Bruce, who sat against the wall, wincing.

"No, no, no," Savage groaned. "You're dead, Bruce. That open neck wound drew air into your veins. You got massive air emboli. You went into cardiac arrest during the commercial."

Two "paramedics" hurried through the door, neither of them carrying any equipment—not even a long backboard. The female medic could not be more than nineteen, and though her uniform looked authentic, the crimson daggers sprouting from her fingertips destroyed her credibility.

"The wounds are pretty bad," said the male medic.

"No shit. His trachea could be collapsing or maybe he's got a spinal cord injury. C-spine him. Control the hemorrhage. Protect his airway. Get him on a board and out of there. Treat him en route. Do something!" Savage watched a moment more, then switched off the TV and went for a beer. She hesitated before opening it. "What am I gonna do? Sit here, drink, and feel sorry for myself? Donny, you bastard! Why can't you just stay home?"

10

Y ou could spend only so much time sitting on a bench and observing people before you drew the attention of mall security. You could, with impunity, spend an hour or two checking your watch and attentively eyeing the passersby. You could fiddle with a notebook computer or one of those pocket organizers. You could read. But Dr. Joanna Boccaccio had spent nearly five hours in the mall. She had window-shopped, listened to samples of CDs, eaten greasy food court cuisine, and repeatedly returned to the same bench facing a circular fountain with an ornate Trojan horse at the center. The same security guard, a young Hispanic guy, probably an undergraduate night student at the local community college, had passed her three, maybe four times. Now he caught her gaze and ventured over, looking a little nervous as he scratched his stubbly jowls. "I'm wondering if I can help you, ma'am." His voice came in a rhythmic baritone that Boccaccio found enticing. "You've been here a real long time."

"Are you supposed to kick out loiterers?" she asked, conscious that her cutoff jean shorts, worn tennis shoes, and Nike T-shirt hardly reflected her status as an attending physician, though she doubted the guard had mistaken her for a homeless IV drug user.

"They got all these rules about loitering and soliciting," explained the guard. "Most people don't even know about them. You waiting for somebody?"

"No."

"Just killing time?"

"Sort of. I'll go now, so you don't get in trouble."

"You can stay," he said. "Lot of people who come here don't come to shop."

"Really?"

"I got a call earlier from my buddy who patrols the garage. Guess it was about noon. He said the only thing happening down there was that some lady had fallen asleep in her car."

"Really?" Boccaccio asked, feigning innocence.

"He described your hair, which is really . . . well, it's black and curly."

Boccaccio forced a thin smile. "You were going to say 'a mess.'"

"I was going to say 'beautiful,' but that might get me fired. So I didn't." The guard blushed. His name tag read SANTIAGO.

"Well, Mr. Santiago, thank you for your kind assistance. I'll definitely shop here again."

"You're welcome, ma'am."

Boccaccio lingered a moment more, then walked

away, wrestling with the desire for a final look at the guard, who was probably ten years her junior. Maybe what the emergency department really needed was a new scandal. She could already hear the nurses clucking:

Boccaccio's with some young galleria stud. Yeah, she picked him up there. The boy has an incredible ass.

Key word is boy.

Ten years isn't a big difference.

Unless he's sixteen and you're twenty-six.

At her Grand Cherokee, Boccaccio covered a yawn as she keyed open the door. A security guard rolled by in a golf cart. She made a point of stepping out and waving to him—which sent the overweight young man's nervous gaze darting away. She grinned as she returned to the Cherokee, started the engine.

And sat there.

I'm thirty-two years old. That's my apartment. I'm going home. I'm asking her to leave.

You won't do it. Within five minutes, she'll have you feeling guilty and running around like a servant.

But you're a doctor. You save people's lives. You can't handle your own mother? And hey, maybe she left already. Her last page was over two hours ago. Call her.

If you call and she's there, you'll never hear the end of it. Your mother's in town and you just leave her, she'll say.

With arms tightening into steel, Boccaccio threw the Cherokee in gear, squealed out of the parking space, and followed the winding course out of the garage.

The drive back to her apartment took a scant three minutes, barely enough time to brace herself. The trip up in the elevator lasted the better part of thirty seconds. The walk to her door? Eight seconds.

She fumbled in her purse, found her keys, but the door suddenly opened.

"It's about time," cried her mother. "At least you can still come to dinner, but you can't come looking like that."

Boccaccio's eyes widened and her jaw fell slack. "Mom?"

Charti Darunyothin turned sharply left, into the freshly paved parking lot of Club Morgana. He glanced up at the club's unlit neon sign, its phosphorescent night skin peeled back to reveal ugly metal bones. The place always looked better at night, but today he needed an early fix.

He parked, then started for the bar's darkly tinted glass doors. Before he went in, he checked his reflection. He hardly recognized the drawn face staring back at him.

The club's sudden gloom, pierced by the incessant rhythm and vapid lyrics of top forty dance music, wrenched him inside. The familiar scents of cigarette smoke and beer-stained rug and fruity body sprays coaxed him farther. Small tables clustered around a main stage twinkling under a varicolored glow. Runways curved away from the stage, and two old men, Club Morgana's only patrons, sat along the right rail, nursing two-for-one drafts and inch-thick stacks of five-dollar bills. On the left runway, a tall, dark-rooted blonde drew circles in the air with her tattooed ass. Another girl, a curly-haired brunette with pink eyes that failed to focus, strutted onto the main stage, arching her back in a futile attempt to add a cup size to her unenhanced though large-nippled breasts.

Most of the first shift dancers were single moms who couldn't work at night for the big bucks. Charti had once believed that the girls were beautiful, sex-starved nymphos who worked there because they wanted to pick up young guys like him, take them home, and perform acts on them that would make porn stars jealous. The owners of Club Morgana wholeheartedly promoted that fantasy because they knew what young guys like Charti wanted to believe. The butt-shaking blonde probably drove a fifteen-year-old car with two hundred thousand miles on it, lived in a low-rent apartment, and was about as interested in her customers as a nurse working with a patient suffering from a sexually transmitted disease. She killed time on slow days by poking fun at the lonely dorks who, under the influence of long legs and liquor, exercised a level of generosity they hated themselves for later.

Charti caught the attention of another dancer, Brittany, seated at the long bar in the back. A professional men's club entertainer (working for tips only, gentlemen), she was lean, poured into a green evening gown, and had long, naturally blonde hair that partially veiled the image of a large-winged bat on the small of her back. She turned from the bar, exposing the small condominium that was her salon-tanned cleavage, and took Charti into her arms for a friendly hug. "What are you doing here so early?"

"Bad night."

"Come on," she said, leading him toward a private table in the back. "I got the first round."

•   •   •

Dr. Joanna Boccaccio gawked at the apparition standing in the doorway.

"What's the matter with you, Joanna?"

Boccaccio's fifty-seven-year-old mother had zippered her chunky frame into a black leather skirt and a matching halter top that buckled under new breasts. She had strapped on a pair of black heels so high that she towered over her daughter. Her face was hidden beneath a thick layer of foundation, and the shades of her eye shadow and lipstick were at odds: the eyes light pink, the lips candy apple red. Her once graying brown hair had been bleached blond, and large hoop earrings were turning her lobes to taffy.

Beyond her, seated on the sofa, beamed an olive-skinned man about Boccaccio's age. His short locks had been freshly moussed, and he wore gray polyester pants and a blue silk shirt unbuttoned nearly to his navel. Thick gold chains struggled to glimmer through a carpet of chest hair. He suddenly stood, appearing as gangly as an extraterrestrial. Boccaccio could not believe that a man would dress like that—unless he was headed to one of those retro clubs popular with some of the interns.

"Sweetheart, I want you to meet Drew. He's such a darling. He came all the way from Vegas with me."

"Joanna, Joanna," Drew said, in an accent that Boccaccio could not quite place. "Your mother, she tell me what special kind of girl you are. And doctor? Very good. You are special girl. And you have special mother." Drew shifted around her mother and abruptly hugged Boccaccio. Then he tightened his grip around her torso, lifted her into the air, and carried her into the apartment.

"Drew works at Bally's," her mother said proudly. "He repairs the slot machines. He's a supervisor."

"Just put me down," Boccaccio snapped.

Drew immediately complied, his smile fading slightly. "Special girl."

Boccaccio pushed him away.

"I know that look, Joanna. Don't start with me," her mother advised. "It's been hell for the past two days. I mean real hell."

"What did you do?"

"You don't like?" asked Drew. "You mother, she make herself perfect for you. Everything perfect now. She look young and beautiful."

"I'm not talking to you," Boccaccio said, though she could have silenced him with her gaze.

"All right, I know it's a big change, but I told you all about it. The boobs, the lipo, the hair. I didn't expect this kind of reaction. And you know what? It really hurts. It really hurts to see my own daughter standing there and looking at me like that, condemning me like that after all the sacrifices I made for you." She brought a finger to her eye, getting ready to turn on the waterworks.

"No, we can't have any of this," cried Drew. "We all family here."

"What are you talking about?" asked Boccaccio. "I just met you. We're nothing to each other. As a matter of fact, I'd like you to leave."

"Oh, Joanna, please," the greaseball said, lifting his palms. "I want everything perfect for you. If you want,

I go. But your mother, she love you. You both so special."

"Out!"

Drew shook his hands, then hustled toward the door.

"Stay right there, Drew. You're not going anywhere."

"Maybe I go outside. You talk."

Boccaccio's mother hardened her expression. "There's nothing we can't say in front of you." She closed the door.

"Mom, you never told me you were coming. You never told me about this," Boccaccio said, gesturing to her mother's hair and clothes. "Are you all right?"

"I'm fine."

"I don't think so. There's obviously something wrong. I think we should go to the hospital."

"Sweetheart, there's nothing wrong with me. I just wanted to surprise you." Her tone switched into the half-pleading, half-crying of a child. "I knew you'd be upset, so I thought I'd just tell you I had already said I was coming, and try to make you believe you'd forgotten about me, which I bet isn't too hard to do." Her mother staggered on those ridiculous heels toward the sofa and managed to come in for a landing. "I know you hate me."

"She don't hate you," soothed Drew as he rushed to her mother's side. "Everybody love you."

Boccaccio closed her eyes. "Mom, if you would've said you were coming, I would've prepared."

"You wouldn't have invited me. I've listened to you on the phone. You're always so distracted. You don't even want to see me anymore."

"No, I don't. Not when you do things like this. Show

up unannounced with, I guess, your new boyfriend? I don't understand why you act like this. I want to help, but I don't know where to start."

"You can start by wiping that expression off your face," her mother said, suddenly enraged. "How dare you say you don't want to see me—after I brought you into this world, raised you, gave up my whole life for you!"

"Why do you keep saying that? All I hear is how you ruined your life for me. I didn't ask to be born, but somehow that's my fault. I'm sick and tired of apologizing for being alive. I won't do it anymore."

Her mother sniffed. "I wish your father could hear how you really are, instead of that act you put on for him."

"That's not an act," Boccaccio said, closing her eyes. "He treats me like an adult, and so I treat him the same. But you, Mom . . . look at you."

"I don't have to stand here and listen to this." Her mother teetered over to the door and yanked it open. "Drew? Come on."

Wincing under her mother's gaze, the wiry man slipped into the hall.

"You're going out like that?"

"You're just jealous, Joanna. That's what it is. You're just jealous of your mother. And let me tell you something, that's really, really sick. You might be a big-shot doctor, but you still got a lot to learn."

Brittany had been working at Club Morgana for five months, and during that time Charti had developed a relationship with her that some people might find odd.

When they had first met, he, like any other patron, had paid her to dance for him, but that had lasted only a few weeks. Once they got to know one another, Charti would rather just pay her to sit, talk, and drink. He had learned that she had a three-year-old boy in day care, that the boy's father had died of a drug overdose, and that Brittany had been struggling to recover from his death and make ends meet. She rarely dated, despite her devastating looks, and focused her entire life on raising the boy and providing the very best for him. She was pragmatic about her job, figuring she would exploit her appearance and make as much money from it as she could before she finally succumbed to the wrinkles and sags. By then, she planned on having an impressive stock portfolio and a decent retirement fund. Though she had barely graduated from high school, she seemed a lot smarter than some of the interns and residents at SFMC. Which raised the question: Which would get you farther in life—being book smart or street smart? Maybe you needed both.

"You're smoking a lot," Brittany pointed out as Charti lit up his third.

"Yeah," he answered softly, then breathed in the poison, tossed his head back on the padded seat, and slowly exhaled. "I've been trying to catch up on my lung cancer. Fell way behind last week."

She smiled, nudged him with an elbow, then took a long pull on her mineral water. "I got a new car."

"Oh, yeah? What did you get?"

"You'll think I'm stupid."

"Tell me."

"Well, I don't know what came over me, but I got a minivan. It's only three years old, low miles. The other girls here think I'm nuts. I'm twenty-four years old and driving around in a van like it's my mom's and I just got my learner's permit. They said I should've bought a sports car."

"They're probably right."

"I don't want to sound like a granny or something, but I just want my son to have good memories, like some of the ones I had before my mom died and my father went nutty. We used to go on long vacations to the Midwest. I remember my brother and I used to sleep in the back of my dad's van, and there was just something about that. Made us feel happy and secure. I want that for my son."

"You'll need more than a van."

"I know, but it's a start. And it kind of made me feel good, too. 'Course I'll never get a date driving it around. Then again, maybe some guy carrying out my groceries will think I'm a lonely suburban housewife. You never know." She flashed her brilliant teeth.

"You never know."

She took his hand. "You're definitely bummed. That must've been a really bad shift."

He shrugged. "Not really."

"Then why so sad?"

"Tired."

"I've seen you more tired than this. Is it something outside the job? Are you fighting with your brothers again? Your dad call to drive you crazy? Or did you finally find your mother?"

Charti took another long drag on his cigarette, then put it out. "This family got into a real bad car accident this morning."

"Yeah, I heard about it on the news."

"Saw this kid come in. I see a lot of kids come in. A lot. But this one. Little boy. It was just hard to explain."

She frowned. "Did you recognize him from somewhere?"

"No. But I heard about the accident. And when I saw him, it just, you know. . . ." Charti's lip quivered.

"God, that's got to be so hard. I mean, compare that to this. Bunch of lonely, horny dorks who need to be relieved of their money."

He gave her a look.

"Oh, I didn't mean you."

"Sure, you did. That's okay. What's pretty funny is if you saw me at work, I'm nothing like this. I don't talk much there. I focus on the job. I got this one medic who likes to harass me. I just give him the robot routine. Messes with his head pretty well. He doesn't even get the fact that I'm imitating him. He comes across as a real prankster, but I've seen him out in the field. He's cold. Sometimes I wish I could be like him."

"You don't ever want to be like that. People are usually so scared when they go to a hospital. Maybe you just answer the radio, but if I got sick, I'd want you there."

"I guess there's a compliment in there somewhere. You know what it is? I don't think the human psyche was made to deal with the kind of pain and suffering we see every day. Sometimes you just need to shut it out. But when that kid came in, I couldn't do that."

Her tweezed brows came together in a look of utter incredulity. "So you're mad at yourself for caring?"

"I went up to the ICU to see him. Boccaccio caught

me up there. She gave me this look. I knew it was weird for me to check on the kid, but I couldn't help myself."

"So what?"

"When I got off, you know what I did? I went to their house. Gorgeous place in Toluca Lake. Even had a white picket fence."

"You went to that family's house? I don't know, Charti, maybe that's weird."

"The neighbor thought so. He took down my tag number. Thought I was a burglar or something."

"So why'd you go?"

His voice cracked. "Because my sister died."

"What? You had a sister?"

"I guess I was about thirteen. My parents were taking all four of us kids to buy sneakers. Santa Anas were coming in real strong that day. I remember that when we got in the car, I got something in my eye, and I was rubbing that eye for the whole time during the ride. I didn't know what we hit or how any of it happened until later on. Some drunk and senile old lady decided that she needed to get Kitty Litter for a cat that had died two years before. My brothers were banged up pretty bad, but they were okay. My parents sustained multiple fractures but nothing really life-threatening. It was my sister who got crushed. Pelvic fracture. She was sitting right next to me. Bleeding inside. Bleeding so much inside. And talking to me. Wanting me to stay with her. Hold her hand. Just. . . ." He closed his eyes, held back the tears with his thumb and forefinger.

Brittany slid an arm around his shoulders. "Charti," she whispered, "it's okay."

"My brothers were all pissed off because they weren't

getting their new sneakers," he said, laughing to fight off the pain. "They didn't understand that our sister had died. But I guess that's how you are when you're a little kid. My sister was fourteen, the oldest. She really wanted me to do something to help her. She kept telling me she was freezing, but I didn't know what to do."

"What was her name?"

"Angelica."

"So you saw that boy, and he got you thinking about your sister and the accident and everything."

"He got me thinking about me. Go out one day to get some new sneakers, and your whole life's changed forever. The world's pretty mean, pretty nasty. But you got a family that'll help you take it on. Or at least you think you do. After my sister died, my whole family fell apart. And sometimes I think that's the real reason why I wanted to work in a hospital. I can't fix shit in my own life, but there. . . . Okay, so I'm not a doctor, but coordinating incoming calls is how I help out." He glanced at Brittany, whose expression had gone distant. "Sorry. I didn't mean to come in here and cry on your shoulder."

"Then let me cry on yours. I never told you the whole story of my son's father."

"You don't owe me a confession."

"No, but you owe me an ear. And a drink. So pay up, mister."

Charti mustered a slight grin and dug into his wallet.

Abe Kashmiri parked his late model Jeep Wrangler about half a block north of the apartments, jammed some quarters into the meter, then swore as he read the sign indicating that there was no parking charge after 6 P.M. Perhaps his mistake was an omen. He should not have dinner with Lisa and her precocious three-year-old.

But for the past day and a half she had possessed his thoughts. Even during the critical incident stress debriefing that Savage had strong-armed him to attend, he had been caught daydreaming about her:

"Are you with us, Abe?" Lieutenant Martinez had asked.

"Yes, sir."

"Because for a moment there—"

"Leave the boy," Fitzy had cried. "If he wants to think about his TV award, that's okay."

Guffaws had answered Fitzy's teasing, and Abe's cheeks had flushed.

Thankfully, he had been very discreet about the dinner invitation. If the other firefighters had known that he had been thinking about a woman, even Lieutenant Martinez would have joined in the razzing.

Abe reached the stairs that would take him into the pool area and paused to make a last inspection of himself: khaki Dockers, black polo shirt, black loafers with tassels. He had tried on four different outfits and had, after an hour, returned to the first one. Clearly, he was sartorially challenged, but at least he wasn't wrinkled. He swallowed his nerves and reached unit 119, wishing he had brought the bottle of wine and flowers that he had agonized over while dressing. However, arriving with the accoutrements of romance might be too forward. This was a thank you dinner, not a date. The door opened before he rang the bell.

"Right on time," Lisa said, wearing a smile and a dress that could easily trigger a mass casualty incident.

He winked. "I'm a fireman."

She led him into a living room furnished in Southwestern style, with bleached wood furniture, paintings of mesas and adobe homes, and lamps made of miniature wagon wheels. Candles burned on a small table with service for two, and the wonderful scent of hickory emanated from the adjoining kitchen. "Have a seat. Can I get you something to drink? I have beer, wine, soda, Scotch. . . ."

"Where's your daughter?"

"She's up in Newhall with my sister. I need a break once in a while, you know?"

That's interesting, Abe thought as he lowered himself to the sofa. *No kid. And I don't see any signs of a boy-friend.* "Do you have any bottled water?"

"Thought you were off tonight," she said, opening the refrigerator.

"I've never liked the taste of beer. And I don't really drink. Maybe champagne on a holiday. That's it."

"A fireman who doesn't drink? That's like a cop who doesn't steal."

"Ouch. That's cold. Back at my old station I knew a lot of police officers who didn't—"

"Just teasing," she said, handing him a fancy square glass brimming with water and ice cubes. "Dinner's almost ready. I made hickory-smoked chicken. I was worried that you might be a vegetarian, so I have a backup plan if that's the case."

"Chicken's fine," he said, then realized that as he had taken a sip from the square glass, water had spilled all over his crotch. He brought his legs together and found a coaster on the end table.

"I see you just spilled your drink all over your pants," she said teasingly as she tugged open the oven door. "Want a napkin?"

"I'm fine," he said, his voice a little too high.

"Went out on a blind date a couple years ago. Guy ordered spaghetti for me—even after I told him I didn't want it. So I'm wearing this low-cut blouse and a piece falls into my cleavage, but the end of it is kind of hanging out. He doesn't say anything. The waiter doesn't say anything. But both of them keep looking at my boobs, and I'm thinking they're both pigs until we get out to the car, and I see it hanging there. Pretty stupid, huh?"

"I guess so. Can I have a different glass?"

She smiled broadly. "Sure."

They continued the small talk for several minutes as she brought him a round, Abe-proof glass and finished preparing the meal. He took his place at the table, and as she served the food, he remarked that this would be the best meal he had had for a long time. Being single and too lazy to cook, he survived on take-out from Jerry's Famous Deli and from a couple of the Thai and Chinese places along Ventura Boulevard.

"Oh, this is heaven," he said breathing it all in before putting his fork and knife to work.

"Hope you like it," she said, haloed in flickering candlelight.

A strange rumbling came from above, and the light hanging over the table swung slightly.

"Tremor?" Abe cried.

"Relax. The bastard upstairs has a rowing machine, and he works out every night. The joys of apartment living."

"That's pretty loud," Abe said, furrowing his brow at the ceiling. "You complain about it?"

"Yeah. This is the solution. He used to work out at midnight. I'm sorry. I was praying he wouldn't be home."

"It's all right. If we were at my place, we'd be listening to this little Italian woman having sex with her pro wrestler boyfriend."

She grinned crookedly. "Sounds more interesting than rowing."

"First few times it was funny. But when you just get off a twenty-four-hour shift and you're trying to sleep while some girl is yelling through the walls, that gets old pretty fast. And this chicken is great."

"Thanks. So, Abe, I hate to play the old interview trick, but I'm curious. You got the dark hair and the skin, but I can't tell where you're from."

"Get that a lot. I'm one hundred percent Angeleno. My parents were born in Pakistan. They moved back there."

"Do you read Urdu?"

"No, but my parents do," he said, mildly astonished. Rarely did he encounter anyone who could find Pakistan on a map, let alone refer to the country's official literary language. "How do you know about Urdu?"

"I was a linguistics major. Four years of undergraduate work and two more for my master's. I taught composition as an adjunct for a while, but the low pay and combative students just wore me down. Now I manage a Thoreau's Bookstore in Glendale. It's a great job. I like helping people, but I'm not doing anything as admirable as you."

"Some people think I just drive an ambulance. I get out, I put the sick person on a stretcher, then I drive like hell to the hospital. On the way, I'm having fun making all kinds of funky noises with my siren."

"I hear you. I manage a bookstore. All I do is sit around and read all day, right?"

"No, you bust your ass. Same as me. People don't have a clue about medics. I stick tubes down people's throats. I punch holes in their necks so they can breathe. I zap them with electricity. I can administer twenty-one different medications, including narcotics."

"And those people don't know how dangerous your job can be," she added soberly. "I wasn't going to bring that up, but maybe we should get it into the open. I don't want any hard feelings."

"I told you it was all right. I wouldn't be here if it wasn't."

"The living room phone is locked up in a drawer now. And I had a long talk with my daughter. She said she called because she thought I needed help waking up, which most mornings isn't far from the truth."

A moment passed. Just the clanking of silverware and Abe's faint groans of appreciation over such delicious food. He thought about mentioning the hearing he and Savage had attended earlier, but decided that would only darken the mood.

"So, do you have any brothers or sisters?" Lisa asked as she brought her glass of water to her lips. "Oh, God, I'm sorry. I sound like an interrogator."

"I have a sister, but I've never met her. It's a long story. My parents are in Pakistan because of her."

"You don't have to talk about it." She reached across the table and touched his hand. "My life's been so simple. Raised in New York. Migrated west with my sister after my parents passed away. Married an idiot who cheated on me, but all my relatives live out here, and they helped me get through that. Being alone has to be hard on you."

"Sometimes. I just became a NREMT–P, a Nationally Registered Emergency Medical Technician–Paramedic. I'm doing the fire department's three months of probation. The pressure's really on. Makes me think about what my parents say."

"How long have you been doing this?"

"About six months before my parents left, I joined the fire department because, no offense, I found college so boring. Every fireman has to be trained to the EMT-I level. That's about a hundred hours in the class and ten of supervised clinical experience. There used to be an EMT-II program, but it got phased out, so the only thing left was the EMT-P, which requires over a thousand hours of training for a marginal pay raise. I got my state licensure and my accreditation from Valley Fire Rescue. And that was way more than you needed to know. What was the question again?"

She graced him with that perfect smile. "You answered it. And for someone with second thoughts about his job, you sound pretty ambitious. You could go back to college. Tough it out. Then take the M-CAT and apply to medical school."

"I think I'm set in my ways. I'm not sure I could take all of those general education classes because some college wants to produce well-rounded individuals who can weave baskets as well as they dribble basketballs."

"That's pretty glib."

"It's not mine. Guy I work with said it. Some guidance counselor told him he had to take gym and a crafts class, and that's when he dropped out. He wanted to be a lawyer, but he absolutely refused to take anything that wasn't related to his major. He said the whole system was bullshit and just designed to make students spend more money on their degrees."

"Well, it felt a little like that when I went to school. I guess you can look at those classes as barriers or stepping-stones. It depends on your attitude." She pointed to the ceiling. "He stopped. Maybe he got a phone call. You know, I'm an idiot. I should've put on some music. It's been a while since I've entertained."

"You're doing a good job," he said. "I'm entertained."

She crossed to her stereo and hunkered down to turn on the receiver placed on a bleached wood stand. "Do you like hip-hop?"

"No," he answered sharply. "Sorry. It's okay. Whatever you want to hear."

"Wow, that lit your fuse," she said. "I'll put on something else."

"You know how you can listen to a song and remember a whole time in your life, maybe a summer or a person?"

"Sure. So you've got an aversion to hip-hop? Brings back bad memories?"

Abe left the table and crouched down next to her. "What's your greatest fear?"

"You know, Abe, when I invited you here, I figured the conversation would focus on sports or some other macho subject. You're really surprising me."

"Is that good or bad?"

She pinched his arm. "Good."

"So what's your greatest fear?"

"Losing my daughter, I guess. Sometimes I have dreams about that. She's dying. And I can't help. What's yours?"

"Kind of the same: causing someone to die because I screwed up. Even when you do everything right, you still lose patients. Part of the job. When I got to my first firehouse, there was this sweet lady who was retiring. She'd put in twenty-five years as a medic and had outlasted all of her friends. At her party, she came up to me, and it was a weird moment, like she was passing the torch or something. She told me, 'They're all your children, Abe. Don't ever quit or become cold, because they need you.' I thought that was a strange thing to say until I spent some time in the field. Funny saying we have: When people are hurt, they revert. Think about how you act when you get a really bad cut or something. I'm the same way. And when I'm out there, sometimes I feel like a parent."

"Which brings us back to hip-hop?"

"Right," he said, feeling his cheeks grow warm. "First patient I ever lost belonged to an amateur hip-hop group. Kid got caught in a gang war. Typical stuff you read in the newspaper. When I got to him, he was lying on the pavement."

"God, I can't even imagine. . . ."

"The thing I remember most isn't all the blood or this little-boy expression he had on his face or the way his friends were screaming for me to save him. It was this boom box playing this hip-hop song. I remember screaming for someone to shut it off. That song stayed in my head for maybe a year. Every once in a while I hear it on the radio, and I just shiver." He paused, expecting her to say something. She didn't. "And you're looking at me now like Wow, this guy is way out there. Inviting him here was a huge mistake."

Lisa did not move, and her face seemed blank.

Which made her sudden lunge for his lips all the more surprising. In fact, she knocked him onto his back, cupped his head in her hands, and moaned faintly as they kissed.

With the engine of her seven-year-old Pontiac Grand Prix idling a loud plea for a tune-up, Isabel Vivas and her daughter, Consuela, waited in the market's fire zone for Mama to come outside. Several customers made hasty exits, and Consuela played a little game of trying to guess which cars they drove.

A bony old woman wearing a stained corduroy jacket and puffing on an unlit cigarette, pushed her shopping cart in front of Vivas's car. As the woman neared the open window, she scowled and said, "This is a fire zone. Can't you read?"

"Yeah, I can. And I happen to be a firefighter."

"I don't see you fighting any fires." The woman screwed up her face in an ugly knot and trundled off.

"What a day, what a day," Mama groaned in Spanish as she tugged open the door and plopped inside. Nearly a dozen badges hung from her red smock, some service awards, others sporting lame promotional slogans like

Ask Me About the New Spam. "He put me on express again. I've been working in the same place for nineteen years, and he puts me on express. He's got his eye on those three blondes he hired. He figures he'll get rid of the gossiping old lady by putting her on express. Maybe tomorrow I'll talk to the shop steward. We'll see if Mister Manager likes me getting the union involved."

"Mama, don't make trouble. You have one more year. You'll get your pin, your party, and your pension. Why do you want to make your last year your worst?"

"I don't. But I'm not going to let some young kid with a JCPenney's shirt and a college degree push me around." She glanced to the back seat. "Now, how is my beautiful granddaughter?"

"Okay," sang Consuela. "Today, um, at school, Miguel, he, um, he pushed me, right? And my teacher, she, um, she had to come and put Miguel in time-out, which is for babies."

"You tell that boy to stop pushing," insisted Mama. "And if he does it again, you tell your teacher right away, okay?"

"I will."

Vivas pulled out of the parking lot and hung a right onto Sepulveda, heading north toward their apartment building. She repeatedly checked her rearview mirror and silently swore over the black sports car riding her ass.

"Why are you going so slow?" Mama asked.

"I'm doing the limit."

"Louis's show is on at eight-thirty. You keep driving like this, we'll miss it."

"I set the VCR."

"I don't care. My youngest son finally gets an acting job on NBC, and I'm going to miss it because my daughter drives like an old lady. Come on."

"This is as fast as I'm going."

"Grandma, this morning, um, Mommy drove really slow to school," said Consuela. "There was people honking at her, and she said bad words."

Mama placed a hand on Vivas's shoulder. "Isabel, do you want me to drive?"

"No! Just be quiet and let me concentrate. And it's not like you haven't seen the show. Were you asleep when we went to the taping?"

"I want to see what it looks like live on TV."

"But it's not live. They're just playing a tape. We saw it live when we went to the studio."

"But this is the first time the world is seeing it."

"Okay, Mama."

Ahead, a lowrider pickup truck with the chrome silhouettes of naked women on its mud flaps barreled around the corner of Sherman Way and cut in front of Vivas. "Son of a bitch! Why do people drive like that?"

"Because they see how slow you're going and they don't want to get behind you," groaned Mama. "You're so worried about getting into an accident, you'll cause one."

"Mama, please. I drive a rescue at work. We'll get home in time."

And, with five minutes to spare, they did. Vivas pulled into the subterranean parking garage of her two-year-old building and found her usual spot. Mama and Consuela were already out of the car and waiting for the elevator before she shut off the engine.

Vivas knew better than to speak to her mother during the elevator ride up to the fourth floor. Disgust lined the woman's face, and her gaze would not lift from her antique gold watch.

Frowning at the sound of the TV coming from inside, Vivas opened her door. Consuela charged into the three-bedroom apartment, passed the kitchen, and cried, "Daddy!"

"What's he doing here?" Vivas asked, grabbing Mama's arm.

"So I invited him to see Louis's show. So what? He *is* your daughter's father."

Rolling her eyes, Vivas stiffened as she closed the door, then dragged herself into the living room, where Manny Nuva sat, scuffed black boots propped on the glass coffee table, blue mechanic's shirt probably getting grease on Vivas's sofa. He wore his customary smirk and had, for some reason (probably on a bet or during a drunken binge) shaved off his thick black hair, making the three scars on the right side of his head stand out like whip lashes against the stubble. The new cut made the tattoo of the tarantula crawling up his throat look even larger. Though he would turn thirty this year, not a speck of gray lightened his goatee. He flicked a quick glance at Vivas before taking Consuela into his arms. "Oh, I missed you, my baby," he cooed.

"You're just staying for the show," Vivas said.

"When Mama called, she said she'd make coffee afterward," he replied, pressing Consuela's head into his filthy shoulder. "And I want to see my daughter."

"Come on, Manny. You have her all day Sunday. I don't want to confuse her."

"Don't," warned Mama as she scooped up the remote from the coffee table. "Not in front of the child."

Vivas glared at her mother, then took a deep breath before facing Manny. "Maybe we should talk."

Manny pried off Consuela and followed Vivas into her bedroom. Two weeks before, she had bought a new bedroom set, liberating herself from the black modern pieces Manny had insisted they buy. Warm, bright pine created a much more airy and livable environment, but it returned to its darkness as Manny nodded his head and curled his lips in a twisted smile. "Got rid of the last of me, huh?"

"What did you expect? That I'd set up a shrine to a man who divorces me because his parents don't like me or my family?" Vivas gripped the edge of her dresser. "You're not even a man."

He stroked his goatee, wandered over to the window, and stared down at the street. "Not this conversation again."

"Manny, why can't you just leave things as they are? We're trying to make a life here. We have a routine for Consuela, and now you're messing that up."

"What? I can't even drop by? That's my daughter in there."

"You should have thought of that every time your mother told you I'm not good enough for you. You should have thought of that every time your father said I'm a latent lesbian because I'm a firefighter. This is the twenty-first century, for God's sake. I don't want a penis. I wish your stupid father could understand that."

"This argument is so old."

"Look, the next time Mama calls you and tries to get

us together, you ignore her. This routine is the best for Consuela. I know you love her. I know that. And you'll do this for her."

He glanced back at the window.

"You listening to me?"

"I used to stand here a lot, looking at that corner down there and thinking about you riding around in that rescue all night. I spent a lot of hours right here, just waiting."

"Hey, in there, it's on," hollered Mama.

Manny shrugged. "We'd better go in."

"Every time I see you, you're giving me this look like you want to get back," Vivas said, feeling her eyes glaze over. "But it won't work. You'll never change. And neither will your parents. You'll never grow up. You'll never be a man. And you'll never take charge of your life. That's why you lost us."

"There it is again," he said, lowering his voice to a growl. "You asking me to choose between my family and this one. That's not fair."

"Tell that to your parents."

"They don't have anything to do with this."

"You're the way you are because you lived your whole life with a domineering mother and a father who's the most petty man I've ever met. I don't have a meal on the table every night, and suddenly I'm no good. Then you start acting like your old man, and you wonder why I won't have sex with you."

"Maybe I don't want to get back, Izzy. And our sex was never that good. Your mother's living in some kind of dream world where she thinks she can put a Band-Aid on this. She couldn't fix your father's stroke, so she's working out her frustration on us. It's so obvious.

But I don't care, because I get a chance to see my daughter. Consuela can handle an unexpected visit."

"You people are missing this," shouted Mama, a laugh track punctuating her words.

"Just do what I said and don't listen to my mother. You come here, you pick up Consuela, you take her for the day, you bring her back. That's it. There's no coffee. There's no socializing. Once you have what we shared, you can't go back. It's all or nothing. And now we have nothing."

"You're wrong. We have five years of memories. We have a daughter."

"And we could've kept making memories and our daughter wouldn't have to explain to her friends why her daddy doesn't live with her. We could have had something—if you would've been a man. Ask Mama about it; she'll tell you. She has two sons. When a boy leaves the nest, he leaves his family behind and starts a new one. It's the girl who never leaves her family."

"What does your mother know about raising boys? She's got one who's a flaming homosexual and another one in jail."

"She tried her best—which is more than I can say for you. Why didn't you ever defend me when your mother made all those remarks? Even at our wedding, she stabbed me in the back, and you just let it go because you didn't want to hurt her."

He muttered a curse.

"Come on," came an urgent shout from the living room. "This is Louis's big scene."

"Mommy, Uncle Louis is on TV," shouted Consuela.

Vivas narrowed her gaze. "Look, maybe with you sitting around here it feels like we never broke up. It's hard, you know?"

"Yeah, it is. It's hard for me because you blame it all on me and my family, like you came into our marriage with no baggage, like your mother isn't as domineering as mine, like your father isn't draining every cent out of your family by lying in that home. You think it was easy telling my parents that Louis is gay and Ricardo's serving a life sentence for murder? I never told you what they said. Maybe you should've heard it. I stood up to my parents. I did."

Gritting her teeth, Vivas shook her head and went back to the living room. A commercial blared on the TV, and her mother dialed the cordless phone, probably calling her girlfriend Juanita, who lived two floors down. Consuela sat on the edge of the couch, mimicking her father by kicking her shiny black shoes up on the coffee table as she combed her long hair. Vivas went to the refrigerator, snickered at her cans of Ultra Slim-Fast, then pulled out a cling-wrapped slice of pizza, tore off the plastic, and sank her teeth into cold cheese.

How dare he ridicule her family? All those years he had smiled and been pleasant at family gatherings? All those nights she had cried over her brother's sentence, with him lying next to her and saying all those supportive things? Just lies. Why had he even bothered to marry her? Why did he waste five years of her life? Why did he want to make a baby? She had always told him how she felt about his parents and had repeatedly urged him to put his new family first. He had always known exactly where she stood. But she had never known what went on inside him until it was too late.

"What's this show about?" Manny asked Consuela, then dropped onto the sofa, making himself way too comfortable.

"Uncle Louis works at this chicken place, and, um, he, um, has to dress up like a giant chicken or something. There's like this pretty girl he wants to see, but he has to wear the giant chicken costume even though, um, it's not Halloween. I have a Halloween costume. Wanna see it, Daddy?"

"Sure."

Consuela ran out of the room.

"Manny, is your sister still working for Ralph's?" asked Mama.

"Yeah, but she got transferred to Sun Valley."

"And your parents? How are they?"

His gaze found Vivas's. "They're fine."

Vivas set down her pizza. "Manny, I can't do this."

"Isabel . . ."

"Shut up, Mama."

"That's okay," Manny said, getting to his feet. He checked his watch. "Sorry, Mama. I can't stay for coffee."

"Oh, yes, you can. Don't let my daughter intimidate you."

He hurried to the door. "Kiss my baby good-bye for me."

"Manny," Vivas began, feeling the guilt tighten her stomach, "it's just—"

Consuela came rushing in, carrying her costume. "Mommy, where's Daddy going?"

"I'm sorry, baby, I have to go now," Manny said.

"No, Daddy, don't go! I want to show you how I look

in my costume." Consuela jerked in frustration, then tugged on Manny's pants.

He hunkered down and smiled. "Don't worry. I'll see you Sunday."

"No, Daddy, don't go!"

"I'm sorry, baby, I have to." He straightened and pried her off.

"Daddy has to go now," Vivas said, then draped an arm around her daughter, holding her back.

"I'll call before I come," he said.

"Okay." Vivas had to look away.

" 'Bye."

" 'Bye." She closed the door after him.

Consuela's face looked so tearful and wounded that it tore a huge gash in Vivas's heart. "Mommy, why did you make him go? He wanted to see my costume."

"I didn't make him go."

"Yes, you did."

Shaking her head in disgust, Mama came up behind Consuela. "Daddy will see your costume on Sunday. Now go put it away and come back quick so we can watch Uncle Louis, even though that ungrateful boy went to a party instead of being here with his family." Mama squeezed Consuela's shoulders, then nudged her toward the hallway. Once the little girl was out of ear-shot, Mama *tsk*ed and said, "Your father and I have been married for thirty-eight years. Kids today are lucky they can last thirty-eight minutes."

"Mama, never do that again."

"What?"

Vivas glanced at the door. "Invite him here."

"You're telling me what I can and cannot do in my

own apartment, the place where I pay half the rent and more than half of the other expenses? You'd dress Consuela in rags if I didn't take her out once a month and buy her some decent clothes. Kids grow. Styles change."

"You spoil her."

"She's my granddaughter. She deserves the best. But maybe I should get my own place."

"Oh, don't start with that."

"Maybe I should. We don't agree on how to raise that child or anything else."

"*We're* not raising that child. *I am.*"

"You think you are. But she needs a stable family. She needs her father."

"So I should get back with him because Consuela needs her father? Never mind if I'm miserable for the rest of my life because his family treats me like a second-class citizen?"

"When I married your father, I knew I would have to make sacrifices. And then when you were born, I made even more. Sometimes I wanted to leave him, but I knew if I did, that would hurt you. So I stayed. And even with all of Ricardo's problems, it all worked out for the best."

"You stayed in a loveless marriage because of the children. You think that was smart?"

"It was the right thing to do."

"Mama, you couldn't convince me to stay with Manny, and you won't convince me to get back with him. You wanna call that selfish? Go ahead. But I don't want my daughter saying to me what I'm saying to you: if you didn't love Dad, you should have left him."

Throwing her hands in the air, Mama wandered back to the sofa. "You teach them as much as you can," she muttered to herself. "And you think they understand life, but they don't understand. They really don't."

Vivas and Mama watched the rest of the sitcom in silence. Not a single line or situation brought so much as a faint grin to Vivas's lips. She cracked open a can of Slim-Fast and guzzled it, then headed off to the shower. Afterward, she tucked Consuela in, then went to bed, willing herself to dream about another life. She had married a man who put her first. She had become a doctor in a small town in northern California where she knew her patients by their first names. She had bought an expensive home for her parents and had hired a private nurse for her father. She had put Consuela in a private school with no metal detectors or drug-sniffing dogs.

Then, one night on their way home from vacation, her husband fell asleep at the wheel.

13

After sleeping away most of Wednesday and moping around for the better part of Thursday, Doe was resigned to the fact that Geneva was not going to call. Time to get his depressed ass out of his apartment and divert his attention from her and the pregnancy. He took a long, hot shower, slipped on a pair of jeans and designer crewneck shirt, then jetted off in his vintage Corvette.

He spent nearly an hour just cruising around the valley and listening to the EMS frequency on his scanner. Slow night. Couple of fender benders, couple of girlfriends getting beat up by their boyfriends, and another in a string of Dumpster fires behind supermarkets. Probably a couple of kids raising hell. Valley PD would catch up with them sooner or later.

Growing bored, he wound up north of his apartment, at a blues club in Encino. A six-piece band roared from the stage as he threaded his way to the empty bar, sat, and ordered a vodka and grapefruit juice. Although it was a weeknight, couples jammed tables near the stage. In fact, Doe spotted only two people sitting alone: a dark-suited man in the rear, who seemed more interested in his pager than in the band, and a husky woman with straight brown hair wandering down to her waist. She met Doe's gaze, smiled, then reached for her drink. Doe turned back to the bar, sipped his greyhound, then eyed the band's lead singer, a spirited black woman of fifty belting out a song about a man who had left her at the altar. Within a minute, Doe imagined Geneva on stage, maintaining a white-knuckled grip on the microphone as she sang to the audience about a relationship gone sour because of a selfish man.

"Mind if I?"

Doe glanced over his shoulder. The husky woman's eyes sparkled. He half-shrugged.

"You waiting for someone?" she asked.

"Don't you mean *looking*?"

She grinned coyly; not a bad grin, but not one Doe would pursue. "I'm a little more subtle."

"Sorry. I'm not exactly good company right now."

"No problem." She lifted her drink and stood.

"You can stay."

Her eyes widened. "You don't know what you want."

"Got that right."

"I'm Cheryl Livasse."

He sighed. "John Smith."

"That's my real name. What's yours?"

"John Smith's my real name. Most people call me Doe."

"As in John Doe?"

He rubbed a finger on his sweaty glass. "They used to call me Smitty when I was a kid. I hated that because it turned into 'Shitty Smitty.' "

"But Doe's better?"

"They call me the Pillsbury Dough Boy, the Dough Boy, the Dough Man, the Pillsbury Pickle, and Doe the Toe, as in John Doe's toe tag."

"Why don't they just call you John?"

"Because they know me too well. And John's just plain wrong for a guy like me."

"What kind of guy are you?"

"I'm a selfish egomaniac who never wants to grow up and assume responsibility. I'm a sex addict, a lush, and probably the most inconsiderate and uncaring man you'll ever meet. People are tools for my pleasure. It's all about me. The whole world revolves around me."

"That's quite a pickup line. I'm not sure if you're going for the sympathy lay or just being honest."

"Ma'am, you're very nice, but I don't want to waste your time."

"That's so polite of you, *sir*. I'm used to being blown off with a *honey* or a *sweetheart* or a 'Look, you're very nice, but you're just too fat for me.' "

"Force of habit."

"You always go to bars and call women *ma'am*?"

"I work for Valley Fire Rescue."

"A fireman. . . ." She sounded intrigued.

"And a medic."

"So you drive the ambulance?"

"Right," he answered. *I drive the ambulance.*

"Bet you've seen a lot of stuff. Why don't you tell me a story?"

Here we go. . . . Doe used to love telling stories because of the attention it garnered him. Then, after a while, he realized that some people listened to him not because they enjoyed his company but because they wanted to hear the story and couldn't care less about him as a person. Of course, when he was among fellow firefighters, medics, and cops, he always spun a good tale or two because his colleagues understood the emotions and complexities of the incidents without explanation. The shorthand of the street was an amazing thing, one this woman might never know. "Trust me," he told her. "This is *not* going to happen tonight."

"I don't really care. I'm a lonely woman who's been divorced three times. I had a hysterectomy when I was nineteen, so I'll never have my own kids. My father died last year, and all I got in the world are my mother and sister."

"You're a little weird, aren't you."

She tapped her chest. "Me?"

"I don't want to hear your life story. I just came in here for a drink."

"No, you didn't. You got something on your mind. I've seen that same look on a thousand guys. Three of them I married."

"You want to hear a story? I'll tell you a story," Doe snapped before she pried any further. "My partner and I get called to an MVA: motorcycle versus car. Apparently this biker ran into the car's rear bumper on the passenger side. There's substantial damage to the bike and the car. Driver of the car is this college girl, maybe nineteen, still got her high school graduation tassel hanging from the mirror. She's crying but showing no signs of injury. Biker's a guy about thirty, and he's lying on the grass about twenty feet from the site. Our engine beat us to the scene, and two of my buddies logrolled the guy onto a long backboard and C-spined him. Guy's helmet is sitting right there with a huge crack in it. My buddies tell me the guy's been unresponsive since they got there."

"So what did you do? Rush him to the hospital?"

"First me and my partner assess the guy. He's bleeding from his nose and one of his ears, and I'm thinking periorbital ecchymosis is on its way 'cause he's probably got a skull fracture. We have to keep suctioning him to maintain a patent airway. His ventilations are irregular, and we're hearing snoring sounds. His skin's pale, and I'm seeing early signs of cyanosis around his lips."

"You mean blue lips?"

"Right. Lack of O_2 in the blood. So while we're assessing this guy, a cop who looks like he's already a couple of years past retirement comes up and *firmly advises* me that it's rush hour and that traffic needs to be reopened ASAP. What he's really saying is shovel this loser into the back of your rig and get the hell out of here. Nine times out of ten, cops work really well with us, but this guy has no patience. When I get to a scene, I have to take into account my own safety, then look at the physical evidence like the impact to the car, the motorcycle, the guy's helmet. I have to be thinking about whether or not the biker's got life-threatening injuries based on the kinetic forces involved. I'm thinking the guy sustained multiple impacts. His airway's screwed up. He has an altered LOC, level of consciousness, and then there's the blood from the nose and ear, which is telling me he's probably got, like I said, a basilar skull fracture. Just saw another one of those this week. Little boy. Anyway, you see what I'm doing? I'm thinking about why the accident occurred, how it occurred, judging what I see, and considering the possibilities of what I don't. There's a lot of stuff going through my head while I got this cop telling me to move my ass. And while I'm considering all of that, I got a rapidly deteriorating patient who needs aggressive airway care and rapid transport in under ten minutes."

"Wow. You sound like a doctor. I never knew you guys had to do so much."

"I'm not done. I have to intubate this guy—"

"Stick a tube down his throat to help him breathe," she happily translated. "Saw that on TV."

"Yeah, but as I'm setting up, the cop starts yelling at me to move the patient into the rescue and tube him en route. I don't like tubing people while we're driving. I figure I can get the tube right there, bag him, finish packaging, and get him loaded. The whole thing might take a minute, two max. So I tell this cop that, and the old bastard won't have it. I get so pissed off that I think about throwing down my tube and blade and getting right in this guy's face. But if I do that, I'm abandoning the patient. I can't turn him over to my partner, because at that time she was only an EMT-I. The biker's lawyer would hang me. So I just go about my business while the cop is screaming his head off like a goddamned drill instructor." Doe sucked down the last of his drink, then faced the husky woman, whose name he had already forgotten.

"There's a gleam in your eye," she said. "What happened?"

"You won't believe it. Maybe I'll stop here."

"Did you punch him?"

"Didn't have to. He's standing over us, still hollering, and I mean you can hear him above all those diesel engines. His face is beet-red. Spit's flying everywhere. He's squeezing his billy club, getting ready to start swinging. I get my tube, auscultate for good breath sounds, and when I look up, the cop is down, supine, clutching his chest, had an AMI right there."

"A heart attack?"

"Acute myocardial infarction. I can laugh about it now, because the old prick made it."

"So this cop wants you to move out of there fast, and he gets so pissed off when you won't that he suffers a heart attack, which probably delayed traffic even more."

"It took twice as long to clear that scene. He really got his, didn't he? Rescue Nine rolls up, and two more of my buddies get a history and blood glucose from him. No documented chronic obstructive pulmonary disease, so they put him on O_2, start a line, and get baseline vitals."

"You lost me there."

"Doesn't matter. Bottom line is he had a heart attack. We saved the bastard. And we saved everyone else who worked with him, because he retired after that. Cops from his precinct bought us pizza. They couldn't wait to see him leave."

"That's quite a tale."

"Still pretty tame as trauma cases go. I could tell you about the calls we dream about, MVAs with decapitations and dismemberment, cases that really let us shine."

"You dream about decapitations?"

"I didn't mean it that way. I'm not trying to be morbid. See, when something really bad happens, we want to be there. Situations like that are what we train for. That's why I never joined the Marines, like my father wanted. I couldn't bear to go through all that training and not get to use it. There just aren't enough hot spots out there. The chances of me *not* fighting were too great. But with this job, I'm always busy because there's always some kid getting stuck in a railing or some gang-banger getting stabbed or some guy getting on the freeway going the wrong way."

"You sound as cynical as me."

"Hard not to be when all you see is how stupid people can be. Guys getting their girlfriends pregnant because they use the rhythm method instead of condoms."

"So there's no hope for humanity. . . ."

"There's hope, I guess. Just hard to find. I gotta go." He slid off the bar stool.

"How 'bout a phone number? I promise not to bug you. Maybe we can do this again. Just talk."

"Okay." Doe headed for the door.

"Hey," she called after him. "What about that number?"

He glanced back and winked. "You already know it."

As Doe pulled out of the blues club's parking lot, a fire engine streaked by, xenon strobes ablaze, siren ministering to the brethren of bad drivers. He switched on his scanner and learned that a call had come in from one of the local nursing homes. White female approximately seventy years old and complaining of dyspnea, trouble breathing. If Doe had a dollar for every raisin run that turned out to be a false alarm, he could have retired long ago.

He stopped by Fire Station Ten and chewed the fat with a couple of buddies, who urged him to get some sleep. The 8 A.M. shift sneaked up on you, and according to their primary assessment, he looked like hell. But Doe ignored their advice and instead drove to SFMC.

He went in through the ambulance entrance and nodded his hellos to Bellows, the triage officer on duty, and some of the ED nurses. Charti's medic controller station was manned by a new dispatcher whom Doe had met only once. A lot of activity surrounded C-booth. From snippets of conversation Doe gathered that a patient with a gunshot wound to the head had been brought in, and would probably not last more than a few minutes. Sparing himself that grim happening, he left the emergency department and ventured into the seeming maze of passageways that was San Fernando Medical Center.

Four halls later, he found an elevator and rode up with a custodian, a gray-haired man no more than five feet tall whose ID badge read PADRE. The guy got off on the third floor; Doe rode up one more and entered a hall terminating in glass doors marked Women's Center. He moved through a large lobby with at least half a dozen sofas positioned below a pair of ceiling-mounted TVs. When he reached a security door, he plugged in his ID. Yet another corridor led him toward a nurses' station with a placard that said OBSTETRICS. According to another sign, the nurses working the ward had over two hundred years combined experience in labor and birth, nursery and postpartum care, and were specially trained to meet patients' needs.

Dr. Joanna Boccaccio rounded a corner, tugging off her gloves and looking as bedraggled as ever. Nevertheless, Doe still felt an electric something for her. She frowned. "Hey."

Doe swallowed. "Hey."

"What're you doing up here?" She pinched his sleeve. "And on your off time?"

"What're you doing up here?" he countered. "Unless there's something I don't know about." Doe wriggled his brow.

She didn't smile; she looked too tired. "Got paged to a cardiac arrest. My resident wigged out. I got in there, worked that infant for over an hour. Nothing. Lost her. Another half-hour talking to the parents. And here I am. I'm thinking the postmortem will show us what we missed. Maybe a birth defect or something. Bums you out, you know?"

"I definitely know."

"So what's going on?"

"What?"

Her mouth fell open, then she gestured to their surroundings. "Duh. Somebody you know having a baby?"

"Yeah, that's kind of right."

"So she's kind of pregnant?"

Doe felt stupid. "Oh, she's pregnant."

Boccaccio nodded. "And how do you know her?"

"Why do you ask?"

"Just curious."

"She, uh, cuts my hair."

"Oh, Doe, the whole sad story is standing here, right

before my eyes. I'm seeing it so clearly now."

He snorted slightly. "I'm seeing it all end. You know what I mean? Have you ever thought about settling down and having kids?"

"People are always asking me that. You want the stock answer?"

"How 'bout the truth?"

"I have. Creating a life—God, that's power. We're always trying to save lives, but creating one. . . . Yeah, it has crossed my mind. But I don't know if I have that much commitment. The job takes so much. And when it comes to being a mother, my own is a bad role model."

"Yeah, it's definitely a commitment thing. And you gotta be a good role model. It's not fair to bring kids into this world unless you can give them a hundred percent."

"You don't have to convince me. So, do you have a choice here?"

"I'm not really sure. I told her . . . oh, man—I told her stuff. I screwed up."

"You told her to get an abortion."

He flinched. "Yeah, I kinda did."

"And knowing you, you spelled out the procedure and told her how easy and 'painless' it is."

"Whoa. How'd you know that?"

"I've overheard you bitching to my RNs about all those pregnant junkies you're always hauling in here. How do you expect to take care of another life—"

"When you can't take care of your own," he said.

"Well, I hope it works out for you."

"You, uh, wanna get a coffee? I'm buying."

"I'm not good company right now. I need to get some distance from this place. Maybe another time."

"Really?"

"Yeah, really."

"All right. And hey, do me a favor? Will you keep this. . . ." He put a finger to his lips.

"You're not my patient, but yeah, I will."

"Thanks."

He watched her vanish through the door, then turned and walked past the nurses' station, drawing the gaze of the nurse manager, a black woman of about forty-five, broad in the beam, with massive breasts swaddled in sea-green scrubs. Her cherubic stare tightened into a frown as Doe moved toward the nursery at the end of the hall.

To his disappointment, only one baby slept quietly in the wide room. Rolling carts, sinks, scales, rocking chairs, and an impressive collection of stuffed animals lined the walls. Doe studied the tiny face peeking out from beneath a pink cap. Eyes closed. Chubby cheeks. And one serious pout.

"Excuse me. I noticed you had a code to get in here," said the nurse manager as she lumbered toward him. "And I saw you talking with that doctor."

"Yeah, I'm a medic with Station Ten." Doe pulled out his wallet and showed her his photo ID.

"You also a relative?" she asked, lifting her chin toward the newborn behind the glass.

"No."

"Just like looking at babies?" she teased.

"Old instructor told me that when the job got rough, he used to go to the maternity ward and just stare at the infants. Said it was therapeutic. I don't know. I look at that little baby, and all I see is stress."

"You're not looking at stress; you're looking at a miracle, a new beginning, the greatest wonder of the universe."

"Wow. Someone who likes her job. I'm impressed."

"Twenty-four years in OB, last ten as nurse manager here. Yeah, I like it. We have our good days and our bad—like we just lost a little one today—but most of the time this is a place that reminds us of how innocent we begin, how beautiful life really is, and how there's still hope. We teach parents how to nourish and care for a brand-new person. Can't beat that."

"Preach it, sister."

"I do," she said with a grin. "Every Sunday. First Baptist of North Hollywood. It's on Victory. Why don't you come? It's a real diverse congregation. You'd like it."

"Ma'am, if I set foot in a church, God would send down a bolt of lightning and fry me right there. You're pretty much lookin' at the devil himself."

"Satan wears many faces, and he thrives on fear."

"One of these days I'll get back into a church. I was baptized a Catholic, received my first Holy Communion, but I started playing baseball on Sundays." Doe regarded the glass. "Must be slow here, huh? Just one baby?"

"Try eleven. Wish I could show you more, but they're all with their mothers. It's not like the old days when we had them lined up and people would crowd around the window and exchange cigars. Mothers like their babies in their rooms. We bring them here only when they need special attention or when Mom wants to sleep. It's all part of the bonding process. Do you have children?"

"No. I've seen what kids have done to my sister."

"Probably brought her a whole lot of joy."

"Don't know about that. And I've seen firsthand what losing a child does to people. You put your whole life into raising a kid, building a family, and for what? So some drunk asshole can mow them down. I've pulled kids out of pools and from the bottoms of cars. Why bother?"

"Oh, I see the devil's got a bind on you."

"It's not the devil. Just the world."

"Come with me."

"I really have to go."

"You really have to come with me."

Doe mumbled an okay and followed her down an intersecting hallway, past a half-dozen birthing suites. She paused at one.

"You're going to show me some mother with her baby and tell me that this is why we should bother," Doe said.

"No, I'm not." The nurse manager went in and spoke quietly with another woman while Doe waited impatiently.

A tall man emerged from behind the door, cradling an infant wrapped tightly in a blanket and wearing a blue cap. The guy looked a little older than Doe and wore business attire.

"This is Mr. Stone," said the nurse manager.

"And this is my son, Patrick," the father added. "Nine pounds, three ounces, twenty-three inches long. Born at two fifty-five yesterday morning."

The nurse manager raised her brows. "A big baby."

"Look, I'm sorry to bother you," Doe told the man.

"You don't need to be showing your child to strangers."

"You kidding? I'm ready to parade him around the hospital. He's five years in the making."

"That's the irony," Doe said with a sigh. "People who really want babies have a hard time."

"You and your wife trying?" Stone asked, his gaze never leaving his son.

"I'm not married."

"Oh. So Margaret here tells me you're a medic. Ever deliver one of these?"

Doe shook his head. "Came pretty close. But we always got her to the hospital in time. Well, sorry again." Doe pursed his lips at the nurse manager. "And thank you, ma'am." He left abruptly and reached the nurses' station when she called for him to wait.

"To be a father is to be divine," she said, catching up to him. "There's no more important job in the world. And there's nothing more worth doing."

14

C lutching a thirty-two-ounce cup of 7-Eleven coffee in one hand and safety glasses in the other, Stephanie Savage walked across the apparatus floor. In deference to the previous day's crew, she usually arrived at least a half-hour early. As Murphy's Law would have it, calls came in during the last hour of your shift, forcing you to work overtime when you were already exhausted. Savage and Abe would take any early call, allowing yesterday's people to leave on time and avoid "getting burned." Tomorrow's crew would do the same for them.

Most firefighters rotated service on the apparatus—one shift you rode the engine, the next the squad, the next the rescue. Since Savage was Abe's FTO during his probationary period, Lieutenant Martinez allowed them to ride the rescue during every shift, thus reinforcing Abe's medic training. Though the other medics of Station Nine did not exactly appreciate that, they sympathized with Abe's goal to get as much experience as possible. Besides, all of them had begun as firefighters, and you needed to keep those skills as well-honed as possible.

"Hey, Beast," called Daniel Lombardi, a tall medic with a chestnut crewcut, a Fu Manchu moustache, and droopy, puppy-dog eyes. Lombardi was about to turn forty and celebrate twenty years as a firefighter. He signed out in the rescue's drug log, then handed it to Savage, so she could sign in. "Heard about that big MVA near Roscoe. You follow up?"

"Called the hospital last night. Boy's out of the woods. Rest of the family's still critical. Mother and daughter are the worst off. It's a miracle they're still hanging on, especially the daughter. I heard she coded on the flight in."

"That's some shit, huh?"

Savage gave a faint sigh. "Yeah."

"Heard about that shooting, too. I'm surprised you didn't take a personal day."

"Wasn't the first time I've been shot at. Couple years back I was working down in Compton."

"Think I read about that one."

"Stays with you. Hey, you run anything good last night?"

"Nah. Another Dumpster fire. Another kid with croup. Picked up a middle-aged woman complaining of chest pain. Turns out she ate nine stuffed jalapeño peppers at a party. She could have told me that up front."

"Like that lady I picked up last week. Tells me she's never had any major surgeries. Breath sounds absent on the right. We get to the hospital, and she tells the resident that she had a lung removed. Guess that doesn't qualify as major surgery anymore."

Lombardi smiled; he'd been there. "Well, you try to have a nice weekend. See you."

As the medic hiked off, Savage crossed to the rear of the rescue. Abe had the doors open and sat on the bench seat, truck checkbook in the crook of his arm. The checkbook allowed new medics riding the rescue to easily identify the location of any item, from scoop stretcher to pediatric bag to cribbing. His gaze switched between the book and the overhead compartments.

"Two shifts, and you still don't have it figured out?" Savage taunted. "What time you get here?"

"Seven."

"Damn. I'm not sure I was ever that eager."

"I'm just going over a couple things. I'll get started on the check sheet."

At the beginning of every shift, Valley's medics were responsible for inspecting the equipment on board their assigned unit. They also needed to fill out a daily apparatus maintenance report detailing, among many things, their vehicle's odometer reading, engine hour reading, fuel and oil levels, radiator coolant, hoses and belts, tires, gauges, lights, batteries, warning devices, and radio. Something as seemingly trivial as worn-out windshield wipers could result in a delay or loss of life. While Abe climbed down to begin inspecting the rescue, Savage set her coffee on the tailgate and started a methodical inspection of the equipment. She began with the first compartment near the driver's side door.

Unlike some other fire department rescues, Valley's rigs were equipped with two hundred-gallon water tanks and L-shaped 250-gallon-per-minute pumps with built-in Class 1 foam capabilities. Rescue Nine's pump unit sat in the left corner of the first compartment, its many dials and handles within easy view and reach. The unit's orange attack hose had been folded accordion-style into a nearby slot. Atop the pump sat a wall-mounted air pack or self-contained breathing apparatus, one of two sophisticated green oxygen tanks with 4500 psi and rated for one hour rather than the usual thirty minutes. The tanks strapped on like backpacks and came equipped with regulators and personal alert safety system (PASS) devices. About twice the size of an average pager, the PASS devices clipped onto the harness near the shoulder and enabled firefighters to throw a switch and sound a piercing alarm should they get lost or trapped. The device would also automatically sound the alarm should the firefighter lie motionless for more than twenty-five seconds. Beneath the tank rested the standard face mask, whose hose connected to the regulator.

A pair of rectangular cubbyholes above the air pack contained the long backboard and the scoop stretcher that divided in the center and allowed medics to scoop up patients from the ground. Savage had used it more than once on people with pelvic fractures. A rolling chair stretcher or "stair chair" was stowed in a slot to the right. The chair unfolded and allowed them to transport, for example, elderly patients who weren't really hurt but felt uncomfortable lying down. With everything else in the compartment present and accounted for, Savage checked the air pack, saw that it was full, then moved on to the next bay.

She tugged open a pair of tall, narrow doors to reveal

four metal shelves crammed with stair-step cribbing, bunker gear, extra safety helmets, a chain saw, and a two-inch supply line to hook to a hydrant or to a truck to fill their water tank. Someone, probably Lombardi, had gone through the compartment, had cleaned the shelves, and had neatly arranged the equipment. Everything looked good.

A small, square compartment above the rescue's rear tire held three life vests (personal flotation devices); a pair of kiddie pools and scrub brushes for decontaminating people; flare tubes; a reciprocating saw stowed in a blue metal toolbox; an extrication bag filled with simple cutters and other tools; tarps; and a yellow isolation tent used in the back of the rescue when carrying contaminated patients. A plastic pouch that bulged with lockout devices used for breaking into cars rested next to bolt cutters, a ratchet set, and another toolbox. Once again, Lombardi or someone else had carefully rearranged all of the items. Savage slammed shut the pair of small doors.

The bay behind the tire included more safety helmets, containers of absorbent materials or "speedy dry," twist lock adapters, more tarps, safety cones, and a portable electric generator. The bay looked fine, so Savage checked out the interior compartments. Lombardi had done a decent job of restocking. The IV fluids were okay, and the airway bag's O_2 bottle was full. Savage turned on the cardiac monitor. The unit's battery needed changing. She fetched a spare from a side cabinet, then slid it into the monitor. She folded back the unit's display, shaped much like a notebook computer's, then switched on the device. A tape recording the patient's cardiac activity advanced at a speed of twenty-five millimeters per second across the moving stylus (a heated writing tip) and recorded heart activity. Savage advanced the tape until the current date appeared. This would inform the next shift's medics that she had checked out the machine, in case it was not used during her shift.

Back outside the rescue, she pulled open the passenger's or officer's side rear bay doors, one of them emblazoned with a gleaming black 9. Adult and pediatric traction splints in plastic, color-coded bags lay on the top shelf. Head-ons (head blocks) used for packaging patients, the c-spine bag loaded with cervical collars for immobilization, an orange trauma box brimming with supplies specific to those cases, and spare fire extinguishers completed that bay's inventory.

Level B splash suits and gloves for working with hazardous materials, as well as two HAZMAT drug boxes, were stowed in the compartment above the wheel. The IV fluids and accompanying equipment were kept in the orange box; most of their drugs specific to working with hazardous materials were kept in the gray one, including calcium gluconate for acid burns and a cyanide antidote kit. With so many different drugs and protocols to remember, Savage was thankful that charts detailing the management of exposure to a plethora of toxic materials were included in the box.

In the compartment nearest the door lay another air pack and bunker gear, with the pediatric bag, a nitrous oxide unit, and portable suction unit stored on adjacent shelves. Savage checked the inventory and functionality of everything in that bay before tugging down its rolling metal door.

"How's it going, Abe?"

"Just waiting on you to pull out," he said, sitting in the driver's seat.

After motioning for him to do so, Savage hurried to the back of the rescue to rescue her coffee before Abe rolled out of the garage. With the rig on the driveway, they inspected all exterior lights and tested the siren, then Abe ducked back inside for paper towels and a bottle of window cleaner. He passed Lieutenant Martinez, who brought a coffee mug to his lips, then came outside.

"Morning," Savage said briskly.

"Hey, Beast. Interesting week we're having."

"Least it's not boring."

"How's it going with the kid?"

"Not bad."

Martinez looked dubious. "Does that mean you've had to pull him away from a patient only once? Or twice?"

"He's just nervous. And he knows it. He also knows the protocol manual inside and out."

"Which won't get him too far in our district," Martinez reminded her, watching as Abe returned to the rescue and began cleaning the windows. "You teach him the street stuff, and he'll be all right. He has to learn that you don't ever *check* windows. You wait for law enforcement. Turns out that guy had a valid license for his weapon, a BFSC certificate, and no priors. I've been surfing the penal code, and since you and the kid won't press charges, I think the judge'll chalk it up to an accident and throw it all out. Read about a similar case in Florida a while back. Medic took a bullet, and they still didn't charge the shooter with anything."

"That's the impression I got from the state's attorney yesterday. I was going to pursue this, but I don't know. Just didn't feel right." Savage nodded with resignation, then her gaze moved to the lieutenant's shiny new belt buckle, a golden fire hat stenciled with a 9.

"You like that? Daughter-in-law had it made for me. Thing's so heavy its making my pants sag."

Savage patted his tummy. "I think it's getting a little help."

"Yeah, from Fitzy's cooking. I swear, that old man has to fry everything in a pound of butter."

"Don't eat it."

Martinez rolled his eyes. "I'll never hear the end of it." He started off, then paused. "Hey, the chief came by yesterday. We're getting a new logo for the rescue." He pulled a slip of paper from his breast pocket and showed it to Savage: a crescent moon beside a number 9 wearing a halo.

"What the hell is it?"

"New logo. Night Angel Nine."

"I was happy with Rescue Nine."

"New community relations policy. They're giving all the rescues the Night Angel moniker and having the apparatus painted. The people over at Ten are now Night Angel Ten."

"Does that mean we don't have to rescue anyone during the day?" Savage asked, unable to repress her smirk.

"Sixty-seven percent of our rescues occur between 8 P.M. and 8 A.M. Guess the director thought that justified the name."

"You like it?"

"Wish my opinion mattered. I'm sure that by the time we're used to it, they'll change it again."

The high-pitched and rapid beeping of an alarm sounded. "Engine Nine, Rescue Nine. Engine Nine, Rescue Nine. Man down with seizures. Twenty-two eleven Woodman Ave. Cross street Riverside Drive. Both units respond code three. Time out: eight-oh-one."

"Gave me a whole minute to spare," Savage cried, then tossed her coffee in a wastebasket. As she hopped into the rescue, Abe revved the engine.

"Maybe it'll be busy," he said, wide-eyed and bubbling with anticipation.

"Are those bite marks on your neck?"

Abe shrank a little as he pulled on his headset. "My cat scratched me."

"You don't have a cat."

"How do you know?"

"Because I'm allergic." Savage picked up the mike. "Rescue Nine responding."

"Rescue Nine," TRO Six replied.

They rumbled off the driveway, lit the strobe lights, and cut loose the siren set to phaser.

"So, Abe," Savage began, adjusting her headset's volume. "What's the practice parameter for seizure?"

"Initial medical care first. We use normal saline for IV solution. Vomiting and aspiration precautions dictate that we place nothing in the patient's mouth during the seizure. If the patient's blood sugar is less than seventy, we should refer to the hypo- or hyperglycemia practice parameter. If the patient is actively seizing, we should administer two to twenty mgs of diazepam slow IV push for adults, titrated to control seizure activity."

"And without IV access?"

"We find large or small muscle injection sites. We also observe the patient's sensorium and airway. We consider etiology of the seizures and refer to the Altered Mental Status practice parameter. If the patient's hypotensive, we'll refer to the Shock Practice parameter. If we suspect substance abuse, we'll administer Narcan in two-mg increments IV push every three minutes if transient response is observed. We won't exceed ten mgs."

Yes, Abe knew the manual all right. And he knew his drugs. Narcan was an effective agent that blocked the effects of natural and synthetic narcotics, alcohol-induced coma, altered level of consciousness, and comas of unknown origin. Its only drawback was its short half-life. After starting an IV, they would administer the drug via syringe through one of the IV catheter's ports. The "push" in "IV push" meant that you injected it quickly.

Of course the whole call could turn into something radically different. "Man down with seizures" could be a cardiac arrest or a father freaking out over his kid who'd just been hit by a car.

"Damn, look at this traffic," Abe said as he slowly forced cars to the side of the road. A black Mercedes blocked his path, then finally pulled over, its driver honking angrily, as though the rescue did not have the right-of-way.

Savage focused her gaze on Abe's neck. "This must be a new girlfriend."

"We're on a call," Abe reminded her.

"Forty-eight hours together, and you never mentioned her. I'm a little insulted." Savage grinned.

•   •   •

A shirtless skeleton of a young white man wearing baggy cut-off shorts lay on the sidewalk at the corner of Woodman and Riverside. As he faked seizures in a display called the tuna dance, a small crowd of bystanders looked on with the usual blend of horror and curiosity on their faces. Behind them stood the broad racks and bright blue awning of a newsstand whose clerk Savage knew. She killed the siren, removed her headset, and hurried out.

"Hey, Raj, what's up?" she asked the bearded clerk from Calcutta whose pink dress shirt bore tawny stains at the pits. Savage did not so much as glance at the patient, and the feigned innocence in her tone amused her more than it did the clerk.

"He's bothering my customers again. I tell you, I shoot this fuck. I will."

She turned to regard Abe, who had ordered the crowd back and now hunkered down to begin his primary assessment. The simplest way to remember that task was to think of one word: SAMPLE. S stood for signs (what you can see) and symptoms (what the patient tells you is wrong). A stood for allergies; M, for medications; P, for past medical history; L, for last meal eaten; and E, for events leading up to the incident. However, the seizing patient would not be able to provide any information—or at least Abe would assume so.

"Is he dying?" a fat bystander asked Savage.

"No," she said, eyeing the young man she had driven to SFMC maybe ten times in the past two years. "Give me a minute."

"He seems almost clonic," Abe reported nervously.

"Airway's clear. No evidence of incontinence. I'll get a BS."

Savage crossed quickly to Abe and used her foot to slide away the airway bag. "Won't need this or that blood sugar."

Abe looked up, giving her the "O sign" like an unconscious patient. "This guy's having seizures. Could be cocaine-induced. Could be ETOH."

"No, they're being induced by something very different, isn't that right, George? Yeah, he looks like a junkie, but he's not on drugs, and he didn't shit his pants. He's Gena Solaris's son. You watch TV?"

"Yeah," Abe answered excitedly. "Gena Solaris was on *Trauma!* for years and years. Played that religious doctor."

"That's right." Savage glowered at the young Mr. Solaris. "Hey, George, why don't you tell my new partner how you grew up watching your mother perform on that hospital show? And while you're at it, why don't you tell him how you developed a fetish for ambulances and hospitals?" Savage dropped in front of Solaris. "Looks like you need some Narcan. And Abe's got a fourteen gauge catheter with your name on it. 'Course you'd just like that, wouldn't you?"

Without warning, George tugged down his shorts to expose his rigid and throbbing penis.

"Whoa," Abe groaned. "Ain't going near that."

"George," Savage hollered. "I've tried to help you. Now I'm done." She glanced at a Valley PD cruiser pulling up behind the rescue.

Out of the car stepped Sergeant Richard Ortez, six feet of graying Mexican American; he smoothed out his mustache and gazed fiercely on the scene like an Old West sheriff. His partner, a dark-skinned woman Savage did not recognize, fell in beside him. Ortez's gaze finally reached Savage, and his lip twisted. "Hey, Beast?" He raised his chin at George. "Think he likes you."

"Hey, I'm fuckin' injured here! I wanna go to the hospital," screamed George.

Ortez motioned to his partner to restrain George.

Engine Nine slowed just ahead of the rescue, shedding Fitzy and Tenpenney while Cannis parked. The two fire-fighters took one look at the writhing man with shorts at his knees and assumed the same silly grin.

"We'll charge him with indecent exposure *again*," said the sergeant. "I'll leave you my new partner to ride along. Looks like you got a new sidekick yourself. What happened to Holiday?"

"Got transferred to Thirty-five."

"Too bad. I liked that guy."

"He should be back when this kid gets off probation," explained Savage.

William "Doc" (What else would they call him?) Holiday had twenty-one years in as an FF-P and was one of the most decorated firemen in all of Valley. Savage had worked with him for about five months before being assigned to Abe. Still, she kind of liked being in the superior position. Although she and Holiday were both paramedics, Savage always felt like an EMT-I around him. He had much more experience than she did, and he wasn't shy about letting her know that. Most para-medics had their own systems for doing things, but when you worked with Holiday, you used his system or you didn't ride. During their first month together, he and

Savage had repeatedly bumped heads. Someone had to ride in the seat, and that someone had always been Holiday. He bitched about her driving. He bitched about everything. He was a paragod's paragod. But Savage had learned a hell of a lot from him.

"How much of the taxpayers' money is this bastard wasting?" said Fitzy as Ortez's partner escorted a handcuffed George to the back of the rescue. "I know the law says we gotta take him to the hospital. And I know they oughta change the damned law."

"Why don't you run for mayor?" said Tenpenney.

Fitzy pursed his lips. "I got a mind to."

The black Mercedes that Abe had forced over came squealing around the corner and skidded to a halt behind the rescue. A tall, lean man with a shock of gray hair burst from the vehicle, his gaze darting to and fro. "Where the fuck is that ambulance driver? I wanna speak to that fuckin' ambulance driver!"

"Sir, you can't park your car there," barked Sergeant Ortez.

Savage approached the irate businessman, whose cell phone was clipped to his belt and ringing. "I'm the ambulance driver," she challenged.

"Well, what kind of fuckin' driving was that? You forced me off the road. I nearly crashed into a meter. You got any idea how much this car costs?"

"Sir," Savage began calmly, knowing her tone would further incense Mr. Mercedes. "We have the right-of-way."

"What you *think* you have is a license to drive any fuckin' way you want. All you bastards whose salaries I pay. I see cops going ninety down the freeway. Firemen doing the same. I wonder how many real emergencies you have. Where's the car *wreck*? Where are the bleeding people? I don't see jack. But I got run off the road so you could get here."

By now, Ortez had placed herself between the man and Savage. She glanced back at Fitzy, Tenpenney, and Cannis. The younger firefighters had paled, but Fitzy's face had flushed. "Hey, mister," he cried. "Next time your house is burning down or you're in a car wreck and bleeding out, I'll make sure I take my sweet ass time getting there."

Tenpenney and Cannis would not have dared to make such a remark. They had careers to consider. But old Fitzy had seen and done it all and took shit from no one. Savage wished she could have cheered.

Abe emerged from the back of the rescue, frowning as Ortez tried to quiet the man. Savage jogged over to him and said, "You made a new friend."

"I see that. What's his problem?"

"We inconvenienced him."

"Hey, while you two are standing around talking, I'm dying over here," shouted George, who lay on his side on the stretcher, tugging at his cuffs.

"Just calm down. We'll be leaving in a second," said Ortez's partner from her perch on the bench.

Savage turned back and introduced herself and Abe.

"This'll be my first time riding in an ambulance," said the officer, Sarah Violet, who had graduated from the police academy only a month prior.

"Won't be your last," said Savage.

"I got it from here," Ortez hollered back, then waved for them to leave.

"He'll lodge a complaint, won't he?" Violet said.

"Won't be my first," answered Savage. "If his house was on fire, he'd get the hell out of the way." She turned her attention to Abe. "Let's go. Code one."

As they left the scene, sans lights or siren, Ortez was still engaged in a heated discussion with Mr. Mercedes, whose blistering expression shrank in the rescue's rear windows. Savage unclipped the mike. "SFMC, this is paramedic Stephanie Savage, Rescue Nine."

"Nine, SFMC," Charti responded.

"Hey, before you call it in, can we stop off for a danish?" George asked. "I'm starving over here. Test my blood sugar. You'll see how I'm dying."

Savage exchanged a look with Officer Violet. "Got any kids?"

"None yet."

"Pay attention. I don't blame him. This is what bad parenting does."

And Savage suddenly thought of how all last night she had been unable to reach Donny. "The cellular customer you are trying to reach. . . ." had reverberated in her head as she had tried to fall asleep. Was he all right? Did he make it down to Miami okay?

"Nine, SFMC," Charti repeated impatiently.

Savage began her report, wishing she could say "En route to your facility with one of our most famous frequent flyers. . . ."

15

"How come you're not my regular nurse?" asked Trent Robertson as he sat up in his bed in the ICU, eyes still blackened by periorbital ecchymosis, lacerations still bandaged. Charti had just finished changing the dressings.

"We have other nurses who work up here," Charti said, dropping the old bandages into a biohazard wastebasket. "I work downstairs, in the emergency department."

"That's why Nancy keeps getting mad at you for helping," Trent said. "So how come you're here? And when can I see my mom and dad and my sister?"

"I don't know," Charti said, moving slowly toward the boy's bed. "They were hurt really bad. It'll take some time."

Trent's lip quivered. "Everybody keeps saying that. They're gonna die, aren't they?"

Charti could lie, but he remembered how his mother

and father had lied to him about his sister. Three days had passed before he had learned the truth. "They might die."

The boy bit his lip, closed his eyes.

"Hey, Trent, I heard you were pretty brave at the scene. The medics told me you must've had your arms wrapped around your sister when the truck hit." No one had said anything of the sort, but Charti knew exactly what he was doing.

"I guess so. I don't remember too well."

"You were probably trying to protect her. You were brave. You did everything you could. You know what that's like?"

"No."

"That's like being a hero. Have you ever been a hero before?"

"Not really."

"Oh, hi," said Trent's aunt, a thirty-seven-year-old named Paula Simkee, whose hair seemed grayer than it had been two days prior. She had just come from the cafeteria with a small salad and half-pint of milk.

"I was just reminding Trent of how he helped his sister," Charti said. "He was holding her when the truck hit."

"Really," the aunt said weakly.

Movement near the door caught Charti's attention. Stephanie Savage and Abe Kashmiri stood in the hall, their expressions tentative.

"Trent, you remember these people?" Charti asked, waving the medics inside.

"I think that guy," the boy said pointing at Abe. "Yeah. He was there."

"Just came to see how you're doing," Abe said, then handed the boy a black leather wallet.

Trent opened the wallet to reveal a shiny new firefighter's badge. "Pretty cool," he said.

"They only give 'em to real firefighters," Abe said.

"Does that mean I'm one?"

"It means that when you get out of here, you get to ride in our rescue truck," Savage said. "Lights and sirens and all."

"Only if I can take my sister. And my mom and dad," he said.

"Fine with us," Savage answered.

"Well, it was good to see you again," Abe said, growing visibly unnerved.

"Thank him," instructed the boy's aunt.

Trent made a face. "Thank you."

"You're welcome." Abe shook the boy's hand, then scuttled outside.

Charti followed the medic into the hall, where Abe leaned against the wall, threw his head back, and shut his eyes. His breath came in ragged bursts.

"You all right?" asked Charti.

"I didn't want to come here. Savage has this thing about seeing the outcome. That kid in there is gonna lose his whole family. I can't even imagine that. It's beyond sad."

"He'll go on."

"How can this *not* scar him for life?"

"You're talking like his family's already dead."

"You didn't see that station wagon. And you didn't just talk to Dr. Masaki."

"No matter what happens, the kid will get on with his

life. At least he's got an aunt who loves him. Grandparents. Teachers. Boy Scouts. You wouldn't believe how many people have wanted to see him."

"And that's just it," Abe said, jerking away from the wall. "Some of the most screwed-up and evil people I know will go through their whole lives and never have anything traumatic happen to them. Then you got your average family. They're good neighbors. They pay their taxes. Give back to the community. And they're the ones who get whacked."

"Yeah, but every once in a while some scumbag gets his. And I don't mind saying that I like being there for God's vengeance."

Abe looked at Charti, a peculiar expression coming over his face. "Don't you work in the emergency department?"

"Yeah. I was just checking on him."

"You know, I've never introduced myself. Abe Kashmiri," he said, proffering his hand.

"They call me Charti. I'm the man behind the disembodied voice."

"I feel kind of stupid."

"Happens all the time here. People come and go. It's like you don't want to bother learning that person's name because next week you'll have to learn the new person's name."

"So what's up with you and Doe?"

"It's territorial. I want him out of mine."

"Ready?" Savage asked Abe as she stepped into the hall.

The medic nodded.

Savage glanced quizzically at Charti. "What're you doing up here?"

"Must've got off on the wrong floor," Charti said, then double-timed down the hall.

The nut that Savage and her partner had brought in lay in Exam Two, and Boccaccio held her breath as she entered the room, the "bounce-back" patient's chart tucked in her arm. "Mr. Solaris? I'm Dr. Boccaccio. Even though we've never met, I feel like I know you already. I understand you've been here quite a few times to see us. In fact, just two days ago."

"Hospitals. I love 'em. Can't get enough of 'em. People bitch about the smell? It's heaven to me. And I can't believe our paths haven't crossed until now. My timing has been amazingly bad."

Boccaccio glared at the young man, who began playing with one of his nipples. "The police officer outside said you exposed yourself."

Solaris shrugged. "Well, you know how it is."

"I'm not sure I do. I have another doctor coming down to speak with you."

"Psych consult. That'd be Doctor Zivaga. He works with EDPs like me."

"I suspect he won't be happy to see you."

"You kidding? I think he wants me."

"After that, you'll be leaving with the police."

"No, I'm having all kinds of pains. You have to admit me. I have excellent insurance. I'm a paying customer."

"But don't you think it's a little unfair to tie up valuable hospital services when we both know that there is absolutely nothing wrong with you save for this, uh, this fetish for hospitals?"

"Can you say that again? But just a little deeper, a little more breathy, you know, like buuut doon't youuu think thaaat . . ."

"I know you find this amusing, maybe even sexually stimulating. It's anything but. You have a problem, Mr. Solaris. You need to take care of it."

"Thanks, doctor. You have a keen eye for the obvious. But I bet if you called the medical director for the department of emergency services and told her that you were turning down a patient who needed a zillion expensive tests and had great insurance, she would be more than a little upset. Truth is, doctor, I know the game. You have to see me. And you have to do those tests. Patient is complaining of pain in the lower extremities, pain in the chest, shortness of breath, dizziness, blurred vision, and lower back spasms. Patient exhibiting signs and symptoms of everything in the book."

"You sound like a reasonable young man with, unfortunately, unreasonable demands."

"I wish I could help myself. This is my mother's legacy. This what the famous TV star hath wrought."

Boccaccio nodded and crossed shakily to the door, where one of her residents, Riteman, waited for her. "Sorry, Dr. Boccaccio. I got hung up in Three with that construction worker."

"It's all right, David. I started this one." She handed him the chart.

"Everybody here knows this guy," whispered Riteman, wincing at the name he had just read. "He's a couple fries short of a Happy Meal."

"No, he's your patient."

As Riteman's mouth fell open, Boccaccio hurried off and pulled out her cell phone. She dialed her apartment. The machine eventually picked up.

Mom and Drew had not returned since leaving the apartment on Wednesday night. Boccaccio had no way to reach them. And it was very odd that her mother had left suitcases behind. Filing a missing person report with VPD had crossed her mind, but she reasoned that this was just another of her mother's antics. Boccaccio wasn't sure if she could ride the space shuttle of stress for much longer. She had called her father at his high school, where he worked as a teacher's aide and basketball coach, and asked him to have lunch with her on Thursday, but he had been busy getting his kids ready for a big game that night. So they had agreed to meet on Friday, at the hospital. Boccaccio had not told her father that she needed advice regarding her mother; no need to light his fuse until the last possible second.

"Dr. Boccaccio? Here comes that MI," called one of the ED nurses.

"Page Wong, Simons, and Bruno," she ordered. "I'll meet them in the booth."

Vivas jerked the rescue's wheel, got onto the shoulder, then hightailed up the Ventura Freeway toward an MVA that had occurred somewhere between Laurel Canyon and Whitsett. Though it was nearly 10 A.M., traffic remained bumper-to-bumper, baking in the Golden State's sun. Lookieloos ahead were probably straining for a glimpse of the accident, hoping to see someone lying on the asphalt in a pool of blood. Sometimes Vivas and Doe resorted to contacting air crews to get them through traffic. You needed a cab driver's instincts and knowledge of surface roads to work in the valley.

"Watch that," Doe cried, pointing at a huge piece of a semi's tire lying on the shoulder.

"Too late," said Vivas, rumbling over the debris and jostling in her seat.

A CHP motorcycle unit's flashing lights materialized around a slight bend, and Vivas squinted beyond the bike. Two vehicles were on the shoulder: an old, white Cadillac and a blue, late model Honda. Beyond them was a second CHP motorcycle unit. One officer stood near the Cadillac while another spoke to a young woman in expensive business attire who leaned on the trunk of her Honda.

Upon closer inspection, Vivas sighed in disgust at the fact that she could find no damage to either vehicle. They parked behind the first CHP unit. She went around back to fetch the airway bag and drug box while Doe hastened off to get a heads-up from the cops.

It had been a very quiet morning in more ways than one. Only a single call in two hours, and Doe had barely said a word to her back at the station. When she had asked him why he was so quiet, he had asked her the same. Touché. It seemed they both were preoccupied, and that was a scary thing.

As she trudged toward the two cars, she sized up the scene. Typical rear-impact collision. In this case, both vehicles had probably been moving, perhaps at nearly the same speed. The math in these types of collisions was simple: the greater the difference in speed of the two vehicles, the greater the force of the initial impact.

A parked car struck by a car traveling at 55 mph would sustain an impact far greater than if it were not parked and traveling at, say, 35 mph. The person driving the Caddy might have stepped on the brake and been tapped by the woman in the Honda. Once struck, the Caddy's driver would have shot ahead, and if his or her headrest was not properly positioned, hyperextension of the neck would have occurred, tearing ligaments and supporting anterior structures—your basic case of whiplash. If the headrest was in place and the car moved forward without interference, the occupant would more than likely not have been injured. However, the Caddy's driver could have slammed on the brakes and stopped suddenly, throwing him- or herself forward, following the pattern of a front-impact collision and increasing the likelihood of injury. When dealing with these types of accidents, Vivas always looked for two sets of injuries, those caused by the rear impact and those caused by the secondary frontal impact.

Doe broke away from the CHP officers and flashed his I'm-bored-already expression. "She says the guy in the Caddy slammed on his brakes. She just gave him a little love tap, but he pulled over. He hasn't gotten out of his car. He's just sitting in there, groaning and rubbing his neck. I'll go get us an insurance collar."

Vivas shook her head, not because she believed the Caddy's driver was faking his injuries, the way Doe did, but because Doe had not even spoken to the man before passing judgment. Vivas moved warily to the car and set down her equipment. "How you doing in there, sir? My name's Isabel Vivas. I'm a paramedic. What's your name?"

"Richard Beauazo."

Signs: the patient was a white male about fifty years old, six feet, 250 pounds, with thinning, greasy hair. He wore a dirty white T-shirt, hadn't shaved in a few days, and had a cigarette tucked behind his ear. His headrest was properly positioned behind his head—something Vivas found rare these days. Most people thought headrests were designed as an extra comfort feature, not a safety device.

Symptoms: Vivas asked him what hurt, and he said that the bitch behind him rammed right into his ass and that his neck was killing him.

"Okay, sir. Don't move your head. We'll get a brace on your neck."

"Okay. Just hurry. It hurts real bad."

Allergies: "Do you know if you're allergic to any medications?"

"I'm not."

Medications: "Are you taking any medications? And I mean everything, including aspirin."

"Does caffeine count?"

Vivas smiled. "No."

"Then I'm not."

Past medical history: "Have you had any major medical problems or any major surgeries?"

"This twenty questions or a rescue?"

"Just part of my assessment. It's important."

"I got fixed down there, if you know what I mean."

"Anything else?"

"My cholesterol's up. But it's been up for ten years."

Last meal eaten: "When's the last time you ate something?"

"Had an Egg McMuffin 'bout an hour ago."

Events leading up to the accident: She asked him to explain what had happened and listened to him groan out the story.

With the SAMPLE complete, Vivas moved on to the Glasgow Coma Scale. She gave him a 4 for eye opening, then asked him to raise a hand and flex his fingers. He got a 6 for best motor response.

"What's your name?" she asked.

He gave a little snort. "Forgot it already?"

"It's a test."

"My name's Elmer J. Fudd. Millionaire. I own a mansion and a yacht."

"Do you know where you are?"

"I'm sitting here on the goddamned freeway."

Vivas went on to ask him the day and date, which he gave correctly, earning him a 5 for verbal response. GCS stood high at 15.

Doe returned with the black c-spine bag, dropped it beside the airway bag. "Insurance collar's ready to go," he said, loud enough for the patient to hear. "I'm going to assess that young lady over there."

"You do that," Vivas said acidly.

"So your buddy thinks I'm faking, huh?" asked Mr. Beauazo. "You tell that jerk I'll sue his ass for slander."

"You feeling any dizziness?" Vivas asked, trying to change the subject as she placed her fingers on the man's neck to measure the distance from his trapezius to the side of his jaw. She would use the measurement to select the proper size collar.

"Actually, I'm feeling a little dizzy."

"How 'bout chest pain?"

"It does hurt a little when I breathe."

Maybe Doe's right, thought Vivas. The patient seemed awfully susceptible to suggestion, and the forces he had sustained had probably been minimal. But her job did not include sorting out the actors from the real patients. She tore off the cervical collar's wrapping and gently secured the collar to the man's neck. "Do you think you can walk?"

"I don't think so," he said.

"No problem." She stepped to the rear of the car, caught Doe's attention, and waved him over. "We'll need the stretcher."

"Yeah," he replied, less than enthusiastic. "Maybe I'll get a backboard, and we package this loser and airlift him out. Make a big spectacle of it. That's what he wants."

Vivas pursed her lips and eyed the other driver. "How's she doing?"

"Just got a release from her."

A patient release was printed on the back of every run form. Any patient who refused medical attention had to sign the form in the presence of two witnesses. Doe had secured her signature and the signatures of the CHP officers, but Vivas figured that he was after more than just the woman's name. "You didn't get her phone number?"

Oddly enough, he ignored the jibe. "I canceled our engine. Do me a favor? Make sure you note that headrest."

"He still could've messed up his c-spine. And that won't work in the woman's favor. Think it was Avalty who was telling me how the courts are reducing liability. You hit someone with a poorly adjusted headrest, and

the court now says that the victim's negligence contributed to his own injuries. I think they call it contributory
negligence."

"I know what it is."

"What's wrong with you?"

"Nothing. I'll get the stretcher."

"Hey, paramedic lady?" Mr. Beauazo called.

"Yes, sir?"

"Are you gonna have to stick me with anything? Because if you're going to stick me, I wanna refuse that
part of my care."

"On our way to the hospital, I'll do a blood sugar test.
It's a tiny prick. Won't hurt at all." Vivas slid on her
stethoscope, then measured respirations and took Beauazo's wrist in her hand to get a radial pulse.

"Am I dying?" he joked.

"That usually happens when you get the bill."

"I'm covered."

"How's your deductible?"

"Pretty good."

"Then the prognosis looks good."

He grinned. "You're a funny lady. You married?"

"Divorced."

"Me, too. That's why I'm driving around in this hunk
of junk and my kids hate me."

Vivas recorded the man's baseline pulse and respiration on the back of her glove as Doe rolled over the
stretcher. She opened the car door, then she and Doe
guided the man onto the stretcher and buckled him
down. A couple of college kids hanging from the window of a passing car chanted, "Sue her! Sue her! Sue
her!"

They groaned as they lifted the man into the back of the rescue. Vivas locked down the stretcher as Doe shut the doors and headed around to the driver's side. Normally, Vivas would have assessed the woman and he would have taken the more seriously injured victim. He also would have stayed with that victim in the back. It was unlike him to relinquish his "power" so readily. Yes, he didn't believe that Beauazo was injured, but that certainly would not have stopped him from treating the man. In fact, Doe usually liked to have a little fun with patients who were less than totally honest about their injuries. He would open the stick box and remove a fourteen-gauge needle. He would show it to the patient, then say, "Would you hold this for me? Just in case we need it." He would also quite seriously explain the possibility of administering medications through the patient's rectum—whether that patient needed the meds or not. On several occasions he had been reprimanded for letting his scare tactics get out of hand. This would have been a perfect opportunity for him to vent his frustration.

After pumping up the cuff she had slid over Beauazo's arm, Vivas got a pressure, a solid 120/80. Then she hooked him up to the pulse ox. While she waited for a reading, she asked, "How long you been divorced?"

" 'Bout five years now."

"You ever want to get back?"

"In the beginning, I did. You know, for the sake of the kids. But my two boys were getting ready to leave the house, and my oldest told me that if I wasn't happy, I should leave with them. They went to college. I went to Reseda."

"But you and your wife had already raised them."

"Pretty much. That's one thing we did well. Our marriage wasn't worth a shit, but we raised two good kids."

"So what's more important? A marriage or raising kids?"

"That's a tough one. I look at my boys and I think it was worth it. I look at myself and I think, fuck, I screwed up."

Vivas unclipped the mike and set for Valley General's frequency. She reached the charge nurse there and began her report. "En route to your facility with an approximately fifty-year-old white male, BLS stable, victim in an MVA. . . ."

"Forty-eight," Beauazo corrected.

"Patient was involved in a rear-impact collision and the restrained driver of the forward vehicle. Patient suffering from possible c-spine injury and is dyspneic and complaining of minor dizziness."

"Dys-what? Am I okay?"

She held a finger to her lips, then added Beauazo's vitals. When she finished, she unlocked the drug box. "Gonna give you that blood sugar test now."

"Okay. But before you do, I got some advice. Don't go back to him. People don't change."

"I know some who have."

"It's an act. And it never lasts long."

She sighed. "Maybe you're right."

16

Many people loved to complain about hospital food. The meat had been cut and cooked in a tire factory. The side dishes tasted as bland as plain oatmeal. The gelatin resembled some kind of alien goo. But most people who sampled the cuisine at SFMC were remarkably surprised by the quality and taste of meals supplied by four separate cafeterias, each open twenty-four hours and staffed by a number of well-trained, professional chefs. The main cafeteria had its own bakery that produced a heavenly assortment of fresh rolls, bagels, muffins, pastries, and colossal chocolate chip cookies. Boccaccio swore she could smell them baking all the way from the emergency department. A world class salad, pizza, and taco bar, as well as fresh fruit and frozen yogurt bars allowed you to rove from a light meal to a thick slice of pizza heaped with toppings. An entrée bar offered an ever-changing menu of pasta, beef, turkey, chicken, and seafood dishes, along with steamed vegetables, baked potatoes, and half a dozen kinds of rice. You could quench your thirst by selecting from over twenty varieties of drinks, ranging from bottled water to herbal tea to Coke to homemade punch. Finally, if yogurt or pastries did not suit your dessert cravings, you could surrender to the gourmet ice cream and cake bar offering too many sinful delights to count.

Despite all of their epicurean magnificence, Boccaccio rarely ate in the cafeterias. You could usually find her wolfing down a Carl's Jr. burger and side of fries in the nurses' break room while one of her patients wailed in Exam One over a gallstone. On nights with a full moon, you might find her standing near the ambulance entrance and wishing for aerial spraying of Prozac. Or on quiet nights, you might find her shushing nurses who dared jinx them by saying, "Wow, it's really quiet tonight." You could also find her in any of the exam rooms, asking her most common assessment question, "So how come after two weeks of this pain you came in tonight?"

And you would, at the moment, find her arriving nearly forty minutes late for a lunch meeting with her dad. She hurried to a corner table, where he sat alone, his plate already empty, his tall glass of soda down to the dregs. "Dad, I'm so sorry. I got hung up doing this—"

"It's all right," he said, smoothing the back of his curly, salt-and-pepper hair, then pushing his glasses farther up the bridge of his nose. "I like this place. You don't know this, but sometimes I just come here for dinner when you're working. I sit and think about what you must be doing over there. Sometimes I talk to people. Tell 'em you're an attending here. You wanna see eyes light up. . . ."

"Dad, that's weird."

"They got good cookies here."

"You're right." Boccaccio smiled and settled into her seat.

"So, this is nice. My little girl wants to have lunch with her old man. You going to eat?"

"I'll get something later."

"You look a little tired. You getting enough sleep?"

"Sleep's not the problem."

He leaned forward, as though other people could hear them. "You got a new boyfriend?"

"I wish I had time."

"So what's going on? They putting pressure on you for the research again?"

"It's not work."

"My God, you're not sick, are you?"

"In a way I am."

He lost his breath. "Oh, Jesus. Don't tell me. What is it? Breast cancer? Not AIDS. Don't tell me it's AIDs."

She reached across the table and took his hands in her own. "Relax, Daddy. I'm not dying. Mom came to see me."

Her father's expression moved into a tight-lipped scowl. "So she finally dragged her fat ass onto a plane?"

"There's something going on with her. She's lying so much now that she's believing herself. Did you know she got lipo and a boob job?"

"I don't keep in touch with your mother."

"Well, she shows up unannounced with this guy who's maybe my age, then she gets pissed and leaves.

Her luggage has been at my place since Wednesday night."

"And you haven't heard from her?"

"No. She said I was just jealous of her."

"That's your mother. So what else is new?"

"Dad. . . ."

His hands rolled into fists. "What do you want from me?"

"I don't know what to do." Boccaccio's throat tightened.

"Put her luggage out in the hall and change your locks," her father said with a snort. "That's all I can tell you."

"She needs help."

"I know. But she won't listen to anyone."

"This has been going on for too long."

He shut his eyes and shook his head sadly. "When you hit puberty, she really flipped out."

Boccaccio's grandfather had died in World War II, and her grandmother had worked. Boccaccio's mother had been forced to take care of her two younger brothers, and consequently had never been a teenager in the traditional sense. When she had her own daughter, she saw the life she had missed and wanted it back—or at least Boccaccio thought so.

"Dad, I can't change my locks."

"Then you have to accept your mother for who she is. I did. That's why I divorced her."

Boccaccio suddenly felt eighteen again, wearing her light pink dress and white heels. The expensive perfume Mom had let her borrow tickled her nose. She waited in her room for Thomas to arrive in the limo and take her to the prom. Voices came from her parents' bedroom:

"So that's it, then?"

"That's it."

"But when we tell her, we're going to say that you're divorcing me. You're the one who's breaking up this family. You're the one making the decision. Not me."

"You want to blame it on me? Go ahead. She's old enough to realize what's happening. She's old enough to understand that I can't live with your lies and your scheming and your highs and lows. Every time we're around other people, I'm walking on eggshells. I don't know what lies you'll tell or what crazy thing you'll do. It's too much."

Boccaccio slammed into her parents' bedroom, eyes awash in tears, a fire burning in her head. "This is my night! My night!" She faced her mother. "Why do you have to ruin everything?" Then she met her father's pleading stare. "Why?" She kicked off her heels, ran out of the house, and was halfway down the block when Thomas's limo cruised around a corner and stopped. With blackened feet and torn stockings, she entered the limo, burst into tears, and fell into Thomas's arms.

They never made it to the prom. Boccaccio drank herself into a stupor and awoke the next morning in a hotel room with a sledgehammering hangover and a crotch so sore that she could barely stand. She thought she had been raped, then she slowly remembered coaxing Thomas. She had wanted him to be rough with her, torture her, inflict as much pain as he could.

"I can't accept the way she is when I know she can get help," said Boccaccio, slapping the table. "I'll drag her kicking and screaming if I have to."

"Joanna, I never told you this, but I tried to get your mother help. I took her to see psychologists, psychiatrists, marriage counselors, priests, every damned support system I could find. Remember all those bowling nights? Those were all me taking your mother to see someone."

"I guess that was a waste."

"Your mother went through this honeymoon phase with counselors. First couple weeks she was real high about the therapy. Did whatever they said. Then it wore off. She'd refuse to go, and I'd have to find a new system. Could never get her to take any pills. She wouldn't put chemicals in her body, no matter what the doctors said. She kept telling me that the drugs would make her fat."

"So you decided that it wasn't worth it anymore," Boccaccio concluded.

"Joanna, you don't just wake up one day and say, 'I'm getting a divorce.' I don't know. Maybe some people do that. It took a very long time for me to step away. Even when we were first married, your mother did a few nutty things. Over the years, her lying got worse, my help wasn't doing any good, so I stood back. Don't think it doesn't bother me. I was married one time. And it was a failure. And I'm pretty sure I'll never get married again."

"Your marriage wasn't a failure. You tried your best."

"Did I? Some days I blame it all on your mother. Makes me feel good. I was just an innocent victim, right? Some days I think I should have been more forceful with her. I should've said, 'Okay, you're screwed up and these are the drugs you need and you're going to take them. Got it?' Maybe that would've worked, because I think deep down she's never really grown up. She needed that father figure in her life to guide her. But I just wanted to be her husband. I tried to listen to what she wanted, but I could never give her that. Some days I think it was no one's fault. The world's gotten too complex for us."

"I just don't know how to deal with her."

"You said she's with some young guy?"

"Yeah, what a joke. He's obviously a gold digger, not that Mom's really got any money. Maybe he's got a thing for older women. Who knows?"

"How long has she been with him?"

"I don't know."

An idea lit his gaze. "Maybe you should find out. Maybe you should talk to him. Maybe that's the way. He's figured out how to deal with her."

"I think he just yeses her to death."

"Maybe. Maybe not. But I'd try to go through him to get to her."

"That'll be weird."

He leaned forward, widening his eyes. "Your mother's a very interesting and difficult person."

"And my father's suddenly a diplomat. Well, if she ever comes back, maybe I'll try that. The trick is getting him alone." She grimaced. "Not that I'd like to be alone with him. He's European or Middle Eastern or something, and likes to put his hands on people."

"Can't be any worse than some of your patients."

She rolled her eyes. "Why doesn't that make me feel better?" Her pager beeped. "It never ends."

He grinned. "You love it."

• • •

For the past two months, Doe had been on a new lunch kick. He and Vivas would order submarine sandwiches from the local Ralph's market where Vivas's mother worked. After the first few times they had returned with the lunch meat masterpieces, the other firefighters at Station Ten had, one by one, jumped on the bandwagon, so that Doe now found himself ordering for eight other people. Who wanted mustard. Who hated olives. Thank God they had written it all down. When he returned to the rescue, Vivas counted the order and said, "We only got eight."

"That's right. I'm not eating."

She turned onto Ventura Boulevard, then pulled out a sandwich and shook it. "If you don't tell me what's going on, I'm gonna club you to death."

His somber expression did not falter.

"You don't talk all morning," she went on. "You let me handle that c-spine. We go to VGH, and you don't even flirt with the nurses. What's your problem? Erectile dysfunction?"

He released a faint snicker. "I wish."

A moment. Just the diesel engine humming, the brakes puffing air as they stopped for a light.

"Usually, I can't shut you up," she finally said.

"Then you should be happy."

"You don't want to talk? I'll talk. You know what's bothering me? Everything. My mother's trying to get me back with my ex, and I'm thinking about quitting this job."

"If you go back to your ex, then you can quit, right? What's he do again?"

"He's an auto mechanic for Sears. And wow, you sound really upset to see me leave."

"It's your life. You wanna throw it away. . . ."

"Forget I said anything."

"Izzy, I'm just really screwed up. Talking is not what I want to do."

"Better to keep it inside, let it build," she said, agreeing vehemently. "Then you can blow up on some patient and make me look like an ass—just like you did with that c-spine. You know what I think? That MVA on Wednesday got to you. You kept saying it was just another trauma case. And while you were saying it, your hands were shaking."

"Because I was so mad. Sometimes I feel like I'm working with a rookie."

"Me, too."

"I don't want to fight. I got a lot of things on my mind, but that car wreck ain't one of them."

"Or so you think."

"Engine Eight, Rescue Ten. Engine Eight, Rescue Ten. Hit-and-run accident. One-two-seven-five Burbank Boulevard. Cross street Coldwater Canyon. Units respond code three. Time out: thirteen eighteen."

Doe breathed a sigh of relief, then switched on the lights and siren. "Rescue Ten responding."

"Rescue Ten," answered TRO Six.

"Engine Eight responding," called the officer from that station. "We're just around the block."

"A real call," Doe said. "I'm amazed. Thought we'd be picking up actors and frequent flyers all day. Maybe we can get Eight to drop off lunch."

Vivas took them toward the intersection of Ventura

and Woodman, then raced up Woodman and hung a
sharp right onto Burbank. Surprisingly, most midday
motorists yielded, though one woman who might be
three times as old as the Dodge Dart she was driving
panicked and stopped dead in the middle of the road.
Hand-over-hand, Vivas turned the rescue's large wheel
and got around the stricken woman—who, Doe mused,
might be their next call: patient with chest pains due to
sudden appearance of emergency vehicle.

Burbank Boulevard looked fairly open, with vehicles
ahead already yielding way. One of the valley's best-
considered features was its road system. Sure, everyone
bitched about the traffic and the inadequacy of the freeways, but most of the surface streets formed a grid, making travel a no-brainer for most people. You could take
any number of avenues or boulevards in straight runs
from the north end to the south end of the valley. Likewise, you could follow a dozen or more streets from
west to east. The pattern made getting to a location a
heck of a lot simpler than in districts in other parts of
the country. Doe had read stories on the Internet of rescuers trying to find a location, only to learn that the
street went by three different names as it swerved around
a lake, doubled back, then finally returned to its original
course. Worse still were the rural neighborhoods of the
Southeast, with their dirt roads, unnumbered houses, and
poor lighting. Although he and Vivas probably ran two
to three times as many calls as those "country" medics,
they could usually count on a paved road, a numbered
building, and streetlights.

Doe pulled up the address on his palmtop. "Veranda

Apartments. Should be on the right." He lifted the mike. "Valley, Rescue Ten."

"Ten, Valley."

"Request apartment number at that address."

"No other information available. Accident occurred on Burbank Boulevard."

That reply meant the caller had probably hung up before giving the unit number. No matter. A "windmill"— a man waving his arms—stood on the sidewalk, marking the scene. In northern parts of the country, Doe had heard, some rescuers called them "snow angels." The frantic man looked about twenty-five, wore a USC sweatshirt, baggy shorts, and sandals. His hair had been bleached white and moussed to indicate all four cardinal points. Just your wholesome, all-American college boy.

Beyond him were the engine and a VPD cruiser, both parked at the curb. Presumably the accident had not occurred in the middle of the road but at the end of the apartment complex's driveway. Two police officers and three firefighters stood there. As Vivas pulled over, Doe told TRO Six that they were on the scene, then ripped off his headset, and wriggled into a pair of latex gloves. He jumped out and retrieved the c-spine and airway bags. Vivas went for the long backboard.

Hit-and-run. Doe hated them. You cause bodily harm to someone, then instead of stopping to help, you drive off because you're scared or think you can get away with it. Doe wished the law included a public apology and required that you drive around for one year with a roof-mounted, illuminated sign that said I HIT SOMEONE THEN FLED THE SCENE. The only time he had tolerance for hit-and-run drivers was when their accidents occurred in the seedier part of his district, where motorists who struck pedestrians feared for their lives because bystanders would pull them from their vehicles and pummel the shit out of them. In those cases, street-smart drivers would leave the scene, then return when police arrived.

Bags in hand, Doe strode toward the group, sorting through possibilities and probabilities, wondering just what had happened. One key element to consider in such trauma cases was the age of the patient. Typically, adults saw an oncoming vehicle and tried to protect themselves by turning away. The injuries were usually on the sides of their bodies or on their backs. Children, not fully comprehending the potential danger, usually faced the vehicle and sustained injuries to the front of the body.

A second element of understanding involved the phases that comprised a motor vehicle versus pedestrian crash. The initial impact was usually to the pedestrian's legs and sometimes the hips. The victim's torso would then roll on top of the vehicle and impact the hood, windshield, or roof. The third blow would occur when the victim fell off the vehicle and onto the asphalt, most often head-first, which caused compression injuries (blunt trauma) to the head, cervical spine, and torso. According to Valley's protocol manual, any person struck by a vehicle moving at more than 10 mph was assumed to have suffered "multisystem trauma" and would be rushed to SFMC.

Despite all of the considerations regarding the mechanism of injury and checking out a scene, your real priority resided with your patient. Doe had been told over and over during his training that he needed to look at his patient and not get too preoccupied with the scene. You did not want to miss a real problem with your patient.

He drew closer and asked the frantic college boy, "What's going on?" Beyond them, a college girl in violet sweat pants and a sorority logo T-shirt jumped up and down on the pavement, screaming at the top of her lungs. "I don't have a fucking car! I told you that! I just need someone to help me get Tobias to the hospital!"

"Come on," cried the college boy. He led Doe through the group, where one of the firefighters from Eight, a trim, balding man with a severe baby face, hunkered down before a black poodle that writhed spasmodically on the pavement and issued infrequent whimpers. The college boy grabbed Doe's shoulder. "Can you do anything?"

Doe returned his most crooked grin. "You called 911 for this?"

"She was walking the dog when he slipped his leash and got hit by one of the tenants," interrupted the firefighter. "I don't know much about dog anatomy, but I think his hind legs are fractured."

"We have to rush him to the hospital," hollered the girl.

"Ma'am," said one of the cops, "calm down. We'll call a taxi for you. I'm wondering why you didn't call one in the first place."

"But isn't there a hospital we can take him to? Can't you give me a ride?"

"There's a veterinary hospital in Van Nuys," shouted another cop, speaking on his portable to the dispatcher.

Doe muttered a curse and marched back toward the rescue.

"Hey, where you going?" called the college boy.

"Yeah," Vivas added, coming toward him.

He neither stopped nor looked at Vivas. "Patient's a fucking dog."

Back at the rescue, Doe stowed the c-spine and airway bags, then wrenched open the passenger's side door and snatched up the mike. "Valley, Rescue Ten."

"Go, Ten."

"Hit-and-run victim is a black poodle named Tobias. No rescue required. Ten is on the air and returning to quarters."

"Copy, Ten."

"That was really compassionate of you," Vivas said, trudging by with the backboard. "Girl's dog gets hit, and you just walk away. Guess that poodle was even one step lower than the usual hunk of meat, huh?"

"That bitch lied when she made the call. She said it was a hit-and-run and hung up. She tricked us into coming so she'd get a free ride to the vet. You don't get that?"

"I get it. And it pisses me off, driving code 3 to a bullshit call. But then I try to see it from her side. That little 'fucking dog' is a member of her family."

"Either way, I think Tobias just had his last bowl of Alpo." He hoisted himself into the rescue.

After securing their gear, Vivas dropped into the driver's seat and swapped her safety glasses for sunglasses. "Lord, if you're up there, cut that poor kid some slack and give her back her dog. Amen."

As they rolled by the scene, Doe cocked a thumb at

his side window. "You see what happens? You see it?"

"See what?"

"That's what all your compassion gets you. She loved that little dog. Now he's gonna die. Just like your MVA last shift. Work your whole life. Build a family. Wham. They're mowed down. It's not fucking worth it."

"So what do you do? Live your whole life like a stone? Never commit to anyone? Never feel anything because you're worried about getting hurt? Is this the old cliché of the medic who likes to help people but can't help himself?"

Doe slammed his head back on the seat. "What it is . . . is the truth."

17

"That's one hell of a rash you got on your neck," said Fitzy, eyeing Abe from across the day room's conference table. "Must be something exotic, come in from Hawaii or one of them islands. I swear it looks just like a woman's teeth marks. What did they used to call them? Hickeys?"

Cannis and Tenpenney glanced up from their slices of pizza and smiled with full mouths.

"Son, you need to have that examined," Fitzy pushed on. "It could spread to other parts of your body."

"He's hoping it will," said Tenpenney.

"Just remember, son, you're on probation. Got to keep your strength up. You come in here all spent and not worth a shit, and you'll make some enemies pretty quick."

Abe nodded politely and lowered his chin. "So how do you tell a woman you don't want her to do this without, you know, getting her upset?"

"Like I said, you just point her in a different direction," said Tenpenney, wriggling his brows.

"No, you just keep her so busy and so satisfied that she doesn't have time to suck on your neck," Savage said as she crossed to the sliding glass doors behind the conference table. She withdrew her cell phone and stood, facing away from them. "Everybody keep it down. I'm trying to call Donny again."

"See that?" Fitzy said, gesturing to Savage. "That's what you call obsessive-compulsive motherhood. Nothing a little diazepam wouldn't cure."

"I feel bad for her," said Abe. "She's worried sick about her son. And he's probably lying on some beach and gawking at T-backs."

Fitzy's brows came together. "T-what?"

"You know those little bathing suits that—"

Fitzy winked. "Got you. Can't get the missus to wear one of them, though she's got this one pair of panties. . . ."

Abe waved him off. "That's okay."

"So tell us about this little vampire you're dating," said Cannis. "What else does she do besides suck necks?"

"She manages one of those Thoreau's Bookstores."

"Then she probably keeps it all bundled behind a heavy sweater and thick glasses," guessed Fitzy. "But you get her into the sack, and you got yourself one untamed beast on your hands. Oh, yeah. I know the type."

"She did kiss me first. And on the first date. Which has me feeling a little weird."

"She been married before?" Tenpenney asked.

"Yeah. And she's got a kid."

"Well, there it is. She's a little older, a little more mature. Knows what she wants and goes for it. Life's too short to play the bullshit games. You're a lucky bastard. She got a sister?"

Abe shrugged. "I just feel . . . I don't know . . . let down. Like there's no more challenge."

"That's normal, my boy. You've tasted the fruit. Now maybe it's time to move on." Fitzy leaned back in his chair and breathed a heavy sigh.

"Is that what you did when you were young?"

"Hell, yes. We didn't have no AIDs back then. I was living up north. Spent a year on a commune."

"Don't get him started," Cannis advised. "He'll tell you 'bout all the weird sex he's had and the orgies, just trying to make you feel bad about how boring your life's been." Cannis widened his eyes at his older colleague. "We don't care, Fitzy."

"I just started with her, and I'm not ready to move on," said Abe. "I shouldn't even tell you this, but we were lying there afterward, and she was asking about my job, and not because she was being polite. In fact, we even talked about it during dinner. She's like this constant learner. She even asked about the Star of Life."

The six-pointed star of life on most rescue vehicles represented the six system functions of EMS: detection, reporting, response, on-scene care, care in transit, and transfer to definitive care.

"Dammit!" shouted Savage.

Save for the faint whispers coming from the TV, the room fell silent.

"Still got his cell off?" Abe asked.

Savage glowered at her own phone. "What do you think?"

"Let the boy have some fun," urged Fitzy. "You keep breathing down his neck, you'll chase him off. Give him a long line. He'll come back. They always do."

"That from a man who's never had kids."

Fitzy turned his gaze skyward. "And I thank you, Lord, for the gift of weak sperm."

An alarm broke over the intercom, echoed by TRO Six: "Engine Nine, Rescue Nine. Engine Ten, Tower Ten, Battalion Six. Engine Nine, Rescue Nine. Engine Ten, Tower Ten, Battalion Six. Structure fire. Two-nine-seven Sumter Boulevard. Cross street Hudson. All units respond code three. Time out: sixteen fifty-two."

Tenpenney and Cannis whooped.

"Finally got a good call," cried Fitzy.

Abe knew that most outsiders would not understand why grown men rejoiced over the possibility that someone could be suffocating to death inside a burning structure. But all those grown men wanted to do was exercise their skills instead of lounging in front of a TV or sitting around a conference table and being called lazy bums who loved to do nothing more than eat, sleep, and watch videos. They celebrated the opportunity to do their jobs, nothing more.

Lieutenant Martinez was out on the squad vehicle with three other firefighters. They had been called to pick up some purportedly radioactive material from the home of a recently deceased UCLA professor. Since no one would be left at the station, everyone began locking up. Abe set the burglar guards on the sliding glass doors, then darted onto the apparatus floor.

"Hatches are battened," shouted Tenpenney as he sprinted across the garage toward the locker holding his turnout gear. Fitzy and Cannis scrambled behind him.

Abe rolled the handle on the bay door nearest the cab, yanked it open, then withdrew his fire-resistant pants with large cargo pockets and reflective yellow strips on the cuffs. Trembling with anticipation, he pulled them on, then stepped into his heavy rubber boots and donned his coat, which also had reflective strips running along the hem and on the sleeves. He removed heavy leather gloves from his pants pockets, squeezed into them, then closed the bay door. Abe would wait until they arrived at the location to put on his air pack, face mask with air-supply regulator, utility belt, and helmet with attached visor and fire-resistant hood.

Meanwhile, Fitzy, Tenpenney, and Cannis had already geared up and were climbing into the engine. Once seated, Cannis, switched on the lights and siren and pulled out, as Fitzy shut his door.

Abe found his own seat, turned the key, and the rescue rumbled to life. As Savage responded over the radio, Abe popped on his headset, then merged onto the road and slipped in behind the engine, his own siren wailing against the wind.

"Engine Nine, Rescue Nine. Engine Ten, Tower Ten, Battalion Six," said TRO Six. "VPD on scene of structure fire. Report two, possibly three victims inside three bedroom residential home. Flames visible from roof at this time. Battalion Six requesting additional rescue unit. Rescue Ten responding."

"Fitzy wasn't kidding," said Savage. "Got a good call." She reached forward and withdrew the personnel identifier sheet that was wedged between the windshield and the dash.

A small slip of paper with lines for the date, unit, shift, name, rank, and position, the sheet—along with matching, color-coded name tags hanging from a key ring—was given to an incident commander and allowed that person to account for every rescuer on a scene. If a unit arrived before a command had been established, the sheet and name tags were placed on the floor of the driver's side of the first engine on scene. Upon arrival, the commander would expect to find IDs of all units there. At the beginning of every shift, Abe and Savage were supposed to create a new list, post it in the cab of their unit, update it when changes were made, turn it in to an incident commander if necessary, and retrieve it and the name tags before departing. Savage was checking to make sure Abe had properly signed the sheet before embarrassing herself by giving the incident commander (in this case their battalion chief) yesterday's sheet.

"Don't trust me?" he asked.

"Don't trust myself. I should've checked this in the morning. And it's not you. Turned in an old sheet once. IC thought everybody was out of this old body repair shop, but me and my partner were still inside. Steel rafters shrank from all the heat and collapsed on us. My partner got trapped, and I was trying to get him out. Thought I'd lose my job over that. Been paranoid about the sheet ever since."

"You save your partner?"

"No. My lieutenant came in to assist. Got him out. Made me look even more stupid." Savage's cell phone rang.

"What're you doing?" Abe asked, gaping at her as she removed her headset and activated the phone. Medics were not supposed to take personal calls—especially when en route to a fire.

"Shuddup. Hello? Yeah, this is she. Okay. Where's Donny?" After a second, Savage reached out and grabbed the dash. "Say that again." She paused. "Oh, dear God, what kind of accident?"

Abe's gaze switched between the road and the look of stark fear gripping Savage's face.

"He was where? Near the swimming pool?"

"Engine Nine, Rescue Nine. Engine Ten, Rescue Ten, Tower Ten, Battalion Six. VPD reports second unit on scene. Power to the residence has been cut. Officers now evacuating surrounding homes. At this time, flames still clearly visible from the roof of the structure. Neighbors report two, possibly three victims inside."

"You say he accidentally what? Forgot to have a second shot? What're you talking about? Is that you, Donny? What the hell is this? What do you mean you're just kidding? What kind of a goddamned joke is this? Have you been drinking? You're lying. I can hear it in your voice. You don't think that's mean, calling up your mother and pretending to be hurt? Jesus Christ, you'll kill me like that. No, I don't worry too much. And listen, you ungrateful bastard, you ever do this again, and I'll get on a plane and kick your ass. You hear me? Donny? Donny, you there?" She swore. "He hung up. The little shit doesn't call me for days. And when he does, he calls up drunk and plays a joke. What kind of a mean bastard did I raise?"

"Uh, ma'am? Steph? Just got another update. Another

VPD unit is on scene. They're evacuating the neighbors."

After several long breaths, Savage finally nodded, clipped her headset back on, then rolled down the window for what Abe assumed would be a breath of fresh air.

Savage screamed and threw her cell phone. It smashed onto the asphalt and skittered toward a sewer grating. "Do yourself a favor," she said. "Don't have kids."

Abe knew when to shut up.

"Aw, look at this," she said as a bus pulled in front of them. "It's probably this idiot's house that's burning, and he's delaying us to the scene."

The odds of that being true were astronomical, but Abe nodded just the same.

A column of smoke, nearly black in the center and swelling to half a dozen shades of gray, rose high in the distance. Abe hung a sharp left onto Sumter Boulevard, having hit every green light thus far—thanks to the Opticom. About seven more cross streets lay between them and Hudson, and the device continued to work its electronic magic, turning red lights to green. Cannis had chosen a different route to the scene, and if he and the engine crew beat them there, that was just fine by Abe, who, at the moment, liked clearing the road himself.

For rookie firefighter–paramedics, the best rush came en route to a scene, especially running code three, lights and sirens. All of your senses tingled. A wail, siren, or phaser heralded your approach. Smart drivers veered off as though bowing in your presence and rolling out an asphalt carpet. Saliva gathered in your throat because you were hungry to work. The sickly sweet aroma of diesel fumes reminded you of the power of your chariot. And the vibration running through the sturdy wheel and into your hands as you guided that chariot across that asphalt carpet kept the adrenaline running even more fiercely. Not many would deny how addictive and empowering it was to get a good call. Abe liked to believe that he was not a yahoo fireman or one of Boccaccio's common trauma Buddhas or monkeys, that he kept level-headed about the job. But at the moment, he felt pretty damned excited. He knew that would wear off the moment they got into their first near crash with him at the wheel.

The two-story house appeared on their left, and Abe brought the rescue across the street, heading straight into oncoming traffic. He timed the maneuver perfectly, pulling up behind the engine and VPD cruisers, the rescue's pump side facing the house in case a backup water supply was required.

As the first rescue unit on scene, Abe and Savage would enter the structure to recover victims while the engine and tower crews concentrated on fighting the fire. Vivas and Doe would staff the treatment sector, and victims found in the house would be removed by Abe and Savage and delivered to them. If the treatment sector became overwhelmed with patients or the battalion chief felt the need for multiple crews, he could call for a third rescue or pull medics like Cannis off one or more of his fire crews. Once the chief knew for certain that there were no more people inside the house, then and only then would he allow Savage and Abe to help out in the treatment sector.

While Cannis walked around the house to size up the scene, Fitzy and Tenpenney went for the inch-and-three-quarter pre-connect line. Abe leaped from the cab and stood for a second, gaping at the burning house. Long tongues of flame extended from blackened shingles and licked the smoke and air; otherwise the house looked in good repair, with a fairly new coat of paint, lush land-scaping, and an ornate stone walkway. Probably cost a fortune. A rumble from behind signaled the arrival of the tower truck, and the battalion chief's Ford Explorer zoomed up a few seconds behind.

"You ready, Abe?" Savage hollered.

Her voice set him in motion. He opened the first bay, found his heavy nylon utility belt, wrapped it around his waist, then fastened it with an attached carabiner clip. The belt carried a small and a large flashlight, a pair of multipurpose pliers, a seatbelt cutter, a loop to hang his radio, another loop with a quick-release latch to hang smaller hammers and axes, and a wide pouch containing an orange search line that glowed when struck by light. The line had a carabiner clip affixed to the end, and Abe would hook the clip on the door of a larger structure (one bigger than an average house), then pay out line behind him so that he could perform his search and have a line back for himself and anyone he rescued.

Next, he fetched his radio from the cab and hung it from the belt. He pulled on the fifty-pound air pack, buckled the harness, and activated and double-checked the PASS device. That completed, he grabbed the face mask, which covered his nose, mouth, and eyes, then attached its hose to the air pack's regulator and opened the line. Oxygen flowed. The helmet came last. He tightened the chin strap and kept the visor up because the mask would do a decent job of protecting his face.

Lumbering now under the weight of almost a hundred pounds of gear, he accepted a pike pole from Savage, who brandished her preferred sledgehammer and was equipped with a new helmet-mounted thermal imager, a FLIR (forward-looking infrared radar) device that flipped down in front of one eye and fed her a thermal-based image. She could see hot, warm, and cold zones, even spot recent footprints through a smoke-filled room because the device differentiated heat levels in fractions of degrees and because infrared traveled in longer wavelengths than visible light. Most important, she could locate a person lying behind a wall of smoke or flames.

With his senses dulled by the mask, helmet, and gloves, Abe followed Savage up the driveway. Two fire-fighters from the tower truck were already ventilating the house by smashing open the first floor windows. Bystanders often mistook the act as an attempt to gain entry, and during a news interview, one infuriated home-owner had called it "a needless destruction of property by those axe-happy bastards." In truth, built-up smoke, heat, and gases could very well cause an explosion. Ventilating a burning structure was necessary. Period.

Fitzy and Tenpenney had busted open the wooden front door and had hauled in the line. Smoke billowed from the entrance. Meanwhile, the tower truck was raising its boom. A built-in hose running the length of the boom would soon belch a frothy stream onto the roof. Cannis and another firefighter from the tower were positioning portable ladders beneath the second story win-

dows. They would climb them, cut screens and break
the windows as necessary, then leave the ladders in place
for escape.

Great arms of smoke embraced Abe as he moved into
the foyer and immediately drove his pike pole into the
low ceiling. He twisted the hook and pulled down;
breaking off a hunk of sheet rock and exposing the two-
by-fours beneath. No fire in this part of the ceiling/sec-
ond floor yet, but the heat pressed on his bunker gear.

Ahead, in a long, rectangular living room, Fitzy and
Tenpenney aimed the hose on a great curtain of roiling
flames that had already turned the furniture into smol-
dering, skeletal heaps. The fire had chewed its way along
a rear wall, and now pushed up, flexing orange talons
across the ceiling.

"Primary all clear on the first floor," Tenpenney announced over the radio.

Prior to manning the hose, Fitzy and Tenpenney had
performed a brief search for people. If they did not find
any, they called a primary all clear. Next came a much
more thorough search by Abe and Savage that included
every kitchen cabinet, the pantry, and the garbage can.
Abe remembered reading a story about a small boy who
had survived a terrible house fire by crawling into the
fireplace. A keen-eyed firefighter conducting her secondary search had found him. Children tended to
squeeze into the smallest and most precarious places,
and you often had to think like a child to find them.

Two masked firefighters from the tower crew entered
the house. Savage told them to begin a secondary search
of the ground floor, then turned back for the stairwell
and keyed her radio. "Savage, IC?"

"Go, Savage," said the battalion chief.

"We're moving up for a left-hand search. Will update."

"Ten-four. Looks like we got the seat in the back of the house, spreading around toward the garage on side 2."

If you looked at the burning house from above, you could divide it into four boxes, with a fifth box in the middle. Beginning with the top left box, you could label the sections A, B, C, D, and call the center box E. You could also label the sides of the house, with 1 for the front, 2 for the right, 3 for the rear, and 4 for the left. You could communicate your location or a victim's to incident command by saying, "I'm on the first floor, side 4, section A," a more concise way of saying that you were on the ground level, left side of the house, in the back. Once on the second floor, Abe and Savage would begin their sweep in section C, moving clockwise through the house until they returned to where they had started.

Savage led the way, sledgehammering the staircase in front of her to test its integrity. Abe shook off an image of Savage falling through the burning staircase and landing on her back as shards of burning wood and carpet rained on her.

18

"**Y**our treatment sector's right over there," shouted Sixth Battalion Chief Daniel Drummond, a six-foot, four-inch lumberjack of a man with gray mustache and bushy brows. "I got Troft and another fella from Eight on their way."

"Good," Vivas cried as she and Doe loaded their stretcher with bags, monitors, and long backboard, then rolled it over to a patch of lawn paralleling the sidewalk.

Drummond had pulled Carla Gomez off Engine Ten's crew to serve as treatment officer. Gomez, a fair-skinned woman who somehow had managed to remain slim despite having six kids, was the most senior medic at Fire Station Ten. She had fourteen years in and had been Vivas's Field Training Officer. Last year, they had had a falling out that had turned into a battle of wills over which patients required immediate treatment. During their sparring, a woman had died, and Vivas still felt that the patient could have been saved had Gomez taken the time to consider the situation fully.

Gomez had already spread out a pair of tarps and had brought over Engine Ten's airway and c-spine bags, as well as the cardiac monitor. Unfortunately, she still held the power to make life-and-death decisions. Her job as treatment officer dictated that she evaluate resources required, report those needs to Drummond, and keep in close contact with other sectors. She would establish immediate and delayed treatment areas within the treatment sector, as well as assign, direct, supervise, and coordinate medics.

"God damn," Doe shouted as a particularly violent flash of flames lit the roof. "Smoke. It's what's for dinner."

"Doe, I'd like you to shut up," spat Gomez. "Then I want you and Izzy to set up on this tarp. Troft and his partner will set up over there. Neighbors say we might have a woman of about seventy, a five-year-old girl, and a thirteen-year-old boy."

Waving the peds bag, Doe shouted, "Heard the update. And you're wearing the vest?" He eyed Gomez, who was not, in fact, wearing her treatment sector vest, which she did not really need. Doe knew her penchant for petty power.

"Just get going," she said, then hustled over to Drummond, probably to ask him for the vest in question. She had become even more threatened by the other medics since the incident with Vivas. For her, it was all about wielding her seniority and authority.

"You don't have to mess with her for me," Vivas told Doe as she set the long backboard on the tarp.

"I'm not. Her power trip's starting to piss me off. Maybe I'll pull the plug." He mimed the act, wearing a tight grin.

"Feeling better?"

"Nope. Just distracted." He opened the peds bag and removed the Broselow tape and tool bag containing the color-coded pouches. "Now if we get something better than a poodle to treat, we'll be all right."

"That is *so* cruel."

"Nah, cruel's coming this way," Doe said, glancing at Troft and his partner, a dorky-looking guy with sideburns resembling black linguini and a funny name Vivas strained to remember, as they tramped over with their backboard and equipment.

"Pooh. Vivas," Troft said. He paused to scrutinize the fire and the great arc of water extending from the tower truck's boom. "Looks like somebody's cookin' Cajun."

Doe cocked a brow at Vivas.

"Somebody could be dying in there," Vivas reminded Troft.

"There'd better be," he answered. " 'Cause I just got dragged away from a rerun of one of my favorite TV shows—*Space: Above and Beyond*. Love that sci-fi crap." He dropped to his knees and zipped open his bags.

Vivas snickered. "That attitude gives us all a bad name."

"What? You think I'm a prima donna? A paragod?"

Doe bared his teeth. "How 'bout asshole?"

"I'm neither paragod nor an asshole, my brethren. I'm a *paragon* of paramedicine. Watch as they deliver the injured and me and my fine apprentice raise them from the dead. Watch and ye—shall—learn."

"Altered mental status?" Doe asked Vivas, lifting his chin at Troft.

She nodded. "Better c-spine him and draw some blood. Have our friends back at SFMC run a tox screen."

Troft's self-assured smile held fast.

"You jokers ready over there?" cried Gomez, radio still held to her ear.

"Jokers?" Troft asked. "Eight years in to be called a joker?"

"Put us to work," Doe hollered, then he leaned back and whispered in Vivas's ear: "Her and Troft are gonna go at it. We'll let 'em pull their own plugs."

"I like it," said Vivas, then turned toward the sound of glass shattering from a second-story window.

"Spreading in this bedroom," called a firefighter from the top of his portable ladder.

"Izzy, I know what you're thinking. You're thinking that could be your little girl's bedroom up there. Could be all her stuffed animals turning into crispy critters. And she's hiding under her bed and coughing and choking. But you know what? Consuela's safe and sound, at home with your mom right now. So don't even give me that crap today, all right?

"There might be an old lady in there. She could be *your* mom."

"My mom ain't seventy."

"Whatever. Hey, look. Must be the father."

A rangy blond man in a white dress shirt, tie, and slacks came sprinting across the street from where he had parked his Lexus sedan.

"Here it comes," Doe muttered.

The man ducked under police tape and plowed by two

VPD officers as though he were trying out for the Raiders. He was about twenty feet from the front door when a third cop tackled him. "Let me go! Mom! Kimberly! Tyler!"

This was not the first time Vivas had seen parents go ballistic at an MVA or other accident or at a fire. Some simply broke down and cried. Others became combative, had to be handcuffed, even sedated. Vivas knew all too well that she fell into the second category. God forbid anything happened to Consuela. Vivas would kill anyone who interfered with her getting to her baby. Yes, she knew that rescuers needed to do their jobs, but she needed to be right there with them, not standing on the sidelines as though her life had become a spectator sport played out and officiated by strangers.

Still screaming for his loved ones and shaking with helplessness, the man was dragged to his feet by all three officers and ushered toward one of the VPD cruisers.

Vivas stood.

"Where you going?" asked Doe.

"Be right back."

His eyes bulged. "You can't abandon the sector."

"I'll be a second."

With the father now safely restrained by the police, Vivas jogged over to the group, knowing that she might be making a mistake—but she sympathized too much with that father to ignore him. "Let me talk to him," she told one of the cops, a black woman with sweat beading her brow.

"You gotta get my mom and my kids out of there!" insisted the man.

"The firefighters are already in the house," said a sergeant, his tone sympathetic. "If your family's in there, they'll get them out. Trust me. I've seen them do it in worse than this. And the chances are, they already got out. Maybe they're hiding. Maybe they're scared. Maybe they weren't even home. You don't know. So you just have to wait."

"Sir?" Vivas called. "My name's Isabel. I'm a paramedic. We've set up a treatment sector. If they bring out your kids or your mom, they'll be taken there. We'll work on them before putting them in the ambulance. I know you want to be close. I know you want to go in there yourself. If you stay with an officer, you can watch us."

"I'll stay with him," said the third cop, an Asian man of about forty who turned an approving glance on Vivas. "Thanks."

Geneva Bowers usually worked at Cuts Plus! until seven, sometimes eight, on Friday evenings. You had your weekend partying crowd who wanted to look chic for their two big nights out. And you occasionally had your wedding crowds, who really put on the pressure. If you screwed up the bride's hair, well, you might hear about it from the entire wedding party. And once in a blue moon you had your firefighter, who would look up at you as you washed his hair, and his eyes would have you jotting down your phone number like a giddy teenager.

Her watch read 5:15 as she said good-bye to her colleagues and left the strip mall, feeling guilty that she would not be there to help her friends battle a Friday night lineup of longhaired nitpickers and poor tippers.

Stopped at a red light, she looked in the car beside hers. A woman in her late twenties yawned and raked fingers through her wispy brown hair. Behind her, a little boy no more than three sat in his car seat and stared in wonder at the storefronts' neon signs, one of them just now blinking into a warm glow.

I know I'm irresponsible. I know I like to have too much fun. I'm Peter Pan. But at least I know exactly who I am and what I'm about. And you know what? I don't really wanna change, because I kind of like me. I know a lot of people just can't deal with that. It's not like I haven't been called a flake or a cocky asshole before. It's okay.

"No, it's not okay," she raged aloud. "You fuckin' jerk. I can't do it alone. I thought I could. But I can't."

Savage felt a tap on her shoulder as she reached the top step. She looked back at big brown eyes shielded by a face mask. Abe motioned with his pike pole toward the ceiling. She nodded, reached the landing, then waited a second as he made his pull. Sparks, soot, and flames spat from the hole.

"God damn it, we gotta move," she shouted, assuming that the fire was spreading rapidly through the attic.

A smoke-clogged hallway leading to several closed doors lay before them. From the ceiling came a muffled pinging from the hose spraying outside. Drummond reported over the radio that the firefighters who had ventilated the second-story bedroom windows had called a primary all clear in the bedrooms.

After studying the thermal imager and noting different

shadings on the walls, Savage went to the nearest bedroom door; its knob had a keyhole and shone hot and brilliant in her display. She tried it. Locked. A bedroom door that locked from the outside seemed a little unusual in a residence. Then again, teenagers were always groaning about their privacy.

With one hand vised around the sledgehammer just under the ten-pound head, and the other near the handle's base, Savage rammed the tool into the door, busting the jamb into a steeple of splintered wood. As the door swung inward, she immediately pivoted to exploit the outside wall as a shield. Abe had already posted himself on the opposite side of the door, pole in hand, his face sewn with tension.

The fire's breath came hot and relentless. Its crackling grew louder, its smoke thicker. Shades of orange and yellow light fell over Savage as she took in the bedroom in one panning sweep. Fifteen by fifteen. Large room. Brown carpet. A half-dozen small fires feeding off a large oak desk with hutch. Posters of music groups hanging all over the walls, some intact, some burned and coiled into black scrolls. Empty beer bottles that had stood on the windowsill but had been knocked off by a firefighter ventilating the room lay on a burning, twin bed amid a freckling of melting glass. Flames mounted the wall behind the bed, fanned by a breeze coming through the open window. Soot stained the popcorn ceiling.

Savage mustered her voice. "Fire department! Anybody in here? Fire department! Anybody here?" She took a tentative step forward, testing the floor with her sledgehammer. The thermal imager showed nothing save the hot spots. No outline of a person emerged through the coiling smoke.

"I'll check the closet," cried Abe, shuffling in behind her. He scampered to the right and tugged open a pair of folding doors, then drove his pike pole gingerly into the gap below a rod sagging under the weight of a teenage boy's clothes.

Dropping to her knees, Savage searched under the bed but came up empty. She quickly got to her feet and seized her radio. "IC, Savage. I'm on the second floor, side 4, section C. Boy's bedroom. Secondary all clear."

"Side 4, section C, boy's bedroom. Secondary all clear," Drummond repeated, then added, "Rescue Five's en route. ETA about a minute."

Sounds like a lot of action outside, Savage thought. They didn't get too many house or apartment fire calls in the valley. Firefighters working the canyon districts probably got twice as many. You arrived on the scene to find some homeowner on his roof, waving a garden hose at an immense wall of flames devouring his backyard. Trauma and medical emergencies comprised about seventy percent of VFD's workload, so when a big house fire like this one occurred, personnel at every nearby station wanted to participate. Two rescue crews had already established a treatment sector. Savage and Abe were conducting the secondary search. A fourth rescue crew would soon be inside the house to assist.

Savage met Abe in the hallway, and they moved swiftly to the next door. It was locked from the inside, and its knob glowed white on the imager. Her glove hissed as she tried it. Locked again. Strange.

"They got some issues with security," Abe said, then stood rigid and ready beside the door.

Rearing back, Savage plunged her sledgehammer home. The jamb cracked but held.

"Watch out!" cried Abe.

Before she could stop him, he lifted his boot and kicked open the door unleashing a sinewy beast of smoke and heat that sent Savage fleeing to the opposite wall. She rebounded, lost her balance, and dropped. Fiery fingers grew from the ceiling and clawed at the door frame.

"Steph!" The rookie hovered over her, grabbed her air pack's harness, then yanked her up.

"God damn it, Abe," she said, then faced the bedroom.

And right there, smack in the middle of her imager, was a figure lying prone at the foot of a blazing canopy bed, out of view from the window. The figure grew more distinct. A woman. Heavyset. White hair. First- and second-degree burns on her lower and upper extremities.

"I think I see someone," said Abe. He started into the bedroom.

Savage grabbed his shoulder.

All four bedroom walls had succumbed to the flames. The nightstand to the left of the canopy bed heaved steel gray smoke clouds. Portions of the carpet had been scorched. The back of Savage's neck tingled as she checked the imager and saw just how hot that rug had become. She dropped to her knees, raised her sledge-hammer, beat once on the rug. A faint cracking answered, then the carpet began dropping away from them, as though it had been stretched over air and Savage had just severed its bindings. Blackened plywood scrolled into view along the entire left side of the room as the carpet and padding continued to plummet.

"Whoah! Whoah! Whoah!" came a shout from Fitzy below as compromised planking cracked off its burned tethers.

A dresser with a large mirror tumbled forward and crashed into the living room below. The gap in the floor widened, spewing sparks and bits of wood and rug. The carpet flapped down now, and flames from below flirted with its tattered edges. The floor creaked again, like the bulkheads of an old ship at sea. Several two-by-fours dropped from somewhere ahead. The canopy bed and woman below it were in the far right corner of the room, on what was left of the floor. About a seven-foot gap stood between Savage and the woman. She could make a running leap for it, but she hardly trusted the rest of the floor.

"IC, Savage. I'm on the second floor, side 4, section A. Woman's bedroom. We got a victim. Floor collapsed. Can't get to her from up here. Need a ladder inside, ground level, side 4, section A."

Below, Fitzy and Tenpenney turned their hose up into the gap and began spraying down the room. "Fitzy? You meet that ladder and take her down."

"We got it, Beast!"

Savage and Abe backed off and headed to the last bedroom door. Standard knob. Hot and locked. This time, Savage swung the hammer like a major leaguer, gaining them entry with a single carefully placed blow.

Wedges of sunlight and a dense spray of water filtered down through a four-by-five ragged hole in the sloped ceiling. Smoke lingered in the corners, furniture was reduced to shadowy rubble speckled by embers and long strips of glowing wood.

While Savage checked the integrity of the floor to the left, Abe poked his way to the right, splashing over the soaked carpet and heading for the closet doors. Savage reached a twin bed whose mattress and comforter had been consumed at the foot by flames. She checked under and behind the bed. Just half-melted Barbie dolls, ruined puzzles, and a few of those kid computer toys. She looked up as Abe pulled open the closet doors to reveal a blonde girl lying unconscious on rows of little shoes.

19

After spending several minutes searching the labyrinth of corridors, Geneva Bowers finally found the nondescript door at the end of a hall. She stepped into a small reception area with the usual chairs, coffee table, magazines, potted plants, and drab artwork purchased at an office supply store. A couple—she a Hispanic girl of about seventeen, he a black boy of maybe twenty—sat near a water cooler, whispering, he with his arm draped around her, she repeatedly rubbing the corners of her eyes. Geneva shuddered a little as she passed them and reached the receptionist's desk behind a four-foot-high wall and a glass partition.

A fifty-year-old woman with bad skin and gray hair razored short by a blind stylist looked up from a computer screen, then slid open the window. "You Geneva Bowers?" she asked curtly.

"Yeah. I have an appointment with Doctor Ratas."

The receptionist frowned. "You're about fifteen minutes late."

"I had trouble finding this place."

The woman rolled her eyes. "My directions weren't good?"

"They were. Look, I'm sorry you might have to work a couple minutes late because of me," said Geneva, disgusted that she had to apologize to this person. "I appreciate it."

"I'm not the only one who'll be workin' late." She handed Geneva a clipboard with a form that posed the usual billion questions. "After you fill that out, I'll send you back to talk with one of our counselors."

"Why do I have to do that?"

"It's required. We just want to be sure."

"Well, I made it this far."

"Trust me, ma'am. That doesn't mean anything."

After a perfunctory nod, Geneva took a seat and winced at the ominous form. Her brow tingled. The couple was staring at her. The girl nudged the boy, who nudged her back. Geneva tried to smile.

"Excuse me?" the boy said.

The girl shoved him hard, her cheeks pinking with embarrassment.

"Yes?"

"This is gonna sound weird, but what would you do if you were us?"

"You asshole," the girl muttered.

Geneva took a moment to consider. "I'm sorry. I don't know."

"How come you're by yourself?"

"Don't pay any attention to him," said the girl. "He's just doing this to piss me off."

"No, it's okay. I'm here *because* I'm by myself. Some women can do the mom thing alone. I admire them."

"Doe? Vivas?" Gomez called. "You got the first victim. She should be coming out any second."

"No, *we* got the first victim," Troft said, marching toward the treatment sector officer. "*They* will assist."

After exchanging a knowing smile with Vivas, Doe stood by his equipment, realizing that he could never share the moment with any of his colleagues because none of them would believe it. No career-conscious medic would ever exhibit behavior like Troft's, especially at a scene. You didn't do that. In fact, the entire group's earlier conversation was pretty rare. Most of the time, Doe's colleagues were all business, wired to the moment. Gomez obviously brought out the worst in everyone.

"IC, Savage," came the medic's voice through Doe's radio. "We got another victim. Little girl. Bringing her out now."

"We'll take the girl," Doe shouted to Gomez.

"All right," she said, then lifted a finger at Troft. "You got the first victim. And a write-up."

Troft threw up his hands. "Lovely." He stamped back to the treatment sector as Fitzy and Tenpenney carried an elderly woman through the front door.

Vivas circled to Troft's tarp and stood ready to help the medic's partner until the second victim came out. Doe held his ground, knowing full well that Troft would not want his help, though if some miracle were to occur and Troft resigned himself to assistance, Doe would be there.

"Okay, let's get her down," Troft told the firefighters.

Fitzy and Tenpenney gingerly placed the woman onto Troft's long backboard, then stood back as Troft checked the woman's airway, breathing, and circulation while his partner cut the woman's dress with a pair of trauma shears. The woman had black soot stains around her nose and mouth—an indication that she had serious inhalation burns from breathing superheated gases.

"Mom," shouted the blond man from behind the police tape. "Mom, it's David. Can you hear me? Mom!"

"No pulses," Troft said after checking the woman's neck and wrist. "And no breath sounds on the right or left. All right, Benjamin, let's go! Let's go! You tube her. I got CPR."

The fire had consumed the woman's oxygen supply and had caused her to become hypoxic, which in turn had probably led to ventricular fibrillation (v-fib), a chaotic heart rhythm that appeared on the cardiac monitor's tape as a line with many randomly packed hills and valleys. Once Troft's partner got the cardiac monitor hooked up, there might be asystole (cardiac standstill) and its accompanying flat line on the monitor. The woman, who probably had other medical problems that contributed to her poor condition, had—for all intents and purposes—passed on, but Doe knew that Troft's ego would not allow him to admit that. He would try to resuscitate her, though chances were high that she would end up a vegetable and/or die a few days later from an accumulation of fluid in the lungs or an infection.

"There's a picture," said Vivas, staring at the house.

"Second victim coming out," hollered Gomez.

Haloed in smoke and clutching an unconscious little girl in his arms, Abe materialized in the doorway—just as a news camera crew reached the police tape. Abe came forward through a sudden downdraft generated by two news choppers circling and thumping overhead. He was having quite a week: news interview on Wednesday, then he had been shot at, and now he would once again be a TV hero. Doe wished his own probation had been as eventful; his forty ALS patient contacts had included gangbangers, law enforcement, MVA victims, and nearly a dozen from assisted living facilities, but Doe had never once been on TV. He waved over the flush-faced rookie, then helped him lower the girl to the long-board.

"Kimberly? It's Daddy? Can you hear me?"

The pain in that father's voice made Doe want to look at the man and offer some reassurance that he would do everything he could to save her. But Doe knew that if he gave in to that voice and glimpsed the agony on that man's face—if he let himself feel just a little of what that father felt—then the job of saving the girl would be that much harder. Vivas kept saying that he treated patients like hunks of meat, biological entities that needed fixing. But Doe knew damned well that a little girl with her whole life ahead of her lay on his backboard and that a father who had spent the last five years caring for and loving her stood there feeling like less than a man because he could not help his flesh and blood.

"Guys, please," cried the father. "Don't let her die. Don't let my little girl die."

•   •   •

"Have you discussed this decision with your boyfriend?" the counselor asked Geneva as they sat in a small, somewhat claustrophobic office.

"Yes, I have," she lied, wanting to end the whole third degree as quickly as possible. "He supports this decision one hundred percent."

Perhaps a few years older than Geneva, with black hair begging for a deep conditioning and decent cut, the counselor leaned back in her chair and nodded halfheartedly. "Your boyfriend can come, you know. He can be with you throughout the entire procedure. Have you thought about rescheduling so he can be here with you?"

"You work for the doctor, right?"

"Yes, I do."

"Well, this is kind of funny, because it sounds like you're trying to talk me out of this, but I know the doctor's here to make money. Funny sales pitch. Reverse psychology or something."

"We just want you to be sure. We'd rather not perform a procedure if a woman's unsure, because when it's done, it's done. We also want you to feel as comfortable as possible. Right now, I'm sensing that you're angry. You got lost coming here, our 'friendly' receptionist gave you her usual scolding, and now you're forced to sit with me. Sucks, right?"

Geneva's lips curled. "Yeah."

"But you know what? That's not why you're mad. I'm guessing it's him."

Closing her eyes, Geneva released a long sigh. "I just want to get my abortion and get out of here, okay?"

"You doing this to spite him? Are you mad because he won't assume responsibility? Did you even tell him?"

"If I tell you, will you let me do what I need to do?"

"Probably."

"I'm not doing this because I'm mad. I just got involved with the wrong person. And I really thought I could keep this baby, but I can't."

"What's stopping you?"

"Everything. Work. Money. Responsibilities. I don't have any family here. There's no one that could help me."

"Not even the baby's father?"

"No."

"Why's that?"

Geneva tightened her lips.

"I'm sorry," said the counselor. "Did he pass away?"

"You could say that. . . ."

The little girl wore a pink shirt with a Barbie logo printed on the breast. Wielding her trauma shears, Vivas cut the shirt straight up the middle.

Doe lowered his ear to the girl's mouth, which, along with her nose, appeared clear of soot. Basic CPR: listen for breath sounds, try to feel them on your ear, and look at the patient's chest for movement.

Nothing in all three areas.

He listened through his stethoscope. No sounds. He checked the girl's neck for a carotid pulse.

Yes! A rapid, bounding pulse.

Wait a minute. Shit! That's mine.

Focusing all of his senses toward the girl and concentrating more intently than he had in a long time, Doe waited several seconds. No pulse. "She's in full arrest."

•   •   •   •

Geneva entered the cold exam room with its pale blue walls, white cabinets, and little biohazard trash bins. As the nurse had instructed, she removed her clothes and slipped into the gown. She sat on a table covered with white sanitary paper that stuck to her skin. The nurse entered and said she was going to draw blood. Then she would need a urine sample. She handed Geneva a plastic cup.

A high school kid had once come for a "ride along" with Doe and Vivas because he was thinking about becoming a firefighter and especially liked the medic side of the job. Strangest string of coincidences had occurred that day. They had received seven calls during the ten hours the kid had ridden with them, and every patient had been under the age of twelve. One of them had been a nine-year-old boy who had been struck by a pickup truck. The boy coded en route, and Doe had been unable to resuscitate him. During that day, Vivas had been fairly diplomatic with their visitor, as had Doe, but by the end, Doe wanted nothing more than to be rid of him. Those young patients had taken their toll. You did not want to see mostly innocent kids in pain, kids who one moment were tossing around a Frisbee and the next were lying in the back of your rescue with their heads caved in and their faces ripped half off. And the crying, all that crying as you tried to start a line and tried to comfort them while a high school kid sat behind you, bug-eyed and chomping on gum.

"Kimberly? I'm here for you. I'm right over here. Daddy's right over here. You gotta fight. Don't give up. Don't you give up, honey."

Vivas already had a pediatric bag valve mask ready to go. She turned on the oxygen, then positioned herself behind the child, placing the girl's head between her knees. She set the mask over the girl's mouth and nose, then held the seal by encircling the mask with her thumb and first two fingers. She hooked her little and ring fingers under the girl's chin to keep it elevated and avoid a loss of seal. She began to hyperventilate the child, keeping the bag between her free hand and her thigh to ensure a consistently high volume of oxygen.

Meanwhile, Gomez performed chest compressions. Although the treatment sector officer did not say a word to Vivas, Doe could tell that criticism was balanced on the end of her tongue. The heat between the two women billowed in waves.

Two hours earlier, Doe would have given anything for a call like this one, but as he shifted beside Vivas, scope in the left hand, ET tube in the right, it all seemed very, very wrong.

Geneva grimaced as the nurse stuck her with the needle, then loosened the tourniquet. "That wasn't so bad, right?"

"I'm hoping I'll say that after the whole thing's done."

"You will, honey. Don't worry, you will. . . ."

"Ready?" Vivas asked.

Doe nodded. "Go!"

She removed the bag valve mask and pulled away.

Gomez continued her compressions until the very last second, then held up so Doe could work.

He assumed Vivas's place behind the girl, inserted the

blade into the right side of the girl's mouth, swept her tongue to the left, then visualized the cords without putting pressure on her teeth. He held his breath and inserted the tube.

Doctor Ratas came into the exam room, his gaunt face and tiny eyes anything but comforting. He donned a pair of latex gloves over his powdery hands. "Ms. Bowers? I'm Doctor Ratas. I'd like to do a pelvic exam before we begin. Just lie back and place your feet in the stirrups."

The father's voice pierced the hum of choppers and diesel engines. "Come on, Kimberly! Wake up! You can do it!"

With the tube in place and thanking God that the girl's throat had not been burned, Doe accepted the bag valve mask from Vivas and attached it to the end of the tube. He began ventilations while Vivas listened to the girl's chest. "Breath sounds bilaterally," she said, then opened a Veni-gard, the tape used primarily for securing IV catheters that she liked to use on ET tubes as well. She finished that task, then took over on the bag.

Gomez had already stuck one of the cardiac monitor's pancakelike electrodes on the girl's chest, over the heart. Doe helped her roll the girl so that she could place the other electrode, the negative pad, near the center of the girl's back and a little higher than the front pad. He turned on the monitor and immediately recognized the chaotic pattern.

"She's in v-fib," he cried.

"C'mon people, let's work her," ordered Gomez.

Vivas glared at being given a needless order. Of course they'd work her. After releasing the bag, she sat up, making sure no part of her touched the girl.

Doe's stricken gaze went to the monitor, where the words DELIVER SHOCK glimmered on the display.

Geneva shivered as the doctor examined her. His movements were abrupt, painful. She winced.

Finished, he peeled off his gloves. "You're a little further along then we thought, but that shouldn't be a problem. You understand what's going to happen now?"

"Yes, I do."

"We'll inject you with a painkiller. You'll feel a wave of comfort wash over your body."

Geneva doubted that the drug would remove all her pain.

The girl weighed about twenty kilograms, meaning Doe would hit her the first time with a forty-joule shock.

"Clear!" Doe announced, then pushed the shock button.

The girl jolted.

They waited several seconds.

"Still in v-fib," said Vivas, who had resumed her ventilations and now checked for a carotid pulse. She shook her head.

"Hit her again," Gomez said.

Doe gave the treatment sector officer a look, then cranked up the setting to eighty joules. "Clear!"

C'mon, sweetheart. You know you don't want to die. You've got your whole life. Your dad's right here. He's right here for you. He's right here. . . .

•   •   •

"You'll just feel a sting," said the nurse. "Same little pain as before.

Geneva's breath grew rapid. She smelled alcohol. Crinkled her nose.

The doctor pushed over a cart with all kinds of tubes and hoses and medical equipment hanging over its sides. He looked bored.

"Still in v-fib," Vivas said, then swore as she jerked her hand off the bag.

Doe reached once more for the shock button. "Clear!"

For a second—or it could have been a year—Doe felt the weird sensation of stepping outside himself.

He now stood over the scene, looking down and watching himself shock the little girl.

She lay there, shirtless, electrode on her chest, beautiful hair splayed across the backboard.

He turned his head, saw the father for the first time, the man's face twisted into an indistinguishable blur by Doe's stress.

Vivas shifted her gaze with underwater slowness as Doe lifted his finger from the button.

He eyed the monitor. His jaw fell slack.

Dr. Ratas muttered medical babble to the nurse. Turned on a beeping instrument. Turned on another one that made a gurgling, sucking noise. The lights over him seemed to grow brighter, to throb in time with Geneva's pulse, to nearly blind her in a glowing orb whose heat made it harder to breathe.

She trembled, clutched the table.

The nurse advanced with the needle.

"Okay," Vivas said, relief flooding her expression. "She converted. Bradycardic. Got a good pulse."

Though the little girl's heart beat less than sixty times per minute, a condition known as bradycardia, Doe was thrilled by the change. If she had not converted, she most certainly would have died right then, right there.

Little person. Little coffin.

The last thing Doe wanted to do was call SFMC and have the girl pronounced right in front of her father; he knew the scene that would produce.

"All right, so she converted?" Gomez asked. "You're out of here."

They lifted the backboard onto the stretcher, placed the cardiac monitor and airway bag between the girl's legs, then strapped her in. Her father would probably follow in a police cruiser. According to Gomez's orders, Doe, Vivas, and Cannis would ride in the patient compartment. Avalty would drive.

The elderly woman had already been hauled off by Troft and his partner. Doe seriously doubted that the other medics had successfully resuscitated her.

"She was still asystole when they loaded her," said Vivas as they pushed the stretcher toward the rescue. "No way she'll make it."

They reached the rear doors and braced the stretcher as its legs folded up. A familiar pain stabbed the small of Doe's back. He grimaced, told himself, *You've lifted way too many of these.*

Avalty ran to the cab and jumped in as Doe and the

others stepped up into the compartment. Gomez shut the doors. Doe got on the intercom and told Avalty to hold up so they could start a line.

In the meantime, Vivas kept her ventilations rapid and even. Doe knew that by the time their shift ended, she would complain of soreness in her knuckles; that discomfort should be a reminder that she had helped save a life.

Though Doe knew Paul Cannis only in passing, he had heard that the medic was a sharp operator. Cannis proved the rumors true by immediately checking the girl's arms for veins. As expected, he did not find access and began tearing open packages for intraosseous infusion—a way to establish an IV in pediatric patients by inserting a needle into the patient's leg, through the bone, and into the marrow. Fluids and drugs administered that way quickly entered the circulatory system.

Cannis readied saline solution, an IV administration set, a special Baxter Jamshidi intraosseous needle with stylet, a syringe with 5 cc of normal saline, antiseptic swabs, gauze pads, and tape. He faced Doe, his expression nearly blank. "It's your rescue."

"Thanks." Doe positioned himself on the bench seat, then palpated the girl's left leg, feeling kneecap and moving down to detect a little bump on her shin bone, just below her knee. He measured two finger breadths below the bump. If he measured wrong, the needle could penetrate a growth plate behind the bump, and that was, in two words, not good.

He accepted an iodine swab from Cannis, rubbed concentric circles on the girl's leg, then did likewise with an alcohol swab. He took the big needle, removed the sheath, and twisted it to adjust the depth. Now came the fun part.

Balancing the needle at a ninety-degree angle from the joint, he inserted it and, using a boring motion, continued deeper. Though the rescue's engine drowned out the usual soft pop, Doe felt a lack of resistance and knew he was in.

After removing the stylet, he attached the syringe and attempted to draw bone marrow to verify the needle's placement. If he failed, he would try flushing the needle with the 5 cc of normal saline. Thankfully, the marrow appeared.

"Nice stick," said Cannis as he handed Doe the IV tubing.

Doe connected the tube, opened the clamp, then secured the needle by turning the needle guard clockwise until the flange was in contact with the girl's skin. He and Cannis then used gauze pads and tape to finish securing the site.

"Let's get some lidocaine on board," Doe said, then spoke into the intercom. "All right, Avalty. Let's whistle her in."

As the rescue pitched into gear, Cannis opened the drug box. He prepped a syringe with 100 mg of lidocaine, which would raise the fibrillation threshold and reduce the development of v-fib. Doe pinched the IV line, took the syringe, and injected 20 mg of the lidocaine bolus into an IV port. That finished, he reached for the radio while Cannis took the girl's pressure, reported it, and continued monitoring.

"SFMC, Rescue Ten."

"Go, Ten," answered a breathless Dr. Joanna Boccaccio after several moments of dead air.

"En route to your facility with a five-year-old female, ALS unstable fire victim. Patient was found unconscious, unresponsive, with no obvious signs of burns to facial area or airway. Initial rhythm was v-fib. BLS procedures initiated. Patient intubated with good bilateral BS and bag-assisted with one hundred percent O_2 at a rate of 20. Patient shocked once at 40. No change in v-fib. Repeated at 80. No change. Repeated at 80 and got a conversion to sinus brady at a rate of 50 with good pulses. Intraosseous line established. Gave her 20 lido, IV. Vital signs are BP 60 palp, pulse now 70, respirations still assisted at 20 via BVM. Pupils midpoint and equal. Updated ETA: four minutes. Any questions or orders?"

"Negative, Ten. We'll be waiting for you."

The rescue cut sharply to the left, throwing Doe into the overhead cabinets. He caught himself, then found a spot on the bench seat. "Don't do that again," he admonished Avalty.

Vivas cringed. "Kid doesn't get to drive the rescue too often," she said to Cannis.

"I can tell." Cannis eyed the little girl. "Guess they'll get her into a hyperbaric chamber, right?"

"Yeah," Doe replied. "Tell you what, she's giving me a good scare."

"She is?" Vivas asked, eyes widening.

"Yeah. Wanna know something weird? For a second back there, it felt like a movie—you know, where you're watching everything around you and so much is going on that you just can't take it all in? Well, I'm there, about to shock her the third time, and then I'm watching myself, and I see this kid's father. And deep down I'm thinking whether at that moment I'd rather be me or that father, because the pressure's killing me, and all he has to do is stand there and watch."

"That is weird," said Cannis. "You're weird."

"So who would you rather be?" asked Vivas.

Doe thought about it. "I don't know."

A be drove his pike pole into a wall just outside the large kitchen with a center island. The Sheetrock gave, and he checked to make sure no fire simmered within the wall. It felt good to be out of his mask and air pack, but his shoulders still ached. Behind him, Savage probed an exterior wall with her sledgehammer. Still more firefighters inspected the second floor. Once you had put out all visible signs of a structure fire, you always followed up with an "overhaul" to make sure no flames were hiding from you within a wall or attic or closet. You did not leave a scene until you were absolutely certain.

"Know what, Abe?" Savage said. "This was one hell of a nice house. Half-million, easy, with probably a hundred grand in furniture. Too bad we couldn't save much. Weird, though. You take this house, you put it way up north in some rural town, and it goes for a hundred and thirty K, which is like almost affordable. I used to dream about owning a house like this."

"Property values in Pakistan are pretty high, too," Abe answered. "My parents can afford only an apartment right now. And I'm paying nearly a grand a month for my little dump."

"Well, there he is," cried Lieutenant Martinez, who had come by in the squad to check on his engine and rescue crews. He picked his way up to Abe and let loose a hearty slap on Abe's shoulder. "Dammit it, son. If you're not giving Station Nine good press, I don't know who is. I'm guessing your picture will be in the paper, and you'll be all over the news tonight. Station Nine poster boy. I love it." He squeezed Abe's neck and chuckled.

"I didn't join to become famous," Abe answered, squirming under all the teasing.

Martinez laughed again. "Well, you ain't here for the money."

Abe's tone grew serious. "So how is she?"

"She was doing a heck of a lot better when they loaded her than when you found her."

"And the grandmother?"

The lieutenant averted his gaze. "That's one I think we'll lose."

"Anybody find an obvious cause?" Savage asked.

"Nope. But the son's been missing. Drummond talked to some of the neighbors, and they said the boy's pretty wild. Thought he might be taking drugs. Grandmother was telling one neighbor that she was afraid of him. Maybe that's why she and the daughter had locked their bedroom doors. Who knows?"

Savage struck a particularly violent blow with her sledgehammer, hacking off a three-foot-long hunk of

Sheetrock. "My question always is, Where are Mom and Dad when all of this bullshit is happening?"

"I heard Dad works for some kind of an import firm, and Mom's a VP of a title company."

"Business types who let Grandma take care of the kids," said Savage, backhanding sweat from her brow. "Grandma was way out of her league. With all their money, they should've hired a professional."

"Sounds like the son needs some serious disciplining rather than a nanny," Abe said.

Martinez nodded soberly. "So, Abe, I bet your new girlfriend's gonna be all hot and heavy for you tomorrow, eh?"

"Excuse me?"

"Come on, now. Old Fitzy told me all about her. Academic. Works in a bookstore. Likes to suck on necks. You guys had sex on the first date." He winked at Savage. "She said you were small."

Abe rolled his eyes. "I think that's sexual harassment."

"You're probably right," Martinez said, heading for the staircase. "Wish someone would sexually harass me. The wife's been pissed off for two weeks."

"Because you keep coming in on your days off," said Savage.

"Yeah, but she's a firefighter. She knows the drill."

Savage waved her index finger. "I'm saying this because I care. If you don't get yourself a life outside of the job, you'll self-destruct like old Timmy and Bell did."

"I know it, Steph. And you'll be right behind me."

•   •   •

At six-forty-five, the fire marshal arrived to begin her investigation. She received a report from Drummond that included information on injuries, speculation on causes of the fire, and even the estimated cost of repairing the damage. She spoke briefly with Drummond and Martinez, asked Savage a few questions, then ventured into the house.

After taking off their bunker gear, Abe and Savage began the anticlimactic task of cleaning and storing their equipment. Still sweating through a fine layer of soot on his face and neck, Abe could not wait to hop into the shower. The adrenaline rush left him hungry, thirsty, and exhausted.

Before he could open the rescue's door, a reporter stopped him, and Abe did his best to articulate what had happened while blinking against the cameraman's powerful light.

"My partner and I found the grandmother, but the floor collapsed, and we couldn't get to her. Another crew came up from the first floor and—"

"Tell us about the little girl," the reporter said, her tone all but screaming her impatience.

"We found her in a closet. When there's a fire, little kids hide under their beds or in their closets. I know they teach 'em fire safety in school, but some of them don't remember—"

"So you found her in the closet and brought her out?" asked the reporter.

"That's right."

"Did you have to battle your way through flames or maybe break down a wall? Did that caved-in floor give you any trouble?"

Abe smiled. "I just walked out. Smoke was still pretty thick, but I could see enough."

"Cut," she yelled to her cameraman. "Mister—what is it—Kashmiri?"

He nodded.

She extended her hand. "Thanks a lot. Appreciate it." She whirled to her cameraman and spoke in hushed tones.

"I don't think she liked me," Abe said to Savage as he climbed into the cab.

"Abe, how can I say this? You should have embellished the tale."

"I got that feeling from her. But I don't want everyone seeing me lie on TV."

"Why not? Presidents do it."

He eased away from the curb. "Right."

"You watch. When your interview appears, she'll do a voice-over with something like . . . 'and firefighter Abe Kashmiri of Valley Station Nine battled his way through this intense blaze to pull a small child from the clutches of certain death.' "

"Wow! I did?"

"Yeah. And pretty soon you'll start believing the lie yourself because it'll become too embarrassing to tell the truth. What drives me really nuts is when we got the fire breathing down our necks and we do something heroic and they ignore us. I damn near died pulling this old man out of his apartment. Anchorman says one resident was rescued and one firefighter was injured. No names. No interview. That's it." She took up the mike. "Valley, Rescue Nine.

"Nine, Valley."

"Nine on the air and returning to quarters."

"Copy, Nine."

"Hey, take us back up this street, but go real slow."

Abe turned his head and found her staring past him, through his side window. "What?"

"I wanna see if we can find my cell phone."

"You kidding? Some kid already found it. He's run up a thousand-dollar bill calling those porno lines."

"That's what I'm afraid of."

"Did you leave it on?"

"I think so."

Abe unclipped his own phone and tossed it to her. "I'll look for it. Give yourself a call."

She brightened at the idea and quickly dialed. "Hello? Who is this? No. *Who* is this? Rafey? Listen, Rafey, I'm the owner of that phone you got in your hand. Why don't you do me a favor and come back to the corner where you found it? I'll give you twenty bucks." She paused. "That's not enough? How old are you? Fifteen? And you want eighty bucks? For God's sake, the phone ain't even worth that much. And you know what? After I turn off the service and report the ID, that phone ain't gonna be worth jack. So just show up, and you'll get your twenty bucks. No, I'm not paying any more." Another pause. "Listen, you punk, you use that phone and I'll. . . . Hello? Hello?" Savage wound up, ready to pitch Abe's phone out the window.

He snatched it from her. "Don't you dare."

She sat there a few seconds, just breathing. "Oh, God," she finally said. "What a pain in the ass this is gonna be. At least I know Donny's all right. That punk said he's been trying to call me. Hey, you mind if I use your phone again?"

Abe narrowed his gaze. "You keep the window rolled up, it's a deal."

Dr. Joanna Boccaccio guessed that before her shift ended, she would see or supervise twice as many cases as she did during any other night of the week. Saturdays were bad, but on Fridays, people exploded like cans of warm soda. Trouble was, they let out all that pressure and angst in the most unpredictable and often stupid ways:

Unsupervised little kid takes dive into bathtub.

Middle school kid designs pipe bomb, lights it, leans over for closer look.

College kid swallows piece of Lego on dare.

Eighty-year-old kid takes Viagra, makes love to pool filter, mangles unit.

Ninety-year-old kid comes in, complains of not feeling "right," is oblivious to ball point pen sticking straight out of his chest.

You had to do three things in your life: pay taxes, visit an emergency department at least once, and die (the latter hopefully not a result of either of the former).

As she finished downing a slice of pizza in her usual record time, Boccaccio wondered just how many overdoses, stabbings, beatings, and gunshot wounds would accompany the stupid human tricks, the minor cuts, the cases of flu, or the poorly disguised drug seekers who had been unable to meet with their "unlicensed pharmaceutical representatives" and now complained of migraines, lower back pain, and numerous allergies to meds—except Stadol nasal spray, a favorite that would provide them with instant narcotic relief sans an injection or pills. She also wondered just how long the wait would become and just how many patients would end up seated on the floor near the triage nurse's room.

One particular Friday night a mother, father, and their two kids had come in. The mom had had their younger daughter a week before and was complaining of vaginal bleeding. They had taken a brand-new baby out into the cold night air, and the ED waiting room had been so full that they had been forced to take "tile seats," near the doors. That little child was in the cold and surrounded by people with hacking coughs. Boccaccio had seen limbs torn off, skulls so fractured that they crunched when you touched them, burns so severe that you could not tell the affected area had belonged to a human. An intestinal fortitude born during her residency allowed her to look numbly on such horrors and think only about immediate treatment. But seeing a brand-new baby sitting out in the cold? That was a sight she could not bear. She made sure the family waited no more than a couple of minutes.

One of the first-year residents, a twenty-eight-year-old Puerto Rican woman named Linda Lopez, stepped outside and came jingling over, her white coat's pockets stuffed with small medical guides, sutures, sunglasses, a little red reflex hammer, and other items she thought she needed to carry. Boccaccio envied her innocence.

"Hey, Linda. Need me?"

"Yes, I do, Dr. Boccaccio."

Her nervous tone sparked Boccaccio's curiosity. They went inside, crossed to the nurses' station.

And there stood Boccaccio's mother and that . . . that Drew guy, appearing as touristy as humanly possible in matching Universal Studios T-shirts and jeans.

"Linda," Boccaccio growled.

"Sorry. She didn't want me to say anything."

Wearing a broad, nothing-is-wrong grin and throwing up her arms, "Mom" came forward. "Joanna, sweetheart, you wouldn't believe what we've seen and done." The hug came before Boccaccio could avoid it. "It's so good to be back."

Boccaccio's gaze met Linda's, then Charti's. Both jerked their heads away and found sudden interest in the floor. "Mom, what are you doing? I'm really busy right now."

"Too busy to see your mother? I heard you were outside eating pizza." She broke the embrace. "I can never get enough of you in your white coat. You've never stopped playing doctor, eh?" She eyed Drew, then chuckled.

Trembling, Boccaccio swept her gaze around the emergency department. She considered taking her mother outside, into the waiting room, then nixed the idea. Mom would only play it up for the audience. Boccaccio saw that a patient was just leaving Exam Three, so she ushered Drew and her mother inside and closed the door.

"Mom, you just take off and don't even call me? Your luggage is still sitting at my place. I don't know what's been going on with you, but I just . . . I don't know. . . ." Boccaccio massaged her sore eyes.

"I didn't think you gave a shit. So I didn't call."

"But you show up here? Don't you realize that—"

"That what? That you don't have time for me? I realize that. I just wanted to see it for myself."

"I'm a doctor, for God's sake. I have a job to do. Why can't you wait until I get off? We'll sit down, and we'll talk."

"Sorry, but we'll be on an airplane by the time you get off. We have a hotel room. I just wanted to get the key from you so we can get our luggage. That's all."

"Where were you yesterday? We could've had the whole day together. Why'd you have to run away?"

"I didn't run away, Joanna. I gave you a break. I was right when I said that you hate me. I just have to learn to live with that. It's okay now. You have your own life." She faced Drew. "Get the key. I'll meet you in the car."

"Mom, wait."

"There's nothing else to discuss, Joanna. Good-bye."

Wringing her hands, Boccaccio watched her mother leave, then shook her head at Drew. "I'm at a total loss. I don't know what she wants from me. I don't even know how to act around her, what to say without getting her pissed. It's crazy. Just crazy."

"I thought maybe we come and make everything perfect for you. But maybe it's not good," said Drew with a pout. "Your mother, she good woman. She love you very much. All she did was talk about you."

"How long have you been with her?"

"Maybe five months."

"Are you living together?"

He winced before nodding.

"I don't know how I did it, but I managed to live with her until I went away to school. I could never live with her now. Not the way she is. How do you do it? Why?"

"Your mother, she very strong woman. That why I love her, I guess. And she want to feel young. That what she want. That what I want to make her feel."

"Sounds like you're doing a good job. And I'm sorry about what happened at my apartment. That touchy-feely thing is just not me. I should feel happy that Mom's found someone, but now I'm feeling sorry for you."

"Don't feel like that. Your mother a sensitive person. She get hurt. That why she go quick, tell me get the key, I'll be in the car. It not easy. But for love, you do it. Nobody perfect, right?"

"Yeah, but what am I supposed to do? I think my mother needs some major therapy."

"Maybe. I talk to her. But you, you are most important person in her life. That why she so angry with you. She want you to make her feel young, too. But maybe when she see you, she feel old."

"So I shouldn't see her? Is that what you're saying? Should I wear a mask? Make myself look older? Don't you see? That's sick. My mother's making me feel ashamed of who I am. I shouldn't feel guilty that I'm a doctor and she's not."

Charti opened the door and stuck his head inside. "Sorry, Dr. Boccaccio. We got another trauma coming in, and Dr. Fuloska is with those two GSWs and Dr. Masaki is with that skateboarder."

"Be right there."

"Maybe I come back later for the key?" asked Drew.

"Know what? I'm tired of my mother calling the shots. You tell her that if she wants her luggage back, you guys will have to catch a later flight and pick it up when I get off. Why don't you come to my apartment at about nine-thirty?"

"Your mother, she be angry, but I think this is good idea. She can't go back to Vegas like this."

"Good. Maybe I'm playing a little power game with her, but maybe I have to. Come on. I'll show you the way out." As she did, Boccaccio called to Charti, "What do we got?"

"Seventy-one-year-old female. Multiple blunt trauma to the head. She's from Woodbridge."

"Another one? We're having some bad nursing home weather."

"At least they come in threes. And she's number three. Rescue's backing in now."

"Just go through that door," Boccaccio told Drew. "You'll wind up back in the waiting room. See you tomorrow."

He gave a curt nod. "Yes, Joanna. See you tomorrow."

21

Fire Station Nine
Studio City
Friday, 11:04 P.M. Pacific Time

"**A**ll right, keep quiet," hollered Fitzy. "Here comes our boy again."

Eight firefighters sat in recliners, hands laced behind their heads, gazes riveted on the TV.

The reporter uttered the words "Abe Kashmiri of Valley Station Nine."

A wall-rattling cheer erupted.

On the screen, Abe uttered all of two sentences before—as expected—the reporter took over and had him "braving the ferocity of a major house fire to bring out a young girl now in critical but stable condition at SFMC."

Savage stood behind the group, tanking down a root beer and trying to taste a Budweiser. She and Abe had gotten only two more calls after the fire. The first had been a domestic dispute. Guy had slapped around his wife, then fled the scene. The woman, an obvious alcoholic and IV drug user, had suffered a few bruises to her arms and neck but had refused to press charges or receive medical attention. She wouldn't even allow Savage to take her blood pressure. The second call had come from the Sportsman's Lodge up the Boulevard. A forty-eight-year old man had been hit in the eye with a tennis ball. Pretty standard and forgettable run. In fact, the only call that would stick with Savage was the fire. Days and people blurred into an amorphous weight growing heavier after each shift. She barely remembered the call to pick up Gena Solaris's kid, but one of those trashy tabloids Fitzy liked to read lay on a nearby end table with the kid's mug splattered across it: SOLARIS'S SON IN TROUBLE AGAIN. The tabloid was more timely than its editors knew. Savage could hand them some serious dirt should she decide to violate patient confidentiality. But she felt so much pity for the kid that exploiting his misery would only heighten her own.

More news had come in regarding the fire. Martinez's brother-in-law worked as a VPD detective and had passed on the gossip. The police had eventually caught up with the missing son. He admitted to threatening his sister and grandmother but had flatly denied setting the blaze. The police had also questioned the boy's best friend, who had eventually broken under the pressure and had revealed that they and one other boy had been responsible for the recent rash of Dumpster fires. You didn't need formal police training to put that one together. The boy or boys had more than likely started the fire. Savage could only grind her teeth over a world where sons attempted to murder their sisters and grandmothers. She wished she could find solace in her own

Donny, but at the moment, his name stood squarely at the top of her shit list.

"Okay," began Lieutenant Martinez, rising from his recliner, along with everyone else except a bewildered Abe. "Mr. Kashmiri, we thought long and hard about a way to express our excitement over working with a firefighter of your caliber."

With that, the firemen reached between the cushions of their recliners, withdrew aerosol cans of whipped cream, held them at their crotches, and zeroed in on Abe.

Knowing that he would try to retreat, they had posted Savage in the rear. She set down her soda, came up behind his chair, seized his wrists, then pulled them back as the others opened fire.

A full symphony orchestra could never reproduce (or want to reproduce) the distinct "music" created by eight gurgling aerosol cans of whipped cream punctuated by the quavering soprano of a young man who had known too much glory. Not satisfied with just covering him in cream, all eight firefighters were determined to empty their aerosol cans. However, Abe wrenched free of Savage's grip and, wiping the white stuff from his eyes, swore and trudged up the stairs, toward the hood and showers beyond.

"You oughta give your vampire a call," yelled Fitzy. "I bet whipped cream is right up her alley." He mouthed his bottle, leaned on the nozzle. "Yeah! Sweet!"

Savage helped the others clean up, then waited another ten minutes or so before hauling herself upstairs. Abe had finished showering and now lay on his bunk, wearing a fresh golf shirt and uniform slacks. "That stuff burns your eyes," he said.

"You wanna call 911?"

"Might as well. We need someone to rescue us from our boredom."

The tones resounded. The siren rose.

"There's your someone," Savage yelled. "You sure you're not psychic?"

"Engine Nine, Rescue Nine. Engine Nine, Rescue Nine. MVA, Lankershim Boulevard, cross street Oxnard. VPD en route. ETA: one minute. Time out: twenty-three twenty-five."

Abe beat Savage onto the catwalk. He slid down the fire pole with the nonchalant grace of youth. Savage scowled at the unforgiving metal, climbed onto it, then dropped.

"Hey, Beast?" Tenpenney called from the other side of the apparatus floor. "Why don't you let Mr. Debonsville ride seat?"

"Mr. who?" Abe asked.

"You're riding seat," she said. "But I'm still chief medic on scene. Got it?"

"Cool. I'm tired of driving." Abe jogged around to the officer's side of the cab and pulled himself in.

Savage slid into the driver's seat, started the truck, then beat the engine down the driveway.

Abe put on his headset, regarded the call on the mobile data terminal, then waited until Savage had donned her own headset. "I get it now. Debonsville. He was a character on the same TV show as Solaris's mother."

"He was the paramedic who got castrated during a rescue," Savage said, deadpan.

•   •   •

Vivas and Doe had just finished listening to TRO Six
dispatch Engine Nine and Rescue Nine when they pulled
behind a Ralph's supermarket—not the one where
Vivas's mother worked, but a smaller store just a mile
north.

A VPD cruiser, its lights pulsing, sat in front of two
trailers backed up to a wide receiving dock. Beside the
dock was a pair of orange Dumpsters, their plastic doors
flopping open, a bare-chested, bearded man of fifty or
sixty standing inside the nearer one. The guy's blackened jean shorts hung loosely around his waist. Two
young police officers Doe recognized were speaking to
him, and a thin Hispanic man in his twenties stood up
on the dock, grinning awkwardly and wiping his hands
on his Ralph's apron.

"Hey, Jon," said Doe as he hit the pavement and
pulled on his latex gloves. "And Lou, you're back?
Thought you were taking off six weeks for that nose
job."

The hook-nosed cop snickered. "This is Roman ar-
chitecture, buddy. You don't mess with Rome."

"So what do we got?" Vivas asked through a yawn.

Officer Jon Gruger cleared his throat. "Receiving
clerk up there is unloading his trailer when he spots this
residentially challenged individual making an unauthor-
ized trash inspection."

"So what's the problem?" Doe asked. "He's eating
food out of the Dumpster, so he's making it less attractive to rats. Ralph's should be paying him for pest control service."

Gruger flashed an approving grin.

"That's pretty good, Doe, but he claims he's not eating the garbage," said Officer Lou Fabiothello. "He says he accidentally threw out a coupon for a free Big Mac."

"How are you doing, sir?" Doe asked, approaching the Dumpster but preparing to duck or dodge anything the guy might throw at him.

"I'm doin' shitty," the old man grumbled, then hunched over and tore open a plastic bag bloated with trash. "Can't find my fuckin' coupon."

"He's got a real nasty cut on his leg," said Jon, as Doe spotted the laceration, which ran from the man's knee down across his calf. "Think he cut it on one of those grape boxes in there. They got nails on them."

"Sir, why don't you come out and let us take care of that cut?" said Vivas. "If you do, I'll buy you one of those Big Mac combos."

He cocked his head so quickly that he probably pulled a muscle. "Ain't the fuckin' point. I lost the coupon, and now I gotta find it."

"But if my partner buys you the food, you won't need the coupon," said Doe. "If you're hungry and you don't have a place, we can get you to a shelter. But first we'll have to take you to the hospital to get that leg stitched up."

"I ain't goin' to no fuckin' hospital. Get the fuck outta here. Mind your own business."

Fabiothello sighed. "We can't do that, because you're trespassing. Those Dumpsters are being rented by the market. They're not yours. You don't belong in 'em. You gotta come out. Why don't you let us help you?"

"Fuck you."

"Well, I ain't jumping in there," said Fabiothello, regarding his partner and pinching his collar. "Eight bucks for dry-cleaning."

"What's your name?" Doe asked the old man.

" 'The fuck you care?"

"What's your name?"

"My name is Jesus Christ. I'm your lord and savior. And I'm a little busy. So don't fuck with me."

"Why's that coupon so important?"

He ripped open another bag and dumped out egg shells, empty milk containers, balls of stained paper towels. "Shut up."

"You didn't lose your coupon in there. We both know that. And your leg's gotta hurt. Why don't you come out?"

"You wanna be Mr. Fuckin' Nice Guy? Why don't you come in here and help me look for my coupon?"

"Touché," said Vivas. She leaned in close to Doe. "I don't think this guy is that nuts. I think he's just mad and maybe a little drunk. Why are you so mad, sir?"

"You're pretty fuckin' slow for an ambulance driver, Missy." He held up a plastic bag, letting its contents rain through the ragged hole he had torn. "I lost my fuckin' coupon, see?"

"You lose it tonight?"

He shook his head.

"When did you lose it?"

"I don't remember."

"Tell you what," said Doe, "we just did a call not too long ago, and I found a coupon for a free Big Mac."

The old man stumbled to the Dumpster's edge, swung up his good leg, and abruptly pulled himself out. He limped up to Doe, who considered taking a few steps in retreat, but his police buddies where right there, ready to step in. "You got my coupon? Show it to me."

"Come on," said Doe, shifting backward, his gaze never leaving the old man.

As they started off, Fabiothello grabbed the old guy by one wrist while Gruger took the other. Surprisingly, the guy seemed unfazed as he was cuffed.

"Guess I'm riding," said Fabiothello with a boyish pout.

"Uh-huh," Gruger replied. "Just give me a sec for the hold form. You still don't want to go to the hospital, is that right, Mr. Christ?"

"I wanna see my fuckin' coupon is what I want."

"Like I said, give me a sec for the hold form."

Doe pulled open the rescue's rear doors, then helped Fabiothello guide the old man into the patient compartment. Vivas shifted their equipment off the stretcher, unbuckled the straps, and helped Doe as they guided the man down, onto his side. Once again, he seemed strangely more cooperative, his gaze somewhat distant.

"Cut's not too bad," said Doe. "Already stopped bleeding. You'll need stitches. I'm gonna bandage you for the ride, okay? Do you know what hospital you want to go to?"

"Where's my coupon?"

"Soon as I'm done, I'll give it to you."

Vivas glared at Doe as she handed him some 4x4 bandages. The old man would probably explode once he learned the truth. Doe wondered how long he could stall the guy; hopefully, until they reached an ED.

Fabiothello moved to the captain's chair. He knew the drill. "Another exciting ride along."

"We'll take him to VGH," Doe told Vivas, then began treating the man's leg.

Outside the rescue, Gruger gave Vivas the hold form. They now had permission to take the patient to the hospital against his will. Once there, he would be sutured and released. Doe seriously doubted that the market would press charges. Most of those store managers were happy to just be rid of the "bums." They got serious only with repeat offenders. Doe wondered how long it would be until the old man found his way to another Dumpster.

With the bandage in place, Doe asked the man if he was feeling pain anywhere else. No? Good. "Do you mind if I get your pulse and blood pressure?"

"Might as well. You're not gonna show me my coupon because you don't have it."

"Truth is, buddy, I don't."

"That's okay. I've been lookin' for it for fifteen years. No fuckin' medic's gonna find it."

Vivas shut the rescue doors, and a moment later they pulled away from the receiving dock. Doe remained quiet as he got a pulse (84), pulse ox (96), blood pressure (128/82), and respiration (20). The guy even let him perform a blood glucose test. Everything came back in the acceptable range. He alerted the receiving facility, then replaced the mike. For the first time since encountering the man, Doe realized that he had yet to lose his patience (small miracle). He usually had little tolerance for these guys and spoke to them in his most condescending tone.

"Hey, sir?" Doe asked. "You doin' okay?"

"Name's Smith. Mr. Smith. Smith the fuckin' bum."

"That's my last name, too," Doe said with a mild grin as Fabiothello nudged him. "And a few women have used the fuckin' bum part, too. So, you okay?"

"These fuckin' cuffs are killing me."

"We'll get 'em off when we get there. Just try to relax."

"You think I'm outta my fuckin mind, don't you?"

"Who cares what I think?"

"That coupon was the last thing she gave me. And I fuckin' lost it. I LOST IT!"

Doe stood and leaned over the old man, whose face had flushed and whose forehead crinkled in agony. "Take it easy."

"Daddy, here's that coupon for your lunch tomorrow. I promise to bring you back something from the mountains, okay? Okay, sweetheart. You take good care of your mother. I love you. Bye."

After bracing himself with a deep breath, Doe asked, "You talking about your daughter?"

"You mean my *dead* daughter. And my *dead* wife."

"I'm sorry."

"You don't know what you have until you lose it. I used to think that was just a fuckin' saying."

"You can talk to some social workers at the hospital. They can really help you out."

"Unless they can find my coupon, they can't do a fuckin' thing."

Fabiothello stifled a snort. "Hey, Smitty? You ever think of trying the Sunday paper? It's full of coupons and less smelly than a Dumpster."

"I've tried. It ain't ever there."

Doe resumed his seat and attempted to dial into the

old man's reasoning. Maybe losing the coupon meant that he hadn't cared enough about his daughter. Or maybe he thought that if he found it, he could redeem it for a life free of guilt and misery. Maybe using that coupon would allow him to make peace. It all made a weird and painful kind of sense.

"They died on the mountain. Got run right off the road by a bunch of fuckin' college kids," the old man blurted out. "You fuckers don't know what real pain is."

"Maybe I haven't felt it like you," Doe said. "But I know what it is. I see it every goddamned shift. And I'm supposed to go home and pretend the world's all hunky-dory. But it ain't. There's people like you in it. And that's just the way it is."

"Well, don't let me ruin your fuckin' night," he shot back.

"Trust me. You won't. I'm too busy lookin' for my own coupon."

Both drivers involved in the MVA to which Savage and Abe and had been dispatched had suffered "acute checkbook pains" and had been promptly fitted with cervical collars because opportunity had knocked, and they were comin' a-suin'. Abe knew that Savage had worked many more fender benders than he had, that when she checked the eyes of some patients involved in such accidents, she would not describe them as PEARRL: Pupils Equal and Round, Reactive to Light. Their eyes were GREED: Green, Round, Equal, Eclipsed by dollar signs, and Devoid of conscience. Surprisingly, she did not act as disgusted as Abe had expected. She had even joked and flirted with one of the drivers, who was an actor on a soap opera that she watched.

After dropping off pretty boy TV star, Abe bought a couple of frozen yogurts from SFMC's main cafeteria. Then he and Savage stood outside the rescue, spooning down cold heaven.

"Damn, it's after midnight," Savage suddenly said, glimpsing thin clouds frayed by the crescent moon's pale glow.

"Why's that important?"

"This day went fast."

"This week."

She nodded. "I bumped into Boccaccio. She said that the parents and daughter we picked up Wednesday still ain't out of the woods. Mom's the worst off. The boy's doing a lot better, though. I bet the sister we met is going crazy. I know if Donny were up there, they'd be sedating me." Her gaze drifted off. "It's hard being so far from him."

"Tell me about it."

"So you don't have anyone here, do you?"

"No, but somehow I've been okay. I guess my screwed-up life is just waiting to happen. Sometimes I worry, you know? You're supposed to have like a support structure. I know what I have to do to remain sane, but I think you still need a place you can go and get clean and forget about all this."

"But we both go home to our empty apartments."

Abe gave a weak nod.

"We're kind of like trauma patients ourselves," she said. "We do a lot better when we have moral support from our families."

"Sometimes, when I'm home, I keep thinking about work. It doesn't feel like off time. It feels like I'm *wasting* time."

"And sometimes when you're here. . . ."

"I just want to be home and only thinking about work."

"Your new girlfriend should be distracting you a little bit. That always helps."

"Yeah, but it makes me worry even more. I mean, just look at our crew. Only a few good marriages. Mostly divorced people with ulcers and every other stress-related problem. I'll probably mess it up with her. I can just feel it."

"You got choices, Abe. You choose to let this shit get to you and run your life—or you chose to control it. Maybe you find religion or some other way to reconcile. And you just go on. I know my divorce happened for a lot of reasons. The job was one of them, but it wasn't the big issue. More like my husband's job—or lack of one. Still, I was wrong in a lot of ways. Everyone says you have to work at a relationship. And you nod, but you don't do anything about it. For a while there, I thought I could fix anything—even my marriage. But some things are impossible. I once heard a doctor say that when God puts his hand on a patient, that's when you remove yours."

"Believe that?"

"I've seen enough to make me believe."

"I didn't think you were religious."

She chuckled under her breath. "I'm your garden variety of backsliding Christian. And your typical veteran medic, fallen paragod with your stress-related problems and failed marriage. I guess the real question to ask is if I'm happy."

"Well?"

"Yeah, I guess I am. I told you I'm doing this because I want to be remembered. I already know I am." She scooped out the last of her yogurt. "You?"

He sighed. "I'm sort of happy. I still wish my parents were here. But if they were, they'd be trying to talk me out of doing this. If I could show them what I do, maybe they would be proud. I don't know."

"Well, they might show it in strange ways, but you got a family right here who's impressed. And that's all I'm gonna say before I turn you into a paragod. Now let's move. My left breast is aching. We're about to get a call. . . ."

22

Charti stood by Trent Robertson's bed and watched him sleep. The heavy blackening around his eyes had faded a bit, and his lacerations were healing well, as would his skull fracture. He had strong vitals.

Sensing a presence, the boy stirred, opened his eyes to slits. "What time is it?"

"Just after eight in the morning. How're you feeling?"

"Little better. You're not gonna ask me what day and year it is or if I know where I am, are you?"

"Not if you know the answers."

"Like a million doctors have asked me the same stupid questions."

"You have a head injury. We have to make sure you're okay. If your injury gets worse, you might forget stuff. So we have to check."

"That's what one of the doctors said. And you know what I said? I said I was getting worse."

"Why?"

"Because everyone keeps asking me the same stupid questions and giving me a headache."

Charti grinned. *Clever boy.* "I'll try not to do that. So, you like your new room?"

"It's okay. How come they keep sending all these flowers?" His gaze flicked from one arrangement to another.

"You know why. They're supposed to cheer you up."

"My aunt says, Look, this is from your teacher, or this is from your principal, or this is from your den leader. I wish they'd send me a Gameboy."

"Maybe they will."

"I want a Gameboy. And I want to see my mom and dad and my sister."

"I know," Charti said in his most comforting tone.

"I had a dream that my mom died."

"It was just a dream."

"Know what? My mom told me that one time when her grandmother died, she had a dream about it, then it came true. That's pretty scary."

"It was just a dream. She'll be okay."

"So, Charti, how come you've been checking on me so much? I heard one of the nurses say it was weird or something. You're not weird are you? I know about child molesters. We learned about 'em at school."

He began to roll his eyes, thought better of it. "Believe me, I'm not a child molester. When I was younger, my family got into a car accident just like yours. My sister died. It was really hard. When I saw you come in, I remembered that. That's all. Just want to make sure you're okay."

"Did you cry when your sister died?"

"Yeah, I did."

"I don't wanna cry."

Charti eased closer to the bed. "Crying's okay. Sometimes it makes you feel better. And no matter what happens, you have to remember that it wasn't your fault and that you have a lot of people who love you."

"Why are you telling me this?"

"I guess, when it happened to me, I wanted someone to say that. No one ever did."

"How come?"

"I don't know. Maybe someone did, and I forgot. I just kept thinking it was my fault when it wasn't." He consulted his watch and sighed. "I have to go. Maybe I'll see you later."

"Hey, Charti? Would you check on my mom?"

"I sure will. See you."

Figuring he could steal another few minutes and slip up to the ICU, Charti headed quickly to the elevator. He rode up with a couple of people from housekeeping, then got off and found the mother's room.

Her bed was empty.

He frowned and hurried back to the nurses' station, where Nancy Rodriguez brightened in recognition. "You trying to get a job up here?" she teased.

"What happened to the woman in 5? Casey Robertson."

"You didn't hear? She coded about two hours ago. Didn't make it."

Charti seized the edge of the counter and stood there, fighting for breath.

"You all right?"

Had someone asked him a question?

"Hey, Charti? You okay?"

"Yeah . . . ," he muttered, then wandered away. "I'll, uh . . . I'll be okay."

Dr. Masaki had been the trauma surgeon working on Casey Robertson's case, so it was his job to inform the family that their loved one had passed on. However, Joanna Boccaccio predicted that at any moment, he would come down to the ED and, for a number of reasons, ask for her assistance. Anything could happen in that room. A family member could lunge at him for "failing to save" Mrs. Robertson. The news could drive someone to faint or become hysterical. At the very least, there would be a fit of crying, and Masaki, though an excellent surgeon, was not the warmest person working at SFMC. No, it was not a "cultural thing." He was simply a man who kept his emotions in check, perhaps too much so. Boccaccio had observed that his tone was not as sympathetic as it could be; he would probably ask her to do the talking, as he usually did when facing a large group.

Boccaccio had just finished giving Linda Lopez a few pointers on her suturing technique when Masaki showed up. "Joanna? I know you're about to get off, but do you have a few minutes?"

She left Lopez and a plumber who had lacerated his forearm, and followed Masaki into the hall. "Heard about your code."

His lips came together. "You know me. I'm always cautious. Never give the family any false hopes. Better to be the prophet of doom and be wrong. The father and daughter have finally come out of their comas. I really thought mom would. I felt pretty sure of that. I don't know why. It's very disconcerting."

"If you want me—"

"You know I do. Some doctors learn how to do this part of the job, and they do it well. I'm not sure I'll ever learn." His lips turned in a faint smile. "Maybe I'll have it mastered by the time I retire." He led her toward a private waiting room near the back of the department. A hospital security guard stood near the door.

"Has the family been called?"

"Yes. They were waiting for the husband's parents, and they just arrived. There are nine people in there."

"Not the largest crowd. We can do this, right?" she said, already nodding.

"Yes, we can." He opened the door.

Boccaccio took a deep breath and reached inside for a voice she reserved for such occasions, a gentle voice as clear as it was calming.

Two pairs of grandparents sat to Boccaccio's right, their expressions bleak as they reached for each other's hands and braced themselves. The mother's sister sat to Boccaccio's left, a ragged frame of a woman siphoned of life by her sibling's battle for the same. A well-dressed man with thinning gray hair and beard, presumably her husband, sat beside her and draped his arm over her shoulder. Three young boys, ranging in age from about five to ten, sat next to them and, seeing nothing special in the new visitors, returned to their computer games, thumbs jittering wildly.

Boccaccio crossed the room and took a seat at the far end, as did Dr. Masaki. "Good morning. Sorry to bring you all here so early. This is Dr. Joanna Boccaccio, one of our attending physicians."

"Hello," Boccaccio said, listening to her voice, adjusting the pitch and trying to steel herself against all those glassy eyes. "Unfortunately, we have some bad news. As I'm sure Dr. Masaki has been telling you, Casey suffered some very serious injuries in the accident, including a massive head injury. We've been doing everything we can for the past several days, but this morning she went into cardiac arrest. We did everything we could, but we couldn't bring her back. We're deeply sorry for your loss."

Even as Boccaccio had said "cardiac arrest," Casey's sister began sobbing loudly. The grandmothers lowered their heads onto their husbands' shoulders. The boys looked up from their games and frowned.

Boccaccio crossed the room and hunkered down beside the sister. "Ma'am, if there's anything at all you need from us, don't hesitate." She braced the sister's shoulder. The husband reached back and pulled several tissues from the box.

"Where is she now?" said one of the grandmothers through a rush of tears. "I want to see my daughter."

"That'll be fine," said Masaki, rising. "I'll have one of my residents escort you up. Once again, I'm deeply sorry for your loss." He exited quickly.

As she preferred, Boccaccio remained with the family

until the resident arrived. She answered the usual grim questions: Was she in any pain when she died? Was she conscious? Who was there? Why didn't she get any better?

The answers seemed less important to Boccaccio than the way she delivered them. The point was moot. The woman was dead. What those people really wanted was some reassurance that Casey Robertson had slipped comfortably and quietly from this Earth. The only consolation they had was the fact that Casey would be survived by her husband, daughter, and son. Of that much they could be certain.

"Hello, I'm Doctor Zarvina," said Masaki's resident, a bespectacled young man of twenty-seven who tiptoed into the room and scratched nervously at his crewcut. "I'm here to take you upstairs."

After bidding her farewells and reinforcing her condolences, Boccaccio escaped.

The damned tears fell as she pushed open the bathroom door. She had thought about that daughter up there who had just lost her mother. She had imagined that her own mother and Drew had gotten into an equally terrible car accident and that her mother had died while they were still angry at each other. She splashed a little cold water on her face, wiped it, then checked herself in the mirror. *Okay. Come on. Time to go home. Make peace. I can do this.*

Once she had gathered her purse and sweater, Boccaccio stopped at the nurses' station to say good-bye. Charti bid a somber farewell, then said a call had just come in for her. "It's that medic Isabel Vivas."

"Oh, damn. I forgot about her again." Boccaccio took the receiver. "Hello, Izzy?"

"Hey. Sorry about calling at the last minute. My brain really hurts. I'll have to cancel."

"That's okay. Another time."

"Hey, Doctor? I know it's kind of weird for us to socialize. I guess I just wanna say thanks for not being a snob."

"We're not all snobs, Izzy. Yeah, some of us have pretty high opinions of ourselves. I hope I'm never accused of that."

"Hope so, too. Thanks, Doctor. Take care."

Isabel Vivas hung up the phone in Fire Station Ten's dayroom, then told a preoccupied Doe that she was going home. Her partner barely acknowledged her as he sat in a recliner, his brow knitted in thought.

As usual, the ride back to her apartment was a nightmare, with rush hour traffic backing up and red light runners at nearly every intersection. At least her fog of exhaustion somewhat blinded her to the danger. Somehow, she navigated home, parked, and reached her apartment.

Mama was at work and Consuela at day care. Vivas would pick up the little gem at 2 P.M..

The phone rang as she stepped inside. "Hello?"

"Why you home so late?" asked Mama.

"Sometimes I'm late, okay?"

"They're gonna let me go home early today. So you come at three. Got it?"

"Okay, Mama."

"And there's a message on the machine for you. Why don't you listen to it?"

"I will. 'Bye."

With a long groan, Vivas scuffled into the bedroom and punched on the machine:

"Izzy, it's Manny," he began. "I don't want to get you upset tomorrow. I just want to pick up my daughter. That's all. Call me when you get home. You know the number. 'Bye."

She stared tiredly at the machine. "Yeah, I got your number."

As she fell back onto her bed, Vivas remembered a Thanksgiving dinner at her in-laws' house. Manny's mother had made some cutting remarks, and Manny had just sat there, silent.

Then she considered Consuela and how excited her daughter became every time she saw her father. Well, maybe that was because "Daddy" was your typical Sunday father who showered his kid with gifts to win her affection. Spending a day with Daddy always meant you got a surprise. Was Vivas's mother right? Did the child really need her father?

Vivas pulled herself from the bed, grabbed her little phone book from the nightstand drawer, and dialed her ex's work number. Another mechanic answered, told her to hold. Vivas listened to the echoing racket of power tools until her ex picked up. "Yeah, this is Manny."

"It's Izzy. What time you coming tomorrow?"

"Uh, say nine?" he asked, sounding surprised.

"Okay. I'll have her ready. Then when you bring her back, we're gonna make pasta. You can stay."

"You serious?"

"Manny, I'm not trying to get back. I just want our daughter to know that she has a family, a good one, even if we don't live together."

"Izzy, I think she already knows that. Maybe we're the ones who need the reminder."

"You're probably right. See you tomorrow."

"See you."

Vivas crawled back onto the bed, tore the pillow from beneath the bedspread, folded it in two, then lowered her weary head. A siren went off in the distance. She closed her eyes.

Boccaccio's mother shook her head angrily. "It's already nine-thirty. My legs are killing me. We've been waiting in this hall for nearly a half-hour."

"I told Drew nine-thirty," Boccaccio said, sliding her key into the lock.

"I hear it wrong," he said. "I think nine o'clock."

"Well, we're all here now." Boccaccio opened the door, trudged inside, then tossed her keys on the kitchen counter.

"So we'll just grab our bags and go," her mother said.

"Oh, no, you won't."

"We stay for little while," Drew suggested.

"Mom, go over there, sit down, and listen to me," barked Boccaccio, pointing at her sofa.

"If it'll get me my luggage . . . ," Mom huffed, waved her hands, then sat. "Yeah, my legs are really killing me."

"Ever think it's because of those heels?"

"I'm flying today. I want to look nice."

"Mom, you're fifty-seven. You wanna look nice? Let me dress you."

"Drew? Go in her bedroom and find our bags. I want to leave right now."

Boccaccio gave the young man a warning look that rooted him to his seat.

"Drew . . . ," Mom said more forcefully.

"Listen, Mom, I don't want to fight with you. But this is *not* normal behavior for a woman your age."

"There it is. You keep harping on my age. You can't accept the fact that your mother's a decent-looking broad at fifty-seven, or that a young man like Drew would find me attractive. You can't accept me for who I am, can you? You want to make me into something you like, the same way your father made you. Let me tell you something, Joanna. I'm very happy now. And you *won't* bring me down."

"Fine. If you're happy, that's great. But all of the lies . . . what about them? You say you told me you were coming, but you never did. You say you told me about your . . . *enhancements* . . . but you never did. You know you need therapy. You're just afraid to go."

"You hear that, Drew? The doctor has spoken. I should jump up right now and get a therapist on the phone so I can tell this overeducated person that I'm fucked up because my daughter doesn't approve of my happiness."

"Mom, why did you come here?"

"If you don't know that. . . ."

Boccaccio stiffened. "Tell me."

"Because I wanted to see you."

"But we've hardly spent any time together."

Her mother recoiled. "That's not my fault. I'm not the one working so much."

"I had a whole day off, but you ran away. You have to go back and analyze your behavior. It doesn't make sense. And the only reason I'm saying this is because I love you and I'm worried about you."

"You don't love me. And you can keep my fuckin' luggage. 'Bye." With surprising speed despite her heels, her mom crossed the living room and made it to the door.

"Mom, don't. . . ."

"Drew? Let's go." Her mother stomped into the hall.

"Joanna," Drew muttered as he rose to follow, "I'm so sorry."

"Wait," she said, then hurried into her bedroom and returned with their luggage. "Maybe you can talk to her. She needs help. She really does."

"I do what I can." He accepted the bags. "I wish you and her could make up."

"Not until she gets help. I just . . . I can't handle this right now. It's too much." She led him toward the door. He whispered good-bye and left.

Boccaccio's eyes grew sore as she looked absently around her apartment, appointed with the artifacts of a hard-fought life. She shouldn't feel bad about what she had become. She shouldn't feel bad that she couldn't save her mother. She shouldn't cry over the remnants of her childhood.

But she did.

• • •

"Who is it?"

"Me. Can you buzz me in?"

"Why should I?"

"Just because. . . ."

Long pause. Very long pause. Finally: "We need to make this quick. I'm getting ready for work."

The lock buzzed, and Doe grabbed the front door's handle. He arrowed straight for the stairwell. Geneva lived on the fifth floor, but to hell with it. Maybe the stairs would help him to shed some of his anxiety. He took them two at a time, listened to the thumping of his boots and his labored breath. One landing. Another. And another.

He reached her door, swallowed, and paused a moment more before knocking.

Her long face appeared in the crack, then she let him in with hardly a glance. "I'm doing my makeup," she said, tightening the sash on her bathrobe. "So you'll have to talk to me while I'm in the bathroom."

"That's all right. I'll sit. Give you a minute."

"Whatever."

Doe slid onto a barstool at a kitchen counter facing Geneva's living room. He laced his fingers, tapped his foot, then his glance wandered left, to the far end of the counter, where he spotted some Post-it notes on the back of an envelope. Scribbled on one was a phone number and the words VALLEY HEALTHCARE. DR. RATAS. ABORTION.

He seized the envelope and, nearly falling off the bar stool, headed for the bathroom. "Geneva?" The door stood half open. He pushed his way in. "What's this?"

"I don't believe it. You're going through my stuff?" she asked, applying mascara to her lashes.

"It was right there on the counter. What's this about an abortion?"

"What do you care?"

He grabbed her wrist. "Did you?"

"I'll say it again," she said, pulling free. "What do you care?"

"Oh, God." He fell back against the door frame. "I thought you decided to keep the baby. We couldn't even say the word abortion, remember?"

Her expression seemed odd, as though she were repressing a smile. Weird. "Maybe I didn't want to do it alone. So maybe I fixed the problem."

"Yeah. That's my fuckin' luck. I came here to tell you . . . aw, shit, I don't even know why I'm here."

She set down her makeup and faced him. "What did you want to tell me?"

"I guess that it was okay."

"What? My pregnancy? Like it needed your approval?"

He looked away, swore under his breath. "That's not what I meant. Just that I was okay with it. I wanted you to have the baby." He snorted. "Like that means anything now. . . ."

"Well, it does. I'm still pregnant. I almost had an abortion. I was like this close, but I couldn't do it. I just couldn't do it."

"Thank God."

She grinned, clearly dumbfounded. "Is this the same guy I left in the bagel shop? You forget about how kids scream through movies? How you give up all your freedom?"

"No. I've been thinking about it."

"Me, too. I've been thinking that I'm gonna have this baby and that you're the father, but I'm not so sure I want you in my life. I don't know if you're responsible enough to have a relationship, let alone a child. I just don't know."

"You won't know unless you give me a chance."

"I didn't think you wanted one. You're too wrapped up in your job and your toys."

He edged up to her, put his hands on her shoulders, looked her squarely in the eyes. "I want you. I want our baby. That's what I want."

"You don't know what you want."

"Listen to me. When I first became a medic, this old-timer told me that you get into EMS because you're running from something or running to something."

"Sounds like somebody I know."

"Yeah. Well, I think I know what he means now. And Geneva, I'm not kidding myself. I know this won't be easy, but I got a feeling that running is even harder."

She nodded slowly. "Let me think about it. People don't change overnight. I'm sure you still like yourself the way you are. And you'll screw up. I know it. It's just a matter of how far you go."

He drew a deep breath, nodded. "Okay, think about it. For as long as it takes. I'll be here. And hey, you want a lift to work?"

"Why? So you can pick me up when my shift's over? See, I know your little ploys. No, thanks."

"Then I'll go. Maybe I'll see you tonight." He lowered his head and started out.

"Hey, Doe? You really think we could be a family?"

He glanced back, his tone never more earnest. "As strange as it sounds, yeah, I do."

And now,
an excerpt of the second novel in the
NIGHT ANGEL 9 series

NIGHT ANGEL 9
Playing with Fire

coming in May 2001 from Berkley Books . . .

San Fernando Valley
Los Angeles
Sunday, 9:05 P.M. Pacific Time

The row of abandoned stores jogged back into the rainy
night's swelling gloom. Sheets of warping plywood
hung over shattered windows and bore the bloodred
curves of territorial graffiti best translated by gangbangers or police officers. Above this ramshackle file rose
a thorny cluster of dilapidated apartments whose paint
peeled in long lashes. Duct tape spanned many of the tenement's broken windows and formed a loose gray web.

"What a shithole," muttered firefighter-paramedic Abe
Kashmiri as he came around the rescue truck. "How do
people wind up in places like this?"

Stephanie Savage regarded the skinny rookie for a
moment, his dark skin paling in the flashing lights, his
black crew cut glazed by drizzle. She wiped her eyes
and shrugged. "Fitzy'd tell you that the government
wants them here. Doe'd tell you that they're all just lazy
fuckin' crackheads and deserve to lie in their own shit.

But I don't know. Guess I've stopped wondering. Come on. Code four. We're good to go in."

At the corner ahead, two Valley Police Department cruisers idled, lights wheeling. A third car from the VPD's special gang-control unit rolled to a squeaky halt. Savage wasn't sure whether the unknown-emergency call involved gang activity, but she felt all the more comfortable with two additional officers on the scene. Only two weeks prior, she and Abe had responded to another unknown-emergency call at an apartment building. A resident had mistaken them for intruders and had exercised his right to bear arms. Thank God he'd been a poor shot. At least this time law enforcement had arrived first.

"Somebody up there made the call," said one of the cops, a middle-aged black man with biceps large enough to warrant a second look. "No one's coughing up an admission. Got a little boy who looks sick. Mom says she didn't call."

"Yeah, we heard the update," Savage answered the big guy.

"God damn," said the cop's partner, another square-jawed military type with sooty eyes too small for his shaven head. He smirked at the tenement. "Guess they don't validate parking. Franco, you got a quarter for the meter?"

Savage rolled her eyes at Abe. She didn't have much patience for glib cops. The rain had something to do with that. Damned rainy nights. Always made her blond hair go frizzy. Always reminded her of that dark Friday when Tim, her ex, had wrapped their Ford Escort around a lamppost and had walked away without a scratch. In truth, he hadn't walked away but had been hauled off in cuffs and charged with DUI.

Rainy nights in Los Angeles. Had to hate them. Always set off her trick knee and made the arthritis in her back act up. Always increased the number of MVAs because Angelinos did *not* know how to drive on wet roads. Always made the job harder when you were husky, over forty, and responsible for the field training of a rookie medic doing his three-month probation. Way it was. Accept it or get out.

They mounted a rickety wooden staircase and ventured up toward a hallway between units. For a second, Savage thought the staircase might pull away from the wall and send them toppling to the pavement. Her paycheck failed to compensate for this brand of shit.

A pair of beer bottles sat on the landing, collecting rain through their open tops. Muddy footprints left their marks across the empty condom wrappers and cigarette butts that had fallen out of a black garbage bag, one of a dozen others piled along one wall. If the hallway had lights, they didn't work. A chute of darkness lay before them until the big cop pierced it with his Mag-Lite. The powerful stench of cigarettes and piss and something gone bad in the trash had Savage grimacing as they ventured deeper into the hall. She ran her gloved hand along one rough wall, then rubbed paint chips between her fingers. Although none of the requisite rats darted from the big cop's light, they undoubtedly lurked in the crevices, sniffing and waiting.

"Manager says every unit's got a good view," said the comedian cop. "You can see right down into the Dumpsters out back and plan your dinner."

"Don't laugh," Abe said. "Bet that ain't far from the truth."

"There it is," sighed the big cop, focusing his beam on an old wooden door whose metal number had long since fallen off to reveal the dirty outline of a "5" broken by nail holes. Hip-hop music thrummed from inside, and Savage wondered why the cops had not turned it off. First thing you did when entering a residence—silence those damned TVs and stereos.

The big cop lumbered in, followed by Abe, Savage, and the comedian cop. A narrow foyer led to a filthy kitchen on the right. Ahead was a living room jammed by two frayed and stained sofas and a battered oak-veneer coffee table that supported a trio of heavy glass ashtrays overflowing with butts. Several gaping holes had been punched in the Sheetrock to Savage's immediate left, just beneath a large wooden cross. The rest of the decor suggested "contemporary ghetto garage sale," with chairs, artwork, end tables, and lamps that were cracked or mismatched or hanging at tremor-inspired angles in the sparse light. Two Hispanic men in their early twenties had claimed one sofa. Both wore expensive sneakers and jogging gear. Bright gold earrings dangled from their ears as they nodded to the music, the rhythm establishing a barrier between them and the authority figures milling about. A third man, white, gaunt, perhaps thirty, with matted brown hair and the hazy gaze of an addict, sat on the floor and leaned back on the other sofa. He tugged violently at the collar of his faded black T-shirt, then unabashedly scratched his crotch through worn-out boxer shorts. Above him sat a bony black woman of about the same age, her hair heavily beaded in varicolored strings, her glare as heated as they come. She wrestled with the five-year-old boy on her lap. Her kid's cries broke into a spasm of coughing.

Savage crossed to the boom box on the floor near the sofas. She punched a button.

" 'Da fuck you do that for?" cried one of the Hispanic men.

"We keep turning it off, and they keep turning it on," said a young cop who came from a hallway that appeared to lead to the bedrooms. "*Don't* turn it on again. Hear me?"

"Don't fuck wit my jams," said the guy, his lip twitching as he bolted from the sofa toward the boom box.

Abe moved faster. With one powerful stroke, he ripped the power cord from the back of the boom box and threw it at the Hispanic man, then he thumbed open a panel to check for batteries. None there.

The bug-eyed gang-banger waved the power cord, which had frayed. "You broke my fuckin' radio!"

Abe nodded. "The county will pay to have it fixed."

Savage grabbed Abe's arm and pulled him up and away, toward a window. "What're you doing?"

"I got a thing about hip-hop music. I'll tell you about it sometime."

Swearing under her breath, Savage headed back to the mother. She introduced herself and added, "Your son sounds sick. Can we check him out?"

"I'm a go to the clinic tomorrow. Nobody called 911. This is my apartment, and I want y'all to just go before I sue your asses for trespassing."

"What's your name?"

"None of your business."

"Her name's Shonica," said the junkie in an eerie lilt as he placed a hand on her knee. "And she's got her mind made up. You won't change it. She'll go to the clinic. Now, if everyone would just stop watching us and giving us the third degree and get the fuck out, we'd be happy." He closed his eyes, his jaw jerking involuntarily.

"Shonica, are you sure you don't want us to check out your little boy? Only take a couple of minutes."

"You listening? I'm a take him to the clinic tomorrow. I don't know who called 911. Wasn't us."

Savage leaned closer to the woman, and they locked gazes. "You sure? Really sure? We're talking about your little boy. He could have a respiratory infection. Lot of that going around. If he has, it could be life threatening. Seen a lot of kids with that."

"He ain't got that, and I didn't call. I don't want your help. Leave."

"Okay. You just have to sign something."

The mother gritted her yellowing teeth. "If it'll get y'all out."

Savage tossed a glance to Abe; he would handle the refusal-to-be-treated form.

As she turned away, the big cop gave her a resigned look. "She says these other two traveling salesmen are her friends. Show me lots of gold and hundred-dollar sneakers, and I'll show you two crack dealers. But I don't know these guys. Must be from up north."

"So who made the call?"

"Dispatch couldn't get an ID."

Savage frowned. "The call came from this apartment?"

"Yeah. Phone's right there."

"What's that?" Savage asked, spotting the leg of a doll sitting on the kitchen counter. She crossed to the toy— a Barbie in full beachwear regalia. "Hey, Shonica? Does your little boy play with Barbies?"

"That's my daughter's doll."

"Where's she at?"

"She's down the hall in my sister's apartment. Now I signed your form. Get out."

Abe walked up to Savage, the two Hispanic men glaring at him. He cocked his brow and held up the refusal form. "Ready?"

Savage looked to the big cop. "We're out of here."

"What kind of a mother refuses care for her sick kid?" Abe said as they headed for the door.

"I don't know," Savage groaned. "But I've seen a lot of them. Couple more years of this, and maybe you'll stop asking that question. Maybe you won't even care why they refuse. You'll just want that signature so you can leave."

He opened the door, paused, and looked back. "So how come you're not that cold?"

"Who says I'm not?"

"You? I'm surprised you didn't give her a sermon on motherhood. Probably too busy thinking about your vacation. Just a few more hours, and it all begins." He flicked on his flashlight and slipped into the hall, the dispatcher's voice echoing from his portable.

As Savage followed, a tingle rose from the nape of her neck. Were those footfalls behind her? "Abe? Hold up."

His light shone past her to reveal a nine- or ten-year-old black girl cowering against the wall. Bare feet pushed out past grimy corduroys, her soiled purple shirt had a tear in one sleeve, and a daisy patch hung limply at her shoulder. She pulled nervously at the patch.

"Hey," Savage called. "It's all right."

The girl lunged forward.

Savage stood there, stunned, as the little one dropped to her knees. "Please. Take me with you. Please." She clutched Savage's leg.

With a growing lump in her throat, Savage stroked the girl's hair and winced at the dirt and tangles. "Easy. What's your name?"

"Keesa. Can I go with you? Please?"

"Where do you live?"

"Here. But I don't want to anymore."

"Do you live in apartment five?"

"Yes."

Savage shared a look with Abe, who then stared somberly at the girl. He crouched to meet her gaze. "Your mom's in there."

"I don't care."

"You have to go back inside." Savage tensed and shifted her leg. The girl clung fiercely. "Weren't you at your aunt's apartment?"

"I was there. She finished drinking and fell asleep. I want to go with you. Let me go with you. Please." She sobbed into Savage's leg.

The comedian cop trudged down the hall. "Looks like you got a growth." His tone softened as Savage fixed him with a hard look. "She belong back there?"

"Yeah," Abe said.

"Please. Don't take me back."

"Sorry, sweetheart." The cop slipped his arm around the girl's waist and pulled her swiftly from Savage's leg. She kicked. She screamed. Tears glistened in the flashlight's thin beam. Unfazed, the cop hauled her back toward the apartment.

"Jesus Christ," Abe said through a sigh. "I bet she made the call. . . ."

Panting, thoughts being born, colliding, dying, Savage could not bring herself to move as the cop rounded the corner and the girl released a final wail before entering the apartment. That little face burned so brilliantly, so painfully. . . .

"Steph?"

Savage held out a hand. "Don't talk. Don't say anything."

They remained there for a long moment, Abe fidgeting, Savage trying to exhale her anger. She wanted more than anything to march back into that apartment and tell that poor excuse for a mother that she was ruining her children's lives, that her babies deserved better than this, that she needed to get help, that she needed to find some way, any way, to get out of this hole. But that wasn't Savage's job. No more strays. No more other people's problems.

To hell with it. She rushed toward the door, but Abe latched on to her wrist with a remarkable grip. "Uh-uh. Forget it. Let HRS do their thing. Maybe they'll get her out of here. Cops inside got it covered. Mom's getting her lecture, trust me. She doesn't need one from you."

Damn, the rookie had her. She jerked once more but wasn't going anywhere. "I can't shove my morals down other people's throats. No shit. But when it comes to kids . . . Fuck! What is she thinking?"

"Who knows. But I'm thinking we get out of here. Now." Abe had the steely glance of a man twice his age.

"Okay. Okay. Know what? I'm sorry. That was totally unprofessional. I'm supposed to be your FTO, for God's sake. I'm okay now. I'm okay."

He raised his brows and increased his grip. "You'll be okay."

She closed her eyes, tried *not* to see that little girl. "Maybe I'll start my vacation early. . . ."

"Engine Twelve, Rescue Ten. Engine Twelve, Rescue Ten. Code three to an MVA northbound Van Nuys Boulevard. Cross street Burbank. VPD on scene. Report multiple victims. Time out: twenty-two thirteen."

John "Doe" Smith tossed his *Sports Illustrated* swimsuit edition onto the end table and hoisted himself from the recliner. He felt a decent adrenaline rush as he hustled out of Fire Station Ten's dayroom and onto the apparatus floor, where Isabel Vivas climbed into the driver's side of their rescue vehicle. She had been restocking supplies, and you didn't get in the big Latina's way when she did that. Lives depended on them making sure that the equipment not only functioned but that supplies were also well-stocked. She performed the task like an artist who would suffer neither interruptions nor criticism. So be it. She kept the rescue more organized than Doe ever could, despite his "senior medic" status. One peek at his dresser drawers would confirm that. He was the only person he knew who stored ratchet sets beside underwear.

"Done drooling over your magazine?" Vivas hollered as Doe vaulted into the cab, assuming his usual spot in "the seat."

He wriggled his brows, flashed his deep blue eyes, then slipped the headset over his ears, muffling the siren and rumbling diesel engine. "You know, there's a woman in there who looks a lot like you," he said into the attached microphone. "All that long, black hair tied back. Nice chocolate skin. Big eyes."

"And a big fat ass, too?"

"Your ass ain't big," he said in his best politician's tone, then lifted the rescue's microphone. "Rescue Ten, responding."

"Rescue Ten," acknowledged the dispatcher.

"You know, I'm pretty much blown away," she confessed, guiding the rescue away from the fire station. "For the past two weeks you're not as nasty and you're not complaining, and you're even telling me that I don't have a fat ass when you, me, and Jenny Craig know that I do."

"All right. So you got through to me. All that stuff you said about me being a cold bastard and treating patients like hunks of meat? I thought a lot about it. I'm a changed man." The lie warmed Doe's cheeks.

"What's her name?"

"Excuse me?"

Vivas grinned crookedly. "You heard me. You're trying to impress her, and you're practicing on me."

He squirmed. "There's no woman. I just, uh, wanted to stop being such a prick. I don't take too many things very seriously. I figured I'd better start working on myself or no woman will ever want me."

"But now I don't like you anymore. I've created a monster. I need you to go back to your old ways. I want you to be a whoremonger and a sexist pig. I want you to bitch and moan about every call. I want you to look dying people right in the eye and think only about what's for lunch, or whether or not you'll have that sexy little bystander's ankles in the air by midnight."

"What?"

"I want you to start smoking again. Wear T-shirts and roll a pack of Marlboro in your sleeve. Treat me like shit. That's what I want."

"You'd better lay off that Slim-Fast. It's going to your brain."

She chuckled. "Whatever it is, I'm glad you're . . . let's say, a little more sensitive."

"Ouch. Not used to hearing that. Not sure if I like hearing it. And her name's Geneva."

"I knew it."

"You're the only one who knows. Swear to God you won't tell anybody."

"Why the big secret?"

"I don't know. I just don't want everyone knowing my business."

"You mean you don't want to ruin your playboy reputation."

"We're going to have a baby." Why it came out so suddenly, Doe didn't know, but it felt awfully good to tell someone. The pressure had been building for two weeks.

"Oh my God. Really? You were just telling me how your sister's always bugging you to settle down. Congratulations."

"Aren't you going to ask the question?"

"What?"

"If we're going to get married."

"Are you?"

"Don't know yet."

Vivas narrowed her gaze in thought. "How long have you been with her?"

"Little over six months now."

"What? Six months? And you've been cheating on her left and right?"

He sighed. "All those dates I told you about? Lies. I've only been with her. Brace yourself. I've been faithful."

"Let me guess. You found out about two weeks ago that she was pregnant. That's why you were so distant. I get it now. Man, you should've told me. We could've talked."

"Don't be pissed, Izzy. This is just all screwed up, and it caught me way off guard. I mean, *me* a *dad*. You tell that to people who know me, and they'll laugh."

"Doe, a one woman man," she said, testing the sound of it. "Know what? I'm not laughing."

"Yeah, you're like me. Crying over my lost freedom."

"You're growing up, Doe. You're growing up."

"Maybe you're right. Only took thirty or so years. I'm like fine wine."

She made a face. "Cheap champagne."

He shook his head as the light ahead abruptly changed green under the electronic persuasion of the Opticom unit mounted atop the rescue. He wiped condensation from the window and reported "all clear" to the right—his job during code three driving.

Two cross streets later, they pulled ahead of the accident, a three-car fender bender, with all vehicles pulled off to the curb and the three drivers standing near their cars, grimacing into cell phones. VPD cruisers sat at the front and back of the line, and Engine Twelve rolled up behind the twinkling parade as Doe and Vivas gloved up and leaped down from the rig. Vivas went for the long backboard and c-spine bag. Doe caught the attention of a tall, heavyset sergeant, a gray-haired Hispanic woman named Juanita Ramirez who looked less than thrilled to be out in the rain, drizzle or no. "Hey, Juanita. Haven't seen you. Figured you pissed off somebody again and got transferred."

The sergeant rubbed the small of her back. "Nah, I finally got that operation. Six weeks out. First week back. Still hurts like a bitch. Maybe even more than it did before the surgery. But I played. Now I pay."

Like Doe, Ramirez was a big-time dirt bike enthusiast who had taken one too many spills. She and Doe had gone biking together on several occasions, and the sergeant had taken risks that made even a veteran cyclist like Doe cringe. "So what do we have?"

"Got that old lady up front. The gay guy behind her says she jammed on her brakes for no good reason. Got this little Dodger fan in the back who couldn't stop in time and skidded across the wet road. They were all out of their cars when we got here. Jimmy's over there with a c-spine on the old lady. The other two claim they're okay, but now they're starting to rub their necks. Acute checkbook pains, eh?"

Doe shrugged. Two weeks ago he would have nodded. "Thanks." He craned his head back to Vivas and thought of taking the more seriously injured patient for himself, but in deference to her, he opted for the other two. "You got the lady. I got these guys." He lifted his chin toward a young man with a sunken chest and hair dyed blond and then to a much shorter man of about forty with a beer gut and a Dodger's cap sitting high on his balding head.

The three firefighters from Engine Twelve strode toward the scene as Doe approached the shorter driver. "How you doing, sir? I'm John Smith. I'm a paramedic. Can I check you out?"

The diminutive sports fan cupped a hand over his cell phone. "Just give me a minute, will ya, buddy? I got a pizza that's gonna burn in my oven if I don't get my neighbor to take it out."

Though he wanted to smirk, Doe simply nodded and turned his attention to the blond man whom Ramirez had assumed was gay. The guy did not exude masculinity, but neither was he flamboyant about his sexuality. "Hey, sir. I'm paramedic John Smith. You all right?"

"No, I'm not all right," the guy snapped, then smote a fist on the window of his brand-new Volkswagen Beetle, which was crunched both front and back, banana-yellow paint flaking off onto shattered taillights. "Look at my car. I'm freaking out."

"Forget your car. And do me a favor. Don't move your neck. You might've injured your spine." Doe ran a finger over his own c-spine. "We'll put a collar on, just to be sure. What's your name?"

The guy *tsked*. "My name's Liga Thomas. I'm sure my lawyer will be glad you treated me."

"Here's your collar," came a familiar voice.

Doe glanced over his shoulder and nearly lost his balance.

Nicole Cavalier had materialized from the rain. A dozen shades of short blond hair framed her narrow face. Hazel eyes widened with intensity and excitement. Her lean, muscular curves begged for exploration.

It was her all right, Nicole Cavalier, the district's most notorious femme fatale, a woman who snared you in her claws of whimsy and rough sex, had her thrills, and then tossed you into the gutter like so much roadkill. Somehow, she had picked up Doe's scent and now howled at the moon.

"So you're back?" he asked, dumbfounded as he accepted the collar. "What happened to New York?"

Her lips grew pouty. "It's still there."

Doe had to look away. He began fastening the patient's collar. "Okay, Mr. Thomas. This will feel a little uncomfortable. Do you have any pain anywhere else?"

"I got a headache."

"Did you hit your head?"

"No, this is definitely stress related."

"Are you allergic to any medications, and are you taking anything right now?" Nicole asked, diving right into the primary assessment.

The guy flinched as Doe finished with the collar. "I'm not allergic. I'm not taking anything."

"Do you have any history of illness or major surgeries?" asked Doe.

"Nope. Had my tonsils out. That's about it."

Nicole lifted her voice over a passing truck. "When's the last time you ate something?"

"I don't know," the guy said, growing pissed. "All I know is my car is fucked! How am I gonna get to work tomorrow?"

Doe shrugged. "Maybe your insurance company can get you a loaner. Anyway, why don't you tell us what happened?"

"Because I already told the cops. You guys are just medics."

Nicole brushed past Doe, trailing a wave of expensive perfume. Doe's heart sank. She came in tight on the patient. "We just want to figure out what we call 'the mechanism of injury'," she explained. "Just tell us how you moved inside the car when you got hit."

"Like I remember? It all happened in like a couple of seconds. I hit that dumb old bitch, and I got thrown forward, then Danny DeVito over there hits me, and I get whipped back. And you know what? My neck is really starting to hurt now."

Doe nodded and pulled out his portable. "Valley, Rescue Ten."

"Ten, Valley."

"Request second rescue unit to this location."

"Copy, Ten. Requesting second unit your location."

"Sir, come back to our ambulance." Doe looked to the other guy in the Dodger's cap. "And you, too, sir. Just need to check you out."

The guy removed his cap and palmed his head. "Whatever."

"You're going to transport that lady," said Nicole. "Mind if I ride along?"

"I don't need any help."

"I've been meaning to call you."

"How long you been back?"

"About a month. But it's been insane. You know, the move. Settling in. Fighting to get my old job back. For a week there, I thought I'd have to go private. Wind up getting used and abused with all those EMTs fresh out of school. Man, that would've sucked. But I just went in there and told them point-blank what I'm about. I'm a kick-ass paramedic. A goddamn medical machine. I've run more calls in my six-year career than some of these lazy farts have run in their whole lives. No one can touch my skills. Even the guy who thinks he's the best in this district."

"I don't *think* I'm the best. I am the best."

"I was talking about Troft. You're just a standard-issue trauma monkey with decent hands." She grabbed his wrist. "Good. No rings yet. Then again, there never will be, right?"

They reached the rescue, and that saved Doe from an answer. The old lady had already been lowered onto the long backboard, her head placed between the cushiony Head-ons, her extremities secured by straps. Two fire-fighters lifted the board onto the stretcher, then guided her into the ambulance.

"Let's get vitals on these gentlemen," Doe told one of the firefighters who had loaded the stretcher, then he regarded Vivas, who sat inside the rescue with her patient. "Oh, sorry. Isabel Vivas, Nicole Cavalier."

They shared polite grins, then Vivas gave Doe a suspicious look before refocusing on her patient.

Nicole leaned in close. "You fuck her yet?"

Doe frowned.

"Why not? She's got nice tits. Big ass, yeah, but I'm

sure you'd give her a good drilling. Damn, I remember how you used to do me—"

"I got a patient," he said, warding off the chills. "Izzy? You need any help back there?"

"No, I'm good."

Doe gazed restlessly between Nicole and the driver's side door. "You heard the woman. I have to go. Good luck, I guess."

"I'll ride up front. My lieutenant's pretty cool. He won't mind."

"Mine's not. She will. So, I'll see you." He lowered his head and got out of there.

"Hey, you still hang out at Tuba's?"

He froze, didn't look back. "Sometimes."

"We're on the same schedule. Maybe I'll catch you there."

"Yeah, maybe."

Back in the rescue, Doe slipped on his headset, tapped on the siren, then pulled cautiously onto the road.

"Doe?" Vivas asked in a strange tone.

"Yes," he answered, matching her.

"You never told me about her. I'm thinking ex-girlfriend?"

"You're thinking too much."

"I'm thinking you've insulted me by keeping this secret. And I'm getting a weird something from her. Just be careful. You hear me? You listening Doe? You listening?"

About the Author

Peter Telep received a large portion of his education in New York; spent a number of years in Los Angeles, where he worked for such television shows as *In the Heat of the Night* and *The Legend of Prince Valiant*; and then returned east to Florida. There, he earned his undergraduate and graduate degrees, and now teaches composition, scriptwriting, and creative writing courses at the University of Central Florida.

Mr. Telep's previous novels include the *Squire Trilogy*, two books based on Fox's *Space: Above and Beyond* television show, a trilogy of novels based on the bestselling computer game *Descent*, four books in the film-based *Wing Commander* series, and the adaptation of the Warner Brothers film *Red Planet*. You may E-mail him at PTelep@aol.com, visit his Web site at www.earth-netone.com, or contact him via the publisher. He is always excited to hear from his readers.

PENGUIN PUTNAM INC.
Online

Your Internet gateway to a virtual environment with hundreds of entertaining and enlightening books from Penguin Putnam Inc.

While you're there, get the latest buzz on the best authors and books around—

Tom Clancy, Patricia Cornwell, W.E.B. Griffin, Nora Roberts, William Gibson, Robin Cook, Brian Jacques, Catherine Coulter, Stephen King, Jacquelyn Mitchard, and many more!

**Penguin Putnam Online is located at
http://www.penguinputnam.com**

PENGUIN PUTNAM NEWS

Every month you'll get an inside look at our upcoming books and new features on our site. This is an ongoing effort to provide you with the most up-to-date information about our books and authors.

**Subscribe to Penguin Putnam News at
http://www.penguinputnam.com/ClubPPI**